D. HALE RAMBO

BETWEEN
THE
LINES

THE PLANAR PAGES

ISBN: 978-1-7361281-8-3 (Hardback)

ISBN: 978-1-7361281-5-2 (Paperback)

ISBN: 978-1-7361281-4-5 (eBook)

Cover Design by Fantastical Ink

The Planar Page Logos by Grace Lewis

The Book of Larrakane art by Rick Hertel Art

To my Book Wyrms, thank you for supporting my creations and breaking my world. Fiona will take it from here. I have faith she'll be as chaotic as you nerds.

Contents

FIONA THORNE ALWAYS HEARD curiosity would be the death of her. It was curiosity that made her poke her nose into her neighbor's garden when she was young after hearing shouts of anger. This led to her first case: carrot theft. A case she was determined to solve and did moments later, although she let the rabbit get away with it.

Curiosity drove her to meddle in an ongoing investigation over the mysterious disappearance of cacao pods on the farm she and her family had worked. She was promptly accused of the theft and had to clear her name. Catching the real culprit, one she didn't let off the hook this time, pushed her inquisitiveness even further.

And so, of course, curiosity got her, after many years of listening to the little niggle at the back of her head, to say yes without hesitation to a job she knew little about based on a name alone. And that, she reasoned with herself as brisk wind twisted through the leaves and dark curls of her hair, was why she was clinging to the branches at the top of a tall tree, knowing at any moment she would fall to her death. Curiosity was Fiona's first love, and she reckoned if the wind got its way, it might be her last.

A soft, chilly rain permeated the canopy of the mossy trees in the forest and landed lightly on her uncovered face. Piercing wind ripped through the branches, whistling and catching Fiona's many-pocketed scarf. The tug of the wind almost unbalanced her thin body. She grasped the branch tighter, vowing next time to just stay on the ground and hide. *You're an absolute blotter, Fi.*

How could she possibly hope to make an impact in the world if she couldn't even do a proper stakeout? Working her way toward the type of notoriety where she could do more good than not started with the basics. Like being blasted competent. She should've said no to notoriety, no to going out of her depth before she was ready, and definitely no to herself when she thought, *The bushes are too far away. I know. I'll climb that spindly tree for a better view.*

The air shimmered briefly in the clearing, and Fiona stopped chiding herself and focused her attention. The ground and the trees bent inward to the ripple, creating a small fold in the scenery. As the world folded in on itself, another world, dark as a raven's wing with flares of crimson, showed on the other side. It looked exactly like the turning of a page in a book where, for a moment, both worlds showed at the same time.

People with more time to mull over these sorts of things (and for whom book printing had just become vogue) called it "turning the page" when the ability to do so first manifested. Traveling from one world to another put you in the exact same spot in each one, and the worlds stacked on one another like pages in a book. From there the metaphor raged on, pushed forward by the fashionable. Give or take two hundred years later, what was the height of fashion had moved on, but the metaphor lingered. Fiona, a lover of books, enjoyed the comparison immensely.

A short human man with pale peach skin stepped out of the reddish page and into the cold, rainy forest. An acrid scent and a tendril of smoke came with him. As if a reader decided to go back to the previous page, the world unfolded on itself. The shimmer disappeared, and the view of the forest solidified behind him. It all took but a moment in time.

Page turners—people gifted with the ability to move themselves and others from one world to another—traveled this way all the time, and as Fiona was one herself, the unfolding scene didn't faze her. The gift was an ability that manifested the same in all who were given it, but not all page turners were alike. Fiona focused on where he had come from. The darkness with the crimson glow could only mean one thing: the fire page.

The man fanned away the smoke that clung to him. Scraping a hand through his hair, he glanced around. He pulled out a torch, lit it, and searched the area. The small bushes surrounding the clearing cast shadows under its firelight. Apparently confident he was alone, he divested himself of a black cloak and gloves. He wiped a hand across his forehead, then pulled a small round glass and iron jar from within a pocket of the cloak.

A wisp of flame, no bigger than her hand, flitted from one side to the other inside the small cage.

Fiona let out a small gasp but covered her mouth to stifle it. The patter of the rain on leaves and wood would hopefully drown out her lapse in judgment. She hadn't expected him to kidnap yet another creature. *I'll free you soon, little one.*

The man strode out of the woods onto the fresh dirt path that would lead him back into the city. This area of the forest must've become a pagemark for smugglers. Page turners used pagemarks to travel from page to page. Official ones were typically in safe areas, tested by various turners to make sure travel was consistent, and well guarded from issues or blocked access

An unofficial pagemark could lead to a variety of ills if the page turners using it were of a mind to commit theft or murder. Fiona was divided on the policing of who went in and out of a pagemark. People should be able to do as they please unless it hurt others, but she wasn't a fool. Not everyone thought the way she did or acted with others in mind.

Once the torchlight was a speck in the distance but still visible, Fiona began climbing down. A tie from the sleeve of her buttoned velvet doublet caught on a branch, making her fear that her curiosity would kill her all too soon. She took a deep breath and untangled it, then finished her descent. She followed him, keeping close to the trees. Her chest burned, not at the effort, but at the thought of losing him. Her entire investigation hinged on her pursuit. If she lost him, she'd have to go with her backup plan, which meant she wouldn't figure out where he was keeping the other creatures. It wasn't enough to capture him. She needed to free them all.

After a short while, the dirt path gave way to cobblestone streets illuminated by oil lamps hanging outside various homes. She rubbed her face to wick away the rain. The scent of olives was light and familiar after coming out of the muddy odor of the forest. She kept tight to the brick and wood buildings on the outskirts of her home district in the city. The shadows of the night swallowed her lithe body and deep-brown skin.

The district's architecture shifted, more reflective of the citizens who lived there than any one style. She made her way around a large felt yurt, its round shape allowing her to squeeze between it and an A-frame timber building, as she tried to assess where the man was going. If he was taking the creature through this district, it meant he had kept his stolen creatures right under all their noses.

He turned down a quiet street and strode up to a tall wooden home, its size somewhat dwarfing the cottage next to it. He walked inside, the flicking light from the creature he was holding revealing his path through the windows. The light disappeared into the recesses of the house where it became stationary. Another glow, this one more typical of an oil lamp, flared up and illuminated his path back to the front. *He must store the creatures in the back.*

Pulling out a tiny egg-shaped clock hung around her neck as a pendant, Fiona flipped it open and squinted at its hands. It was always trouble to read these newfangled things, but under flickering oil light it was an unneeded headache. She sighed inwardly, stowing it away. In an hour she was supposed to meet this ripper she had been following as a prospective client. Her backup plan. She really hoped it wouldn't get that far. She glanced up and down the street looking for the signs of her preferred plan—a spotted cheetah who would hopefully have the good grace to look ashamed for being late. Her friend Dodger.

His real name was Marcius Festinius Cervidus, but no one who liked him ever called him that. And Fiona liked him well enough for being an authority figure in the Travel Guild.

The Travel Guild regulated all the comings and goings of page turners in the Book. The Book was an easy (or certainly trendy two hundred years ago) way of grouping all the known pages in the universe that could be traveled or "turned" to. Regulating, administrating, and supporting page turners and the Book was the entire point of the Travel Guild. Or so they wrote.

Fiona shifted her weight anxiously as her eyes continued searching the street for Dodger. She couldn't make a move herself. Her target would probably attack her on sight at his home, and that would leave her in no position to help anyone. Did Dodger even get her urgent summons? Leaving it with his workmates wasn't her first choice, but she'd been pressed for time after convincing the suspect that she was a wealthy prospective client who desperately needed an adorable new pet. She'd leaned on all the flattery she could muster and quite a few pricey drinks, but it had paid off. And now all she had to do was be patient, wait for Dodger to show up, and they could apprehend the man.

"I'll just nip around for a peek," she muttered to herself.

Sneaking around the side of his home, she pressed herself to the damp wall and listened for movement. She crept silently toward a window at the back of the house. There was no glass, which was usual for a human home. Still behind the times of other cultures as always. She raised up to the high ledge awkwardly to look inside. Cages and crates were stacked up against the walls, and the small fire creature burned in the glass jar on a shelf. A few more flame sprites were scattered throughout the room.

The small thing looked like the flickering wick of a candle but about the size of a fist. Its color went from rust to crimson and back to rust again as it thrust itself against the glass trying to get out. Fiona waved to get its attention, then motioned for them to wait. Although she had studied how to speak in the language of flame, hand waving as communication was a bit of a stretch between a human and a fire elemental.

The creatures all stopped moving and floated where they were. They were all wisps of fire that burned without any discernible features. Content that they at the very least wouldn't topple their jars and set fire to the wooden floor, Fiona glanced down the quiet alley to see if she was still alone. Hearing nothing but the whistling of the wind and bits of conversation in the far distance, she slid her hand into her scarf, feeling for a rough, heavily stitched pocket.

She found nothing at first, but as she thought about what she wanted, a leather pouch appeared beneath her fingers and she pulled out her lock picking tools. Unraveling them, she gave an appreciative grin at the silver instruments. They had cost her a lot of paper, but they were worth their weight every time she got a chance to use them. Which was more than most in her line of work.

She shook her head, focusing on the task at hand. She slid to the front door of the house and inserted the lock pick, leaning in as she concentrated. It only took a few moments before she popped the cold metal lock. If Dodger didn't show up and she had to do things herself, she needed an exit plan.

Moving to the side of the door, she held her breath to see if anyone would come her way at the muffled sound. There were no footsteps. Fiona slunk down away from the building and ambled quietly back toward the street.

She had been tracking the suspect for the last week. He was slippery at first, but Fiona had caught up with him when he let down his guard. People often did when they thought they were off the hook. It just took a couple of whiskeys and the right proposition. She knew he'd have to go back to where he stored the elementals in order to meet up with her later. She hadn't expected him to go to the fire page in between though.

She tugged at her scarf, ignoring her burning chest. She should've stopped him then. She knew the damage rippers could do. But she had needed to know where the others were stored. She'd release them soon.

A hiss whistled through the air like a cat trying to get her attention, so light she wouldn't have heard it if she wasn't trained to hear such things. She saw Dodger scamper around the corner and make his way toward her. His tawny-furred cheetah body was barely covered by the official-looking tan cloak and hose worn by those who worked for the Travel Guild. Other jackets—officers of the Guild who regulated the Book from page to page—were specks of shadow surrounding the area. Fiona barely noticed them as Dodger slid up next to her. Sometimes she disliked how good they were.

Although Dodger was shorter than her, he never seemed meek when looking up at her. He was lightly built with muscles under thin fur. His long legs were matched by his long tail, which he kept curled around his body, not letting it brush the ground. He looked like a typical smilodon, the catlike people from another page. But his demeanor was a bit softer than those he left behind. Being a page turner had that kind of impact on some people. Heavy was the responsibility.

"Thorne," he said shortly, nodding but looking forward at the house.

"Dodger," she greeted him back in kind but added a wink, more relaxed now that he was here. "Took you long enough."

Though he kept a straight lookout, Fiona noticed his spotted tail sweeping side to side. "I was waylaid by Gilded Evenhell. She wanted an update before we could help out. Apologies."

Fiona shrugged and moved on, not wanting to beleaguer the point when he was already annoyed and other things were more important. "I lost him for a couple of hours. He turned the page to Blaze. Came back in the western forest with a tiny flame creature, and I tracked him here. We're not supposed to meet for another hour or so. He should be surprised."

Dodger bared his teeth at the mention of the forest. "I keep telling the Binder we should patrol the woods more."

Fiona raised an eyebrow at his outburst (or what counted as an outburst for Dodger) and mention of the leader of the Travel Guild. The Binder was never seen, but nothing went on within the Travel Guild without his knowledge, it was rumored. One of the first recorded page turners, he started the Travel Guild. But with power came responsibility, which Fiona felt he wasn't owning near enough.

"This is the third ripper this season smuggling elemental creatures. The pages will retaliate if it's not stopped. I think none of us want another Court of Copper situation," she said. The Court of Copper, a page from which many illustrious fashion and scientific advancements stemmed, refused to allow in turners without a native guide. They banned the Travel Guild altogether. She admired the latter part. "It would behoove your Binder to pay attention to the actual Book around him instead of the one he's decided it should be."

"Fi, you know the Guild takes care of many matters. It's not all or nothing," he said quietly, turning away.

She looked at Dodger for a long moment, then let out a small sigh, dropping the subject. How she had ended up friends with a jacket, she never could quite figure out. They'd been in turner training together, sure, but that training had dozens of other people. Only Dodger still commanded her friendship over the years. She assumed it was because their focus was the same: to do some good, mostly.

"Well, either way, once we capture this ripper it should shut down the pagemark for a while. Others will think twice before using it again to get to Blaze." Official ones were typically helmed by the Travel Guild.

Dodger nodded. "Once we break down the door, we'll rush in and grab him."

"The door *may* already be open," she said casually.

"I'm going to pretend I didn't hear that," Dodger said with a slight smile. He conveyed his orders to the nearest jacket, then trotted silently to the house without a backward glance.

Always the professional. Though Dodger could be a pain in the rear, he was very dependable. He was likely the second-best thing that had come out of her turner training. The first had been learning how not to get stranded somewhere in the Book where you could get yourself killed.

Fiona made her way to the back window, preparing for her signal. She barely heard the front door open. A quick shout as the jackets piled into the house surrounding the ripper was all there was of his capture.

Fiona climbed in through to the room of creatures. The floorboards creaked under her weight and puffs of damp wood clung to the air from the earlier rain. The lights flickered, throwing shadows across the room, but it was enough to see there were more glasses than crates. "So a likening to fire elementals then? I'm sorry it's easier to get at you all now." She sighed, moving over to the flame sprite's jar. They pressed themself against the glass toward her. Grabbing a jar, its cool texture beneath her fingers, she almost dropped it as a crash sounded from the front room. *He must be putting up a fight.*

She put the jar close to her face, eyes half-closed shielding from the bright light. In stuttering Claire, language of the flame, the words difficult to whistle out with her tongue in the way, she said, "I'll get you home, little one. But be careful. You could set everything on fire in this dusty wooden house."

"Worry about yourself, girl," a hoarse voice said from behind her as thick, rough hands grabbed her shoulders and covered her mouth.

Fiona dropped the jar trying to wrench herself from his grasp. Pain blossomed in her shoulder, and she cursed at herself for not surveying the room better. She jabbed her bony elbow back into his chest. He grunted, loosening his hold. She ducked and whirled around to face him.

He was human, with long black hair in a loose braid that swung over his shoulder. The light of all the flame creatures reddened his pale peach skin. He reached out to her, but Fiona dropped to the floor away from his hands. She knew her strength was lacking, so she tried to get to the pocket of her scarf containing her whip, but he grabbed her wrists, jolting her.

She forced herself to still and look directly into his eyes. Now wasn't the time to lose a contest of strength. She needed him to be uncertain. "Honestly," Fiona started with a smirk, "you should think for a moment if this is how you'd really like to die."

"Don't be silly, girl," he whispered, shaking her wrists. "What are you going to do?"

"If you want to think that, it's your folly." She smiled casually, tilting her head as if it was little concern to her. "But consider this. Would I, a slip of a thing, really walk into a room completely alone and unarmed? Would I be so stupid?"

The man hesitated, and Fiona took that moment to shout toward the closed door behind him, "Now!"

He turned to guard against this newly imagined threat. Fiona jumped up and swung her whole body into him, throwing him off balance and into the wall with a thud and shattering glass. Fiona took no time to consider what had happened. She ran to the window and vaulted out as the man screamed, tearing through the hushed silence and still night air.

WITHOUT LOOKING BACK, FIONA ran to the front of the house. She burst through the front door, startling the jackets who were making their way toward the screaming.

"Another ripper. In there," she said, pointing in the direction they were heading.

The jackets quickly assembled their wits and made their way into the room with Fiona and Dodger behind them.

The man who had grabbed Fiona was on fire. He was trying desperately to put it out. He had pulled off his shirt, revealing a blue stripe tattooed on his chest, and continued stripping his burning clothes.

The flame sprite, freed from the jar, rose into the rafters of the home and twirled. Wisps of flame spiraled rhythmically.

The jackets stopped short at the scene. Fiona would've laughed at their confusion if she wasn't worried about the fire catching the timbers of the house.

"Not too high, little one," she called out in Claire.

Dodger moved past his jackets and threw a blanket on the man to smother the fire. "Pat him down and take him out."

The jackets grabbed him as the man continued trying to put the fire out, heedless of what else was happening around him.

Fiona moved out of the way and deeper into the room. She needed time to search for evidence among the clutter but without the Travel Guild jackets noticing. She called out to the flame sprite, "Thank you for the help."

It flew toward Fiona, the warmth causing instant beads of sweat on her forehead even as the cool night air breezed through the window. She shut her eyes at the bright light. There wasn't the acrid smell she attributed to Blaze on it but a cleaner scent like a dry wood fire. She hoped it wasn't an actual wood fire and, with a quick glance around, deduced that it really was coming from the flame sprite.

The creature, wisps of fire in the air, twirled around. :Help,: it said. Though it had no discernable form, Fiona could feel a warm, fuzzy satisfaction coming from it.

Fiona smiled as the feeling cascaded over her. It felt like stepping into a deep, hot bath after being up in the cold air too long. A wonderful sensation. But how could they emit it? They were more intelligent than expected. She had little experience with fire elementals and had to push down her questions and curiosity, refocusing on her mission as the jackets hauled the ripper away.

Quickly she worked her way between the crates and jars, looking for any symbol or evidence on them. They all seemed to be general items except the glass that was used to contain the flame creatures. Imported from the Court of Copper, this glass was stronger than the glazed windows and had become popular. It must've been made specifically to not melt in the fire page. She tucked a piece of the shattered glass into her scarf and kept looking.

Fiona opened the drawers of the desk. Empty. She felt around the top and then ducked underneath. The flame sprite bobbed behind her, showering a glow on a neat slim brown leather journal attached to the underside.

She quickly pulled it from the desk and flipped through it. Lists were scrawled across most of the pages in a hurried hand. A thud came from the front room and voices got closer. Sliding the journal into a soft embroidered pocket in her scarf, she felt it leave her hands and then disappear. The ledger would be more valuable given to her client than sitting in a dusty inventory box at the Travel Guild.

A couple of jackets clattered into the room. Fiona waved. "Just the crates and cages in here, mind you. Help me with them?"

The jackets glanced at each other but luckily were saved from having to decide what to do with Fiona as Dodger pushed his way through.

Fiona put on her best smile to ease her next words. "I'm going to take the flame sprite and the other fire creatures back."

Dodger nodded to the other jackets, dismissing them. He waited till the door closed before saying quietly, "Come on, Fi. You know that's our job."

Her smile disappeared. She stood up straighter and arched an eyebrow. "Yes, but you see, you owe me because I involved you. The Guild would've never found these men if it wasn't for me." She wasn't going to relent, but she softened her tone, reminding herself that Dodger was her friend. "I promised this one I'd get it back safely. If I'm making the trip, I might as well take the others with me."

He glanced at the many crates and cages and tugged at his whiskers. "Fine. The point is to get the pulp all back to their rightful pages, I suppose."

Fiona nodded. "You're a good jacket, Dodger."

Dodger rolled his eyes, shoulders relaxed, but his tail swished to the side. "I don't even want to comment with you on what makes a bad jacket. Here." He opened his vest to reveal a bandolier of vials with swirling variations of color, dark to light. He grabbed a shimmering gold one and handed it to Fiona.

"Thank you," she said and turned toward the crates and cages, avoiding his gaze. She hadn't meant to bring up the sore subject and didn't want to argue with him today. She was grateful, really, that he had come to her aid when she had asked. She couldn't have captured the rippers without him. Or at the very least, not so quickly.

She picked up a couple of containers and began hauling them out of the house. It wouldn't do to release them all inside—the house would go down in fire for sure. While a small sprite could be easy to manage, several fire elementals would be a catastrophe this side of Spine.

Not considered a page itself because it didn't stack the way the others did, Spine connected to every page in the Book. Some thought it was because of the page turners who were bound to live here. Others thought it was a world overlooked by Larrakane, the deity who gave people the ability to travel between pages. Either way, Spine was home to every turner in the Book. It had to be, as the gift to walk the pages came with the inability to tarry too long away from Spine. It operated as a large city with over a dozen districts in the tract of land that made up the livable area.

During her mandatory turner training, Fiona had heeded the lectures of the importance of coming home to Spine. Getting stuck outside of Spine for too long was like falling into a lake too cold for comfort, the body never matching the temperature of the lake as teeth chattering and hypothermia set in. A pain much worse than that and longer lasting too. Fiona believed it. She didn't need to test it herself to see the effects on older turners who didn't have training and had to figure it out on their own.

The jackets moved in, helping to clear out the back room as Fiona took her charges out into the cool night air. She loaded the crates and glass jars quickly onto a wooden handcart from the side of the house. This area, her home district, was small compared to other districts in the city but centralized, and it wasn't yet heavily under watch by the Guild. After this capture, she was sure they'd put a few jackets in the area to ward off any other rippers thinking it was a safe haven.

She knew it was necessary for the well-being and travel of turners to have a network of support. But the Travel Guild moved with the regimented stiffness of an army, and no amount of showboating would assure her they weren't corrupt. They regulated any job that touched being a turner, like tour guides. They tried to have a post in just about every page that would allow them. They made her job as an investigator harder than it needed to be. Anytime she tried to work on a case that might have some tie to the Guild or influential people in another page, they had slapped a rule or regulation on her that made it impossible without giving them all her information or money. So often she avoided the Guild like a plague. Dodger was the only one connected to them she even acknowledged these days.

She hadn't always been an investigator. She used her curiosity to delve into the other pages and often took people with her to safe locations as a tour guide. It was an easy, if competitive, way to earn a living as a turner, but working for the Guild wore her down over the brief time she had done it. She enjoyed being her own boss and doing what she knew was best for her clients.

Or at least, what was best in the moment.

And one day she'd have what she needed to expand her agency, take on more clients, and really start making a difference in the world around her.

Fiona stretched her arms and pulled her many-textured scarf down from her head. Its rough cotton and smooth silk patches brushed against her goose-bumped skin. She let it pool over her chest and stomach and tied it tight, securing it into the waistband of her hose. Its secrets were held safely in its various dimensional pockets. She always wondered which page the pockets all went to but so far had been unsuccessful in mapping them all. It was one of a kind, given to her by her father, the only authority figure she had ever really trusted, and though she didn't understand all of its depths, she cherished it nonetheless.

Fiona called out in rough Claire to the various glass containers: "Not too long before you're home." She trotted back to the pagemark where the ripper had turned the page within the woods. She tried to determine just where in Blaze it would take her. She hadn't traveled often to the fire page and an unofficial pagemark was cause for some concern, but seeing as how the ripper had come through unharmed, she was interested in where it connected with Spine.

The rain had let up, but the fierce, frigid wind had not. The flame sprite swirled in the air above her head, bathing their path in a flickering light. They were a cozy little creature, and she wished she could touch them, shelter them from the wind.

The pulp remained silent. These had to be various beasts of Blaze. None of them spoke besides the sprite. If any of them were page turners like herself, they would've tried to leave already, regardless of whether it was safe or not. Fiona moved faster, pulling the burdened cart with what little strength she had to their destination so she could get them home. While fire creatures were lucky (or luckier than water beings) and could live outside of their page for a short while without help, she knew it wasn't comfortable. There weren't many places in the Book of Larrakane where elementals could easily thrive outside of their own page without accommodations. It's another thing that made Spine. Each turner, no matter which page they were from, had a piece of their home here since it was connected to them all. There was really nowhere else like it.

Fiona finally set down the cart at the pagemark. She ran her hands across her scarf until she came to a leather pocket slightly damp from her sweat and pulled from it a spray atomizer bottle with only a few spoons of a shimmering black liquid inside. She doused herself liberally with the mixture, its sticky spray settling on everything she owned.

She took off her slippers and placed them in a pocket of soft lavender velvet on her scarf, then pulled out thick black boots that clashed against her outfit and were scratchy against her hose. From the same leather pocket she took out a long, thick cloak made from crushed lava rock and mud-imbued fibers original to Blaze. It, too, was scratchy like crushed gravel but a necessity. She shook it out and put it on, fastening the clasps to make sure it wouldn't move and covered her scarf completely. Next she unstoppered the vial Dodger gave her and drank the potion swiftly. Making a face (ash, it always tasted like ash and mineral), she tucked the empty vial into her doublet under the cloak. Lastly she pulled from the leather pocket a thin set of glasses, which she fit snuggly to her face. She pushed them up on her brow for now.

Patting herself to make sure she was fully covered, she looked up at the flame sprite. "You've got quite the easier journey here, you know. We all have to be touching since you're out of the jar. Hold on to me." She motioned to her cloaked arm.

The creature danced on the arm of the cloak, and Fiona smiled. They really were a charming creature. Grabbing on to the side of the cloak, she ran her fingers over the material. It was her bookmark to turn the page to Blaze so that she went there and not a completely different page like the Court of Copper or something.

She hadn't been to Blaze in some years due to its usual inhabitability for non-fire natives. In order to turn the page there, she had to focus on the elemental chapter first (the easiest way to group page types), then the page itself. Turning the page wasn't a science but an art form that one had to practice over time to gain any level of precision.

With confidence she connected to Blaze. Its hot air trickled across her skin. The odor of sulfur filled her nostrils. She bound the thrum of the cloak, herself, the handcart, and the flame sprite to her destination. Staying perfectly still, she blocked out the sounds of Spine and listened for the burble of lava. She gave it a moment. One deep breath in. One deep breath out.

The world around her folded in on itself. The familiar Spine wind gave way to intense heat, and she saw the darkened, smoky sky before her. She took a step toward the blackened world, turning from one page to the next.

SCORCHING FLAMES CONSUMED EVERYTHING that wasn't guarded against the roaring inferno. The splashing and rushing of lava falls could be heard from every corner. Sulfur and choking smoke permeated the air. It was hellish to a few and home to many.

There were three layers, like the colors of a sunset laid one on top of the other, in Blaze. The boiling basin roiled with tar-like lava flowing unabated. Sitting on top of the basin was the cap, shifting volcanic rock that most of the cities sat upon as well as the massive volcano that created it. And high above, blocked by fire, ash, and smoke, was A'shar. She didn't know much about that layer, having never been to it, but bright white light radiated down from there and highlighted small aspects of the page. Like rays through the blockade of fire and tangible curled gray fumes. Where the vast layers ended there was the ink-black nothingness of the page's edge.

But then one day the flames dimmed. It was slowly becoming a wasteland of cooled lava rock and settled ash, the sky no longer filled with flame too scary for tourists—or skimmers, as page turners mockingly called them—to visit. The leaders of the page had been trying to figure out for weeks why the fire was waning. It was crucial to most of their survival and kept the page a nearly unbreachable oasis for them.

Without the proper equipment, even turners had been unable to access Blaze. With the page torn as it was now, it was all too easy for rippers to come in, terrorize, and steal creatures without the strength to fight against them.

How long until the embers died down? A few more weeks? A season? Blaze was dead. The Blazing Wastes, more like it.

Fiona tested breathing in the noxious air without choking. It had the tang of mineral but was harmless with the potion Dodger had given her. When she opened her mouth, ash lightly landed on her tongue and dissolved into a gritty paste. She spit it out. "Really didn't need to end my day with that." She pushed the glasses down over her eyes and blinked a few times, adjusting to the view. The world was a bit easier to see through the lenses. The dark a little brighter, the flames a bit dimmer. Oh, to be a human in Blaze.

The surrounding landscape was a rocky outcrop in the middle of nowhere. Steps, manmade from the looks of them, led down and away from the plateau into the distance. It was not a bad place for a pagemark. Open, devoid of major obstructions, and solid. Lined up nicely with Spine. She had been to worse in other pages. No wonder it was being used by rippers. The Guild would probably take it over as soon as they could.

She hurriedly removed the lids from the jars and small crates in the handcart. Even without an ongoing fire, it wouldn't do to stay in Blaze too long. The heat eroded everything. The cart itself was already slightly smoking, and she tsked at herself, feeling like a blotter for not protecting it from the element.

As soon as they were freed, the elementals soared off without a backward glance. While some had amorphous orange and red fiery shapes like the sprite, there were a couple of small smoke-gray creatures she could've sworn were rats. A creature no bigger than her arm with a scaly hide hurried off into the distance on four short, squat legs. "Hmm, maybe a firesnake?"

The flame sprite danced into her view. The wisps of their body and smoldering fire took on a small humanoid shape.

Fiona smiled at the fire sprite as they hovered near her. "Goodbye, little one."

:Stay!: the creature said in a crackling rasp.

"I can't live here," Fiona said, gesturing to the surrounding area. "I breathe differently than you." It was a sweet thought and a bit unexpected for her.

:Stay.: the creature said again. They flew to Fiona and sat gently on her arm.

They weighed barely anything, more like adding a feather on top than a living being. Fiona looked at the dimmed light of the creature and tilted her head. Curious being, this one. While all the others ran immediately, this one wanted to stick around her.

They moved up Fiona's arm, tendrils of flame wrapping around her forearm like a bracelet. :Stay?:

Fiona became still and stopped fidgeting. She didn't think they were trying to hurt her, but she had never been so close to a fire elemental like this before. The way they were acting was peculiar. "You want to stay with me?"

The flame sprite spun their thin form around her arm in a circle. Wisps of flame shot off from them at all angles.

"But what about your family? Your friends?"

:Gone,: the creature crackled. Sadness emanated from the little fire dancer, washing over Fiona.

"Oh." She hadn't expected. She nodded slowly. What was she supposed to say? She was used to being on her own, or she was on her own and made use of it. Often she figured it was both. In order to make a difference as an investigator she had to work hard, constantly, and that didn't leave a lot of time for friends or family. "I move around a lot, you know, being a turner and all. I'll probably never really be at home."

The sprite flew off her arm and landed on her shoulder. Pinpricks of heat pushed against the protective barriers of Fiona's clothing and the solvent she had sprayed. It wasn't uncomfortable but a warm caress. The light was brighter this close, but the glasses protected her sight.

Would it really put her out to let the sprite stay with her? They would go home eventually once Blaze was sorted out, or to a more suitable district in Spine. But perhaps they weren't ready. She knew what that was like, dawdling about until you were prepared to take on the challenges ahead of you. Fiona twisted the fabric of the gloves in her hand and sighed. "You can stay with me for now. But you have to do as I say until we figure out a way for you to move about safely. It's too dangerous for you to follow me everywhere."

She realized in her puzzlement she had spoken in her human tongue. Before she could repeat it, the flame sprite swirled around her, emanating such a force of happiness that the cart immediately burst into fire.

Fiona jumped back and patted herself down lest she catch fire too. She stared at the cart, eyes wide. "Maybe we should make the 'safely moving about' part a priority for tomorrow, hmm?"

The sprite moved back to her arm and circled around her wrist like a bracelet. Fiona couldn't help but smile at the gesture and movement. Spending time with the sprite would be illuminating at least. She giggled internally at her pun.

"Right, back to Spine then." She looked at the cart as it sputtered a bit and collapsed. "Glad that wasn't a loan."

With the flame sprite on her person, Fiona turned her focus to going home. This was much easier than turning to another page. Spine needed no token for a page turner to find their way. It was like walking from the end of your footpath to the door of your home. Laid out, welcoming, and almost a bit of a relief depending on where you had been.

The world shimmered and folded in front of them. There was no time difference between the elemental chapter pages and Spine, thankfully. The rain was still holding off in the short while they had been gone. Fiona was conscious that without a jar for the sprite any drastic weather changes might be dangerous. She walked away from Blaze and back into the woods. The snap of the page closing behind her was barely noticeable, but the heat and smoke lingered around her for a moment. Moving quickly, Fiona strolled the same path she had skulked down earlier to home.

Fiona walked through the stone streets of Spine giving the sprite a tour. It was best to make them familiar in case they got separated, regardless of how long it may be around.

Although she felt a little foolish, she reasoned that if the sprite damaged anything and it came back to her, it was better to set expectations now.

"This is the turner district. It's where most of us turners live. I suppose we could live in other districts, but not many do," Fiona said rapidly, waving a hand at the various homes, cottages, and habitats on either side of the street. The oil lights flickered, and she noticed that a few places were already lit up. She must've spent more time following and tracking the smuggler than she thought. It was later than she normally stayed out.

The sound of rushing water from the aqueducts overhead made for a soothing background to their journey. The pipes were spread out far throughout the huge city, as the only source of water came from the plateau in the north.

"The piers are just down the side over there. If there's anywhere you should stay away from, mind you, it's the water. They lead you right up to Depth's Door, and it's basically mist and waterfalls from there on out." She pointed. "Those big beige tubes up above are the aqueducts. They're full of water, too, so don't get the foolish idea to go in one." She kept walking on with the sprite following above her. "I haven't talked to someone this much in weeks. I guess I was getting used to nattering on to myself."

:Natter?: said the sprite, confusion tingling into Fiona.

"Talking a bit and going on so. My mother used to say I nattered like a daft hen. But with enough practice I learned I could use that to my advantage. Distract people and the like."

The sprite bobbed to and fro as if they were enjoying the night air. She wasn't quite sure if they understood her, but she decided she had felt silly enough for one night.

Fiona stopped at a two-story brick house on the edge of the street. It was small in comparison to the grandiose marble-columned homes or the stone-walled keeps in the center of the district. The outside was almost an exact duplicate of the same manor houses from her native page. The carved wooden door's sign read, *Thorne Investigations. No Job Too Small. Inquire Within.*

She unlocked the door and opened it wide for the sprite to float in. Closing it behind her, she said, "I hope this is to your liking." She divested herself of her fireproof cloak, gloves, and shoes and padded into her home in bare feet.

The ramshackleness of the manor house always made her feel warm. She had modernized it when she purchased it dividing it up inside. It was cozy now and less like the homes from her native page. She liked that there weren't constant reminders of her childhood within this part of the city. Perhaps growing up in Spine had endeared the place to her. It made the inability to live outside of Spine less of a curse for Fiona than it was for other turners.

As Fiona walked through the open living room, its familiar musty smell enveloping her, she lit candles while the flame sprite bobbed behind her. She wasn't sure what they were doing or looking at, but as they weren't trying to land on anything, she let them be. It's not that she had anything valuable, but the memories of her life were priceless to her. The walls were decorated with souvenirs from various pages that she had toured throughout the Book. Tapestries of great moments in another civilization's history. Statues of historic figures from one page to another. And books, so many books. Fables, history, terrible poetry. It was all precious to her, not just because it was from another page—it was important to study and learn the other pages' culture and history; familiarity bred insight—but because she had picked it all out on her own.

Without the lightness Fiona used to skulk around during investigations, her feet thudded on the bare floor as she made her way to the front room office.

The office was perfunctory. She tried to keep it clean and professional at all times in case someone of note stopped by. None ever did, but she liked to be prepared. A desk for working, a chair for sitting, and a heap of things for coffee. There was no musty scent but a clean woody smell mingled with the roasted beans. Who couldn't love coffee? Fiona started the small wood-burning iron stove she had installed in the office for such things and boiled water while the sprite lingered around viewing things. They finally rested on the stove, making the water boil a touch faster.

"I suppose I'll have to get used to that for a bit." Fiona smiled easily.

With a full cup and a warm countenance she sat down at the bigger desk. When she lit the oil lamp, the flame sprite flew over her head and nestled on to the wick. Their glow caught the window panes of glass in a bright radiance that no candle could ever match.

"Oh. Well, you can stay there for the night if you want," Fiona said, leaning back in the small wooden chair and sipping her coffee. "Probably the safest place for you."

:Safe.: The sprite emanated pleasure, washing a wave of contentment over Fiona.

Fiona raised an eyebrow at the sprite. "I'm not used to creatures like you. Are there others in Blaze such as yourself?"

:One,: the sprite murmured.

Their sadness moved like a wave over her. "I know what it's like to be alone." Fiona stared into the shadows. "Sometimes you have to be on your own though. It makes you stronger." She stopped, hearing herself. Stronger, sure, but by whose standards? She ran her fingers through her thick curls, her face going warm.

:Friends?:

"Of course you can have friends. You just have to know who to trust, that's all. Being a turner can get a bit...weighty. There's nowhere we can't go. But there's also nowhere we can stay. A turner's not penned in by the page we were born on and we're free to travel to any page in the Book." She snorted. "Well, as free as you can be with the Travel Guild watching the comings and goings of everyone and charging a fee. But people expect everything from us, from our time to our knowledge. And the Book is vast. Not every turner will get the chance to walk all of its pages in the span of a lifetime." Although she certainly wanted to be one of the ones who did.

:Help!: The sprite's confidence was overwhelming.

The lamp flame burned brighter, and Fiona yelped. "Yes, you can help, but only if you don't burn the building down." She laughed, some of the somber mood evaporating.

There was a knock at the living room door, and Fiona stopped laughing quickly. It was incredibly late, or early if you were counting. Who would possibly think now was the time to visit her?

She quietly walked to the front door. In the window, with glass unlike some of her outdated neighbors', stood Dodger. She unlocked and opened the door.

"Dodger, what... What's wrong? Come in."

"Ah, nothing's wrong," he said, slinking into the house. He stood in the threshold rubbing the back of his neck, tail swinging side to side. "I was wrapping up the smuggling case and wanted to check that you got home alright."

Fiona shifted from one foot to another. "From Blaze? Yes, I made it back in one piece. The cart didn't, but..." She trailed off. He was acting so skittish. "Did something bad happen with the rest of the creatures?"

"No, no. We got them to the other pages safely. I just wanted to say, it was good to see you, Fi," he said in a low voice. He rushed on before she could respond. "I won't say you've been working too hard because I know that's frustrating. From one workhorse to another. Format has it you closed three cases last week alone. But you should make some time to enjoy yourself. Come around a bit."

"Are you saying you missed me?" she teased, skirting the subject of her workload.

Dodger fidgeted with his whiskers. "I'm saying I'm your friend. I'm around for when you're not working just as much as for when you are."

So he did think she was working too hard. But that was easy for him to say. He made an impact with every case he was handed at the Guild. That's just who he was. She had to stretch if she was ever going to have enough sway to really help people. Not just solve problems. She knew he didn't mean ill, but it was still irritating. She folded her arms. "I appreciate it. Thanks."

He glanced at her and took a step back. "Well, good night. Or, good morning."

Fiona opened the door and smiled to try and ease the tension. "Good morning, Dodger."

She closed the door behind his receding form and leaned against it. Sighing, she ignored the tightness of guilt in her chest mixed with the warmth of gratitude. The only way she got better as an investigator was to focus on doing the work. A few years ago it was just a small dream, but now she was really gaining traction.

She wouldn't have gotten the smuggling case if she hadn't worked with a previous client to find her missing book shipment. That job wouldn't have come to her if she hadn't returned a missing cat. And so on.

She plodded her way back into the office, where the flame sprite was still curled up in the lamp. She reached into her scarf and pulled out the slim dark book she had taken from the smuggler's house. It was formatted like a ledger. She used them herself, but this one was filled with a language she didn't understand tucked in among human words in an odd order. She tugged on her scarf, glancing at page after page of unclear writing, trying to decipher some meaning.

"Whatever they're tracking, I can't make heads or tails of it. I was hoping this would tell me more about the sudden increase in rippers." Her eyes burned, and she rubbed them, yawning. "I'll give this another go later before going to give an update."

She made a mental note to copy the front page so she wasn't traveling with the book and added it to the desk drawer alongside her journal, inks and quills. Locking them up, she turned from the room, calling out over her shoulder, "Good night, little one," and padded up the stairs to bury her head under the covers for some much-needed shut-eye.

FULL DAYLIGHT RADIATED LIKE a beam directly into Fiona's
eyes, making her wince. Grasping with one hand for her
pocket clock that was slung across the wooden chair next
to her bed, she covered her face with the feather pillow in
her other. Her fingers found the chain, and she pulled it to
her, barely peeking from under the pillow to look at the time.
Squinting, she made out the numbers. She was late. Later
than late. Throwing the pillow to one side of the room, she
hopped up, muttering under her breath about early birds and
lost worms.

She danced from one foot to the other, pulling on her hose
and semi-regretting not sticking with the long dresses or
belted tunics humans wore in her native page. They were just
so...open. Climbing through a window in a dress wasn't easy.
She much preferred the hose and doublets that the faekin from
the Court of Copper wore, although she wasn't as fashionably

attired as they tended to be. Hers were wool where theirs were silk. Pairing it with the soft slippers of the nobility and her scarf, Fiona legged it down the stairs. Larrakane help her if she couldn't get a carriage this time of day.

The smell of burnt paper stopped her in her tracks just before she reached the door. She sniffed the air and headed straight into the office to see a pile of ash and soot sprinkled on the desk where last night a few books had sat. Inside the green glass lamp sat the sprite, who bounced around the chamber and then rocketed out toward Fiona.

:Awake!: said the sprite with evident joy.

"Yes, awake. And late. What sort of bind is this?" Fiona said, motioning to the mess. The books had been on loan from the library, and she groaned at the thought of trying to explain this.

:Hungry.:

"Odd, I didn't think elementals needed to eat." Fiona inspected the desk but didn't see any further damage. "You can't just eat anything you like. I'll set something out for you now that I know. In a safe spot. On the stove."

:Sorry.:

"It's okay." She sighed. "They're just books." *At least they weren't mine.*

Fiona grimaced, then remembered what she was supposed to be doing and made toward the office door. "Just stay here until I get back, hmm? I'm visiting a client, and I don't think these particular people would be happy if I brought you along."

:Stay?:

"Yes." Fiona grabbed a piece of wood and thrust it on the stove. "Please," she added in a softer tone. She wasn't used to this much drama right out of bed.

The sprite hurtled over to the stove and with great attention consumed the wood, surrounding it with flames and wisps until it was nothing but ash and black powder. Fiona cocked her head, impressed at how quick the little creature was, and rubbed her face.

"Is it okay if I give you a name? I can't keep going around calling you little one."

:Name.:

"How about Soots? It's easy and I don't know anyone else with it."

:Soots!: The sprite emanated joy. The room grew warmer, and Fiona winced, pulling on the high neckline of her doublet for a little air.

"Soots it is. But do try not to burn the place down while I'm gone." Glancing at her clock again, Fiona threw open the door to find her view blocked by a large wing. It was radiant. The feathers were outlined in tendrils of smoke and white-hot fire. Stretched out as it was, the wing seemed more a wall of crimson with golden flecks than part of a creature.

Shading her face from the bright light, Fiona jumped back. The heat was oppressive. Before she could utter a word, the light behind her hand faded and a cooler atmosphere overtook the small entryway. Peeking, she saw a massive golden-plumed bird flying within the doorway.

Swallowing her surprise, she said, "Can I help you?"

The creature flew past Fiona into the office with a swiftness for their size that made her mouth drop. For a brief moment she felt the warmth of the creature and jerked away, but they were up in the ceiling of the room before it could burn. Switching to Claire, she said, "Excuse me. Can I help you?"

The bird stretched their wings, taking up most of the ceiling space and making a formidable sight. "I am the Ashborn. Has one such as yourself not heard of me?"

Their voice was less a crackle like Soots's and more a roar in Fiona's ears. She winced but covered it quickly. Of course she had heard of the Ashborn: a phoenix alive before the first page turner had been inked some two hundred years ago, long, long before there had been other creatures in Blaze, their native page. The only one of their kind. She had heard that they died and returned at least once every century, but no one knew how or why. They were rumored to have a great memory, but she hadn't known anyone who could speak to it on authority.

Intrigued, Fiona closed the door, all thoughts of her delayed appointment gone from her mind. Having a creature like the Ashborn in her presence was a wonder she couldn't pass up. Curiosity ran through her like water through the aqueducts. Moving quickly, she looked around for something not valuable for the Ashborn to sit on, but almost all the furniture she owned was wooden in some nature, minus the stove. Fire denizens being outside their page was something she had not really prepared for.

With delicate care, the Ashborn settled themself in the air near the iron stove as if reading Fiona's thoughts. The heat baking off of them warped her view, everything a bit fuzzy.

"I'm sorry, Your Eminence," she said, using a word from her native page she hoped would be fitting, "I was surprised. That is all."

They looked to her expectantly, copper eyes like a sunset peering at her, unmoving.

She took a chair from her desk and sat down nearer the stove, giving the Ashborn their audience. Sweat started to bead at the nape of her neck, but she ignored it. *I wonder what they want.*

"Blaze is susceptible to more onslaught than we have previously encountered," the Ashborn launched in. "I have watched over the world as befits my station. However, a crime has been committed that is more than I can abide."

Fiona started to ask questions, but a dramatic wing sliced through the air and she realized the Ashborn was not done.

"Nay, *abide* is too small a sentiment for the atrocity that has befallen me. A stone of great import has been removed from my sanctuary. I have come to your domicile to implore you to retrieve it for me."

Fiona was floored. She tried to gather her quickly swirling thoughts. "I'm honored, but—"

"Nay." They gestured again, outstretched wing knocking wind and warmth toward Fiona. "*Implore* is weak. I charge you with this job, as it has come to my attention that you are no foe to my kind. I know you will not object to such a charge."

"Well, no, I couldn't possibly—"

"Absolutely. Who would reject such an honorable request from one such as myself? And to achieve this insurmountable goal within a week's time is extremely brave of you. You have mettle in your down. That is unquestionable."

"Thank you, Ashborn. It is—"

"Perhaps you wonder where you should begin your investigation? I have laid great thought into a suitable area of start for you. Blaze itself, certainly. The salamanders, the ragnis, and the flarions are all particular groups worthy of being looked into. I take no sides, you understand."

"Of course. But this stone—"

"Yes. The Blackstone flickers with the light of a thousand flames. I have been most judicious in my guarding of it, but lo, it has been taken from my home in Radiance Peak." The Ashborn thrust a wing toward Fiona. "I offer a position within my realm befitting a fire native once it is retrieved. You deserve no less for taking on so perilous and secretive a request." The Ashborn dived, their massive hulk becoming a slight blur, and settled back on the other side of Fiona by the door. "And now I take my leave of you." They looked at her expectantly as only one could who has done it all their life.

Fiona leaned back, unaccustomed to being cut off so rudely. She had her share of royal requests when she was younger, but this one was by far the most obnoxious. Still, the Ashborn was a prominent figure, not only in the history of Blaze but as the only creature of their kind. Perhaps she could bargain for more than just another tie binding her to the whims of a second ruler. She stopped nervously rubbing her scarf and stood, drawing herself to her full height till she wasn't looking too far up to the phoenix. "As I was saying, Your Eminence. I am honored, but I can't take your request at this moment. Far too busy."

The Ashborn ruffled their feathers, fire rippling out. The room got a touch warmer. "You mean to say you would turn down a respectable request from one such as myself? The chance at rank and glory? Absurd."

Pushing off the desire to just give in, she looked away slightly as if unconcerned. "Be that as it may," Fiona said, making her way to the door, "I definitely am." It was a gamble betting on the Ashborn's assurance that she would take the job. But if Fiona had learned anything in her twenty-nine years, it was knowing a self-possessed leader when she saw one.

The Guild could handle it, but they would ask for better pay. Rank and glory were nothing to her. She needed to remain free from ties that could bind her to a power she couldn't direct while she worked to expand her reach. Information and connections were more her speed.

She opened the door and basked in the brief moment of cool air. A fire elemental of amorphous shape floated at the edge of the stone walk as if waiting. Fiona nodded to the phoenix and said, "I hope you have an excellent day." *Now we'll see if I've blundered or intrigued. I'm sure they don't often hear no.*

The Ashborn didn't move. They seemed to grow a bit in size, but that could've been Fiona's imagination. Fiona kept smiling. The Ashborn kept staring. After a moment they said, "As you can ascertain, I have lived many lives within the Book and learned of much through my own ways. Perhaps I could pay you with knowledge of high value?"

Fiona narrowed her eyes. "Are you reading my mind?" Their suggestion was too close for comfort, and although there were rumors of the Ashborn's abilities, they may not cover everything about them.

"Minds are not so easily hidden as one would think. Come, name your price to fulfill this request."

Fiona leaned awkwardly away from the phoenix, trying to see whether they had some ill intent, but she couldn't hazard a guess. While the phoenix reminded her of native birds from her original page, they clearly weren't one. She had a hard time reading them. Besides money, she couldn't think of a thing she needed that this flame creature could possibly provide, but that didn't mean there wouldn't be one in the future.

"A favor," she said.

"A favor?" the Ashborn replied, golden head raised.

"One day I will come to you and ask for something, and you will have to do it. That is my price."

The Ashborn rose a few inches in the air, light warmth radiating from them. The wooden wall behind them creaked. "Easily done. You shall have a favor from me after you successfully procure my stone."

A light giddiness filled her, but she pushed it aside. "And how will I know you'll keep up your end?"

The air grew still, and a crackle hissed through the room before a *whoof* sounded behind them. Fiona could taste ash in the air and swallowed past a lump in her throat. Perhaps she had pushed too far. "Apologies, I am used to dealing in contracts and documents. I believe your word is solid."

Without any perceptible agreement, the Ashborn darted off into the lane and away from her home, the brightness of the day magnified by their golden flamed plumage.

Fiona turned and dashed to the wooden chair that had caught fire. Soots was busy engulfing it in their own flames, and Fiona felt the contentment from the creature. She poured water on the floor around the remaining pieces of the chair nonetheless, careful not to splash the flame sprite. Some modifications would have to be made to her office soon.

Soots floated up and around as she dampened the floor.

She sighed. "Have you ever met the Ashborn before?"

:Many,: Soots said with the confidence of familiarity.

"Ah." It felt odd, but the one word from the sprite spoke volumes. She tried to grasp it, but the sight of a carriage meandering down the lane reminded her of her previous plans. "Here I am standing like a blotter, looking at the sky, as if I'm not late." She shooed Soots back inside, gave a quick glance to the room lest anything else be on fire from the Ashborn, and retrieved the smuggler's journal from the locked desk. She had no time to make a copy. "It's just like me to be late with a great reason but unable to explain it to anyone."

She would have to mull over what the Ashborn said and extract necessary steps from it. Whether she could do the job justice, she'd have to figure out later. Thinking over what just happened and how she had gotten into it so quickly, Fiona made her way to Forest's Edge to meet up with her client.

FOREST'S EDGE WAS THE district that acted as home to the druids of Spine. Secretive they were, yes. Huge fans of nature, of course. The only druids in the Book? Oddly, yes. When turners started coming to Spine, bound as they were to the city, a few things greeted them. Archae, the first page turner, eventual creator of the Travel Guild, and current Binder in charge of it. A rough landscape of hills, valleys, lakes that they could see for miles around, surrounded by a never-ending forest. And the druids. No one really messes with the druids of Spine. No one's sure how to become one, but some wish they could. They were a fixture as old as Spine itself.

On foot, getting to the Edge took hours. Fiona wished she could rent a chariot. It would have been so much faster, but the things were only used by the Travel Guild. Ah well. The druids disliked the things immensely.

The chariot was a recent import from the Kerus page, where Dodger and the other smilodons came from. One of six pages in the earthly chapter of the Book, it was home to a few more species Fiona, as a human, considered barely like the animals she was familiar with. The smilodons always had an eye for innovation, as long as their ruler requested it. Not big thinkers for themselves, those cats, unless they hid it well. The chariot traveled faster than people on foot or loaded-down carriages, but only in certain areas where the horses could run on stone-paved streets. She had always wanted to try driving one.

Fiona ran down the lane to a carriage stand where a few smilodons, their tails kept low so as not to sweep the body of another person, and a gray elephas stood waiting in their daily finery. Elephas were from Kerus as well and resembled a typical elephant (although walking upright and not on all fours) to most humans. Of course it was impolite to compare, and over the centuries the elephas proved to be anything but typical. This one was casually dressed in swathes of creams and mauve silks with large bronze belts tying their ensemble together. A matching ring of bronze adorned the end of their trunk, which they held nonchalantly up in the air and away from the smilodons. A skimmer heading to the market district no doubt.

Since turners were anchored to Spine, it was also a grand travel center for skimmers who wanted to go on holiday to another page or a sight-seeing tour. It was easy to tell a turner from a skimmer, be they human, smilodon, elephas, or even elemental. A skimmer was overdressed, oblivious, and typically had a guide in their hand or paw.

But skimmers brought business not just to turners but to those who could accommodate them. Since the Blessing of Larrakane created page turners, Spine had seen other people settle in as well. People from many pages, earthly and elemental, came to set up shops, begin new lives, get a fresh start. And the Travel Guild took at least a three percent cut from it all, making sure it ran well and was protected. Such was business and life in Spine.

At the stand slightly out of breath, Fiona checked to make sure all her things were together. Feeling discombobulated and a touch peckish, she looked around for a quick food vendor.

Stepping off the side of the road toward a food stall, she pulled a few papers out of her pocketed scarf and waited in line for what smelled like home. Buttery, flaky meat pies. The vendor, a stocky balding man with pale skin, was serving them up from a wooden cart window. He was waving one around, emphasizing his point as he talked to a customer.

"It's always the same with them rock heads," he said, jerking the brown-paper-wrapped pie. Crumbs flew out of the paper as his face reddened.

"You suppose the new hall will ever get built?" said the woman reaching her hand out for her purchased meal. She almost made contact before the vendor waved it to emphasize his next point.

"Not if ya have to depend upon gnomes in the slightest. Lazy workers, that stone guild. Every last one of 'em."

Honestly, acting as if the creatures were lazy when they were constantly working to provide materials to all the other pages. Fiona glared at the man and piped in, "They're able to mine twice the amount of stone as anyone else, actually. And furthermore, the stone guild has more than gnomes in it."

Three heads swiveled toward Fiona. The vendor, the lady who used this as an opportunity to snatch her meal from his stilled hand, and an elephas in a long tan tunic who, up until this point, had been looking a bit uncomfortable. The lady moved away at a brisk pace while Fiona held her papers up for the vendor to take.

The vendor raised an eyebrow. "And they use that importance to dally and delay when they please. New guildhall was supposed to be ready to start building this week. Format has it their stone production's been down the last few weeks. Betcha they got a contract for higher pay and are stringing the Guild along."

"The gnomes don't get paid," Fiona said slowly, "so that wouldn't even make sense."

"It's true," the elephas ventured with a thin grimace. "They work based on absolutely archaic rules because the materials are in their way of living. It's a system that needs to be vastly redone."

Fiona nodded in agreement, noting the Larrakane clerical emblem on the elephas's clothing. She turned back to the vendor. "Perhaps it's best not to spread rumors and stick to what you know."

The vendor grumbled something Fiona wished she didn't understand in her common tongue. She took the flaky pot pie and stepped away, biting into it. His food was good, but his thinking was crude. She'd make a note not to buy from him again.

Demolishing the rest of the small meal, she stepped into the large open-air carriage. The seats were deep and large to accommodate many people, and she fiddled with her scarf as she sat back in one. She began to think a bit clearer about the oddity of the Ashborn hiring her to retrieve the Blackstone. They hadn't particularly asked her name or even seemed inclined to care for one.

Why not go to the Guild? It was a part of what they did, after all. Unless the Ashborn didn't want to pay their higher and higher fees. She was a cheaper option, but how had the Ashborn known about her in the first place? So many questions she hadn't gotten a chance to ask. Next time she'd regain her wits quicker.

She'd have to figure out the best way to go about this. It could be dangerous digging around the denizens of Blaze without more information. Though the Ashborn was held in high regard by most who knew of them, they were still only one ruler in a fiery sea of rulers there.

There was a clang at the carriage door, and the elephas in the tan tunic ambled his bulk into the massive carriage. The smilodons were squeezed between the other elephas, so without more than a thought Fiona motioned to the seat beside her.

"Thank you," he said, voice a deep drawl from beneath his trunk. A light scent of butter wafted as he spoke, and crumbs stuck to the edge of their trunk as if he had hurriedly eaten too.

"Of course." She smiled brightly. Now that he was up closer, she could see clearly a black circle of embroidery on his clothes and belt. The circle was made up of other circles, but she couldn't tell how many without staring. He wasn't just a cleric of Larrakane but one of the Followers, a subset of the church housed in Spine specifically of turners intent on using their ability for Larrakane's wishes. Or what they interpreted her wishes to be, like protesting the new guildhall.

Fiona believed in Larrakane—who wouldn't, with her history of showing off—but thought the Followers a bit preachy. Still, anyone who tried to do some good with the ability to walk the Book was alright by her.

"The name's Fiona. Fiona Thorne."

"Fali of Spine," he said, hairless eyebrows crinkling as he smiled.

"Nice to meet you. Are you on your way to the market then?" she asked lightly. The market district was next to where the new guildhall was supposed to be built. It would squeeze the temple district, removing any future chance of their expanding. The area of the Travel Guild was quite large as it was and butted up against the temple district at the center of Spine.

Though the Church of Larrakane showed up as soon as Spine was settled, it didn't take long for the two organizations to butt heads on how the city should be run. Though both organizations had been started by page turners and publicly said they were in reverence of Larrakane, they worked in two entirely different manners.

Fali's smile fell, and Fiona could see him putting his guard up. "Perhaps. Are you a jacket?"

"Do I seem like I work for the Guild?"

"You have the air."

"That's just my natural aura," she said, waving her hand nonchalantly. "But no. I'm not."

Fali moved his trunk up high and out of the open-air carriage. He leaned back, appraising her. "You're an investigator."

He was either perceptive or gossipy. She inclined her head. "And you didn't always work for the temple, did you?" she said, sidestepping the question and poking. She could be curious and dodgy at the same time.

Fali leaned back as well as he could in the deep leather seat. "No, I did not." He didn't offer anything more. Although he had said it quietly, it was not with any animosity and Fiona realized he was enjoying their tiny tête-à-tête.

"Are the protests going well?"

"Work has stopped, hasn't it?"

"That it has, but was it the work of the Followers or the lack of materials?"

"Every blessing counts the same," Fali said, a smile on his wide mouth.

"I see," Fiona said, unsure of what to think. He had stuck up for the gnomes and called their unpaid work archaic. But he was so…hedgy. All the Followers she had ever met couldn't wait to expound on their work. She lapsed into silence, chewing on the meaning of Fali's words. Perhaps she needed to watch the Followers more closely. The Guild couldn't be the only organization with their own officers.

The carriage stopped to let out the well-dressed skimmers and Fali in the ever-busy market district. It was packed with pulp from all pages in the Book. Skimmers and traders came from all around to shop and sell goods and services here. She could hear a few people hawking guide maps to the elemental pages and underwater gear, the sizzle of meat underscoring it all. The fragrances of incense, fresh herbs, and sugar clashed in the air together with hot stone and mud from the damp ground.

Fiona couldn't remember the last time she had wandered around the market. Case after case had kept her preoccupied, but now as they stopped she had an itch to delay her meeting just a little bit more and grab a brief saunter to see what news had come in from throughout the Book.

"It was nice to meet you," Fali said, breaking into her thoughts.

She pulled back from the window and blinked, focusing on him. "You as well."

He smiled and nodded. "If you ever need a priest, you know where to find me."

"That I do." Fiona waved as the carriage pulled away, empty now save for herself. Fali was clearly someone of talent. She wondered just what he was working toward.

The driver swung his head in the window of the carriage, noting Fiona still within. "Where to then?"

"Forest's Edge, please."

"Are you one of them druids?" said the driver, eyeing Fiona suspiciously.

"Just a visitor," Fiona said lightly, sitting back.

The driver harrumphed. "Right then." And disappeared from the window. He tsked the horses into a brisk trot and muttered, "Judgy lot of 'em, druids."

The rest of the city started to speed by under the lighter weight of the carriage and the pounding of the horses. Since most of Spine was made up of districts and most people in them pulp, each district was more distinct than the page turners' area by far. Immigrants lived in mostly separate neighborhoods where they kept their traditions, architecture, and more from their page together for a slice of home. Those eager to shed their pasts lived closer to the Travel Guild's corridor and headquarters, Larrakane's temple, or the market in the center of Spine.

The carriage rolled to a stop, the sweaty geldings that drew it stamping their feet. They were on the outskirts of Little Cobbles, the district closest to Forest's Edge. Nothing went into the druids' area they didn't approve of, and this included most modes of transportation.

Little Cobbles was a portion of Spine dedicated to all the earth elementals, gnomes, and other earth natives who came from the Cobbles page. Fiona wasn't sure who all lived here. Gnomes never left their page. The few earth elementals who were turners were hard to tell apart from the surrounding area. It was no more than a rocky outcropping. But since it was built by earth dwellers for earth dwellers, she hoped it felt like home to them. It also had the distinction as a known pagemark to Cobbles. Quite a few pagemarks had districts grown up around them to their specific pages.

Fiona jumped out of the dusty carriage, paid the driver a few papers, and gave a cheery wave to his frowning face. Frowning seemed to be the only face drivers knew when coming to Forest's Edge. She made a mental note to just say Little Cobbles next time.

As she strode to the druids' entrance, she marveled at how quickly the paths and nature changed. Broken stone streets gave way to dirt and vine tendrils snaking toward her destination. A bird—no, three—broke out in song as she meandered past. Their high-pitched warbling was like watching rainfall with a mug of warm coffee. Comforting.

The earthy and sweet cedar scent overtook the overwhelming smell of sweat and bodies that could be so pervasive in the city's heart. It was as if the forest was the only thing about Spine that was truly alive.

Fiona tugged on her scarf, straightening it to look a bit more presentable, and brushed invisible specks of dust off her clothing. She walked confidently up the untamed paths to the large forested structure.

The druids lived off the land for everything they had and gave it back to the land in abundance. The first building, and the only known way into the Edge, was entirely made of wood but not cut and stacked. There was an arch of pine branches and garland with doors carved into it. Cedar trees grew close together, and their branches and leaves intertwined to make an impassable wall.

Fiona took a deep breath, inhaling the nutty forest scents, assuring herself that she could handle this, that she had been handling it so far, and that she absolutely was not intimidated. She rapped on the carved wooden door, her solid thuds sounding muted in the quiet birdsong woods.

The door opened and golden light cracked out. A young ursidon's kindly bear face looked out. The ursidon was the last known species from Kerus with the smilodon and elephas, but there were fewer of them walking around Spine. Fiona bit back a startled sound at seeing one so unexpectedly at the druids' entrance. Though many of them were fighters and warriors, they were nature worshippers in general, so she supposed the shock was all on her.

Fiona gave a large smile, ignoring how uncomfortably dry her throat had gotten all of a sudden. "Good day. May I gain entrance? I have an appointment to speak with the Elder."

"The Elder waits for you," he said, voice soft as he opened the door wide.

The golden light cascaded against Fiona's dark-brown skin, embracing her as if in a warm bath, and she stepped inside to a sunny pavilion.

The ursidon inclined his head, stout nose almost to the ground, indicating to follow him. "Right this way."

Fiona followed, noting the soft click of the door behind her as it was locked. The druids didn't love visitors, but the precaution surprised her—a lock seemed very modern for them.

Through the entrance pavilion, many paths crisscrossed in a chaotic pattern, and Fiona could not make heads or tails of which went where. She knew better than to try, having been instructed in the proper manners of the druids' den. It was impolite to walk past your guide unless you were with the Elder themself.

Fiona followed his slow gait through the chosen path closer to the actual forest. The Elder's office and home was within a clearing on the crust of the forest. Sitting in a small circle outside of a tiny hut was the Elder. No one was quite certain if the Elder was human, faekin, or somehow both. And no one was going to ask, that was for sure. Their skin was a warm golden brown, much like an acorn. Their pine-green hair was braided softly to one side and tucked behind their overly large, wilting ear. The dark leather of their attire and blue linen shirt matched the ground below and sky above. Something about them, a thrum of energy perhaps, made them look as if they were ready to move at any moment.

The ursidon approached, head bowed, and stood waiting. Fiona stood perfectly still in the custom of waiting to be called. Nervous about how late she was, she hoped that it hadn't put the Elder too far off their schedule. It wasn't ceremony for ceremony's sake, she knew. Druids thought of time and priority a bit differently than others, although no one quite understood their ideals.

The Elder looked up and flashed a charming grin in Fiona's direction. "Dear Fiona. Please, come. Sit by my side."

The ursidon stepped back behind Fiona, and she walked forward to stand next to the Elder, looking out into the forest beyond. The trees were always green and so tall as to almost blot out the sky.

Fiona sat, the ground warm and cushioned with leaves. She let a moment of silence linger that could only come from being so close to the woods before saying, "Good afternoon, Elder."

"I am delighted to see you return. Good news, I hope," they said, sipping from a cup of coffee.

She licked her lips. "Some, yes. I was able to track down the rippers involved in the elemental smuggling as you requested. I let the Guild handle them, but I think there may be more in play."

The Elder raised an eyebrow. "Not isolated then? I had hoped it was just some ambitious fools."

"With the recent increase of rippers, I think it's a bit more organized than that," said Fiona. She tried to sound hopeful. "I do have a lead. I found this among their things. I think it's an inventory of creatures taken." Fiona pulled out the slim brown journal from a scarf pocket and handed it to the Elder.

Frowning, the Elder flipped through the pages of dark, splotchy writing. "Terrible. I wish we had caught wind of it earlier."

"I think—" She stopped to rephrase her sentence with more confidence. "I know I can figure out who is behind the increased push." It wasn't just one case. There were lives at stake. Creatures who didn't deserve to be taken from their home for who knows what.

"I'll look to you then on discovering that information." Sighing, they handed the journal back to Fiona. "Outside of Spine isn't particularly our area of management, but who could ignore something like this happening anywhere?"

The Guild, thought Fiona darkly. She pushed the thought aside, not wanting to give unfounded opinions to the druid leader. "I'll find out where this leads. You can count on that."

The Elder nodded crisply. "Format had it you were tenacious. I'm glad to see they were right."

Warmth spread through Fiona's body to know that people were saying good things about her. She pulled back from showing a smile on her face. She didn't want to seem smug in front of the Elder. If she could give the druids the leader behind the creature smuggling, then she really would have enough experience to wade into the types of cases that mattered. And possibly go toe to toe with the Guild one day.

"Thank you," Fiona said softly. She started to make her leave, but the Elder laid a light hand on her shoulder to stop her. Fiona worked to control her features and remained still, trying to assess if their next move would be negative.

"I heard that you've taken a new case from Blaze."

She tried to assess exactly what the look said. How in the world did the Elder already know of the Ashborn coming to see her? It wouldn't be impolite to ask, right? "Perhaps I have, depending on your source of information."

"Druids know of many things, dear," the Elder said with a disarming smile. "I've no doubt you'll uncover the missing stone in due time. I hope that when you do, you make every effort to return it to its rightful owner."

"I'll return it to the Ashborn, of course." Fiona said slowly.

"Certainly," the druid said. "The rightful owner will need it the most."

Fiona tilted her head, trying to read between the lines. "Are you saying the Ashborn isn't the rightful owner of this Blackstone?"

"Absolutely not. I would never say such a thing." The Elder removed their hand from her shoulder and picked up their drink. Nodding to themself, they continued, "Please, visit me again when you have a lead."

"I will." Although Fiona wasn't quite sure if they were talking about the stone or the stolen creatures. Perhaps both. She nodded her head again, slightly dazed, then got up as gracefully as she could and made her way to the ursidon to be escorted out of the druids' encampment.

No one messed with the druids of Spine. Fiona was grateful that at least they were on her side.

6

AFTER AN UNEVENTFUL WALK to Little Cobbles and another long carriage ride through the city, Fiona found her home not in flames, for which she was immensely grateful. Walking inside, however, she found Soots within the stove babbling loudly to themself.

"Soots, are you alright?" she said, kneeling down next to the stove.

The flame sprite was within a pile of ash, a soft amber ball of light. :Cold.: Soots emanated a sense of tiredness that almost overwhelmed her.

Fiona hurried to pull a giant log from the wood pile and tossed it into the stove. She hesitated for a moment before she struck a match and lit the stove. The impact of satisfaction from Soots was immediate. The small fire flared, and Soots danced inside of the stove, enjoying and mingling with the fire and burning wood.

"I'm so sorry. I didn't mean to leave you without warmth. You're the first fire elemental I've ever been around so close. Thank you for not leaving the stove and burning the house down." She rubbed her face, feeling awful. They had listened to her precisely, and she had left them without comfort. "I'll see what I can do for you today. Let me have some lunch and we'll head out to the artisan district."

Fiona puttered around in her kitchen fixing what was left in her cold storage. The kitchen was small, which was good enough for her. She wasn't often around enough to do any proper cooking and usually either ate on the go or grabbed what she could where she could. With the paper from the druids' payment she'd be able to take care of the house, which relaxed her a bit. She tried not to worry about paying for this or that, but sometimes the small jobs didn't add up.

After a spot of lunch, Fiona secured the elemental smuggler's ledger back in her desk drawer and headed out to the artisan district with Soots on foot. It was a lovely afternoon. The rushing water from the aqueducts overhead made for relaxing background notes as they walked on. Soots weaved in the air far above the people and houses, but Fiona could still see the flame sprite in the light. Their desire to see things swung over her as they whizzed to and fro. She hadn't realized how little she had seen of elementals who weren't humanoid outside their districts in Spine.

They went through the streets that were a bit less crowded so Fiona could keep an eye on Soots. Not many skimmers were out in this area, as it was a workday for Spine. The Blessing of Larrakane, the inking of the first page turner, threw the way life flowed in many different pages into chaos. Turners were hard pressed to know what time, day, or even season it was in various pages. It could be night on Spine, timeless in Blaze, and morning in Kerus. Decades of work helmed by the Travel Guild went into coming up with a calendar system that most of the pages could agree on, tracking from the inking of the first page turner and Larrakane's pronouncement to present day.

It was made quicker by the advent of diamonnette paper as a currency through the then-burgeoning little Guild. The diamonds were imported from Cobbles, as they were too hard to be easily crushed, melted, wetted, or torn. They formed the perfect travel currency when made into thread (Fiona never understood how that alchemical process worked) and crafted into paper. The Book more or less ran on Spine's time now. Whether that was fair or not she didn't hazard to guess.

The artisan district at the end of the avenue was only rivaled by the market district in sights and sounds. Large banners and signs organized each of the various sections into different types of materials or products made. Sculptures and artwork crowded the entrance on one side, while weavers and looms buffeted the other. Buildings here were permanent and showcased people who came to Spine to stay, work, and sell their wares. Smiths, crafters, and makers of all types from every page. A cacophony of banging, loud splashes, and crashes mixed within a swirl of smoke from one of the many iron smiths in the district. Fiona could practically taste the bitter smell of metal in the air and headed away from it toward the cloth makers.

Weavers sat at large wooden looms near the entrance and Fiona admired their work as she walked through. She always liked tapestries and their ability to tell of stories or deeds in one dramatic snapshot. Looking on, Fiona noticed one of the weavers, a marbled cornflower-and-white sylph, gasp as Soots came into the area following Fiona.

Fiona called out, "It's alright. They won't touch anything. They're quite nice." This became a bit embarrassing when Soots immediately moved toward the sylph. The weavers shrieked as Soots viewed the tapestry. The pleasure emanating from the creature was more than the wooden looms could stand, and they burst into flames. Fiona ran over as people came out of shops at the commotion.

"Soots, back up," Fiona said, shooing the sprite away and throwing regretful glances at the tapestry.

:Pretty.:

"Yes, I know, but you've broken the thing."

:Sorry,: Soots said mournfully and flew back into the sky to hover above the area.

A quick smilodon grabbed pails of water with paws and tail and doused the tapestry. The sylph weaver stood with mouth agape at the burn marks that marred their work.

Fiona pulled at her scarf awkwardly. Surely this wasn't the first time an accident like that had happened here. "Absolutely sorry about that. They just don't know their own strength, you know. Um, here." Fiona pulled a stack of papers out of the velvet pocket in her scarf, wincing. "Hopefully this covers the beautiful tapestry you were making and you can get a new loom."

The weaver, who had been frozen in the moment, took the papers out of Fiona's hand and nodded numbly. Fiona took this as her cue to scurry away from the scene.

"Soots," Fiona shouted, "I'm sorry I didn't think this through. Maybe stay up high until I come for you, okay?"

:Sorry.:

"It's okay. Now we know, hmm." Fiona pulled her scarf down over her shoulders as the air grew chillier. She picked up her pace. "The quicker we're in, the quicker we're out," she said to herself.

Fiona made her way across to the forge. Here she suspected she'd find something suitable for Soots to travel around in safely.

There were a few shops of metalworking, weaponsmithing, and the like, but a small one she had never seen before caught her eye. The new sign was by far the wordiest:

PESTLES AND MORTAR, BOTTLEMAKER, BOOKBINDER, SMITH OF METALS, CREATOR OF CONCOCTIONS AND TINCTURES

Intrigued, Fiona opened the door to take a quick look into the shop. An imposing tunic-clad smilodon, much taller and broader than Dodger, blocked most of her view. The orange fur stood high on the back of her neck, and dark vertical stripes rippled across her muscular arms. She pressed her thick feline body against the wooden counter as she pointed at a small-horned golden-skinned faun cowering behind it. Though the smilodon's hands were bandaged, Fiona could still tell that the claws were out.

"I'm not messing around, you copper-headed dimwit. Vials. Now."

"I'm sorry. So sorry, Petronia. It's not ready yet. It's-it's making its way now. I mean to boil. It's making its way to boil now. It's a very specific formula, you see, so it has to be watched. And-and it's slow going. Otherwise there would be flames and a big boom and, you see, the shop—"

"Stop blathering, Gaili," Petronia said, her furry jaw clenched. "I've had enough of it to last years in the dark edge."

Gaili looked back toward a large cauldron sitting over the fire. "I-I can't guarantee it will work right now. The-the potion might wear off faster or-or not work at all when you get there."

The smilodon grabbed the front of Gaili's brown leather apron, pulling her closer. "Vial now. Or do you need to lose what little you have in this dump to motivate you?"

Gaili's eyes widened.

Fiona cleared her throat, announcing her presence, and all eyes swiveled to her. "I should hope you are jesting, because that sounds like a threat." She'd be sent to the dark edge before she didn't butt in.

The smilodon eyed Fiona warily. "What business is it of yours?"

"As a concerned citizen, of course," she said demurely to the tigress, "it would be terrible to discover that there are those of ill repute threatening merchants when they don't get the answer they like. But I know I misheard." She smiled wide, taunting the tiger.

Gaili took a few steps back from the counter, eyes moving between the two women. She looked as if she didn't know who to speak to—or if she should really speak at all.

Petronia turned around slowly, crossing her arms and flexing. "Did you now? Well, maybe you also misheard the part where I said this was none of your business."

Fiona figured by the looks of the smilodon that she often ended confrontations in one of two ways: beating people up or getting what she wanted. That wasn't exactly how Fiona saw her day going, so she needed an exit strategy that wouldn't get the faun hurt.

There were no doors behind the counter, no windows toward the back. The shop was really small. It would have to be the door she just came in. She summoned up all the guile she had in the world, hoping that she had read Petronia right. "No, no I quite heard that part. I just didn't care. I tried, and then I immediately failed. What is it that you need in such a hurry that you can't possibly wait till it's finished?" She moved a step back toward the door, fingering her scarf. "I bet it's a lovely potion that lets you go someplace. Turner, I presume? That's the only real reason to shake down an alchemist." She took another step, her back to the door as she prattled on. "Or is it a brain tonic? You do seem to be missing some parts."

The smilodon rushed her, but Fiona had gotten her scarf loose enough to pull out her whip and lashed out at the tiger, wrapping it around her bandaged arm. Petronia froze momentarily but then tried to regain her ground and slashed at Fiona with her claws. Fiona took that moment to leap backward, jerking the smilodon forward. With the speed from Petronia and the quick-footedness from Fiona, they both went tumbling out the front door.

WHILE IT SEEMED LIKE a good idea at the time, Fiona found that having a very angry tigress on top of her wasn't the best way to keep breathing. A few people had stopped to stare at them, and she pulled on her whip trying to move Petronia off of her.

Petronia for her part gathered her wits about her and dug her claw into Fiona's shoulder. "You're not very clever."

"Well, I never thought I was particularly clever," she said, grimacing from the pain. "I just thought fighting out here in the open, where everyone could see you, would be much more enjoyable."

A small crowd of people had gathered around them. The smilodon's eyes bounced from person to person, but she tugged her bandaged arm, pulling Fiona closer. A hint of a thick sky-blue stripe tattooed on her chest peeked out from beneath her rumpled clothes.

Fiona said, "Maybe you'll be famous after this. Petronia, wasn't it?" She smiled, hoping to hide her agitation and calculating that someone like the tigress didn't like to have an audience she couldn't fight off.

Growling, Petronia let her go and bounded off and away. Her tail whipped out, smacking Fiona in the face as she tried to sit up, but before Fiona could react, she was halfway across the square. A couple of jackets walked briskly toward the tigress. Petronia looked back once at Fiona, smirked, and leapt to the roof of the faun's building, then jumped to the next building and beyond. The crowd of people gasped, and the jackets split off giving chase.

Fiona got up gingerly and dusted herself off. It was typically gauche for people to do things like running on buildings and attacking shopkeepers. What had happened to her sweet little corner of the Book while she'd had her nose in work these last few weeks?

Shaking her head, Fiona went back through the swinging door of the shop. The faun, Gaili, was nowhere to be seen. "Hello," Fiona called out. "Sorry about that. She's gone now, on what I hope is a brief chase away from some jackets. It's just me."

Two black horns and a crown of curly rosy-pink hair appeared from behind the counter as Gaili got up from her hiding spot. "Oh! You're bleeding."

Looking at her torn doublet and undershirt, Fiona winced. Rusty blood stained all the way through and the tangy iron scent of it filled her nostrils. Darn it, this had been her best doublet too. There was no way she'd be able to get the velvet repaired. Still, she moved her arm, a bit relieved that nothing appeared to be broken; she had only taken a few cuts from the claws. A few bruises from the brute landing on her. Not enough to damage anything internal. Just enough to get Petronia's message. She would be happy if she never saw her face again.

"Here," Gaili said, moving over with a wet cloth and bowl. She applied the cloth to Fiona's shoulder .

It burned, and Fiona yelped, moving away. "Are you trying to hurt me more?"

"Oh my gosh, I'm so sorry. No, absolutely not. It's simply some vinegar to wash the wound. I'm sorry. I should've warned you first."

Fiona sighed, controlling herself, and said softer, "No, I'm sorry. I didn't mean to be so rude. Thank you."

Gaili took a deep breath and a step back. "That should stop any bleeding at least. Rub this on it twice a day and it should look like it never happened." She pulled a small jar from one of the many shelves.

"I appreciate it," said Fiona, eyeing the pot warily. She didn't understand much about concoctions, but Gaili seemed alright enough. Her wound had in fact stopped bleeding after the initial burn. She sniffed, wondering if there was now a moldy smell coming from shoulder, but determined that wasn't the source. She looked up, saying, "I hate to deliver bad news, but your pot is boiling over."

Gaili shot over to the brew spewing over onto the small fire. The faun bent over the boiling pot and fanned the smoke. Grabbing mittens and tongs, she eased the pot off the fire and onto an iron rack. "Oh, cracks and crucibles. It's definitely gone off now. There's no way I'm going to be able to save this but for the grace of Larrakane." She cast off the mittens and palmed her face in her hands, her golden skin deeply contrasted by her small black horns. Stamping her hooves, she started to mumble to herself: "But if I can cool it and mix it with a little powder, it may at least be a half-time potion. Yes, I—" She cut off and started to whizz around the room pulling bottles and plants from shelves and chucking them into the pot.

Fiona watched with wide eyes at how fast the faun could move. She held her tongue, not wanting to distract Gaili from what was obviously an important affair, and shifted her focus to the shop itself.

By the door were several overstuffed shelves of bottles, vials, and what Fiona assumed were vaporizer pumps, their squeeze bottle handles dangling. On the walls hung various contraptions of metal, though what most of them did she couldn't even guess. A long sword looked particularly lethal until you got to the end of the blade, which seemed to be dripping something that looked an awful lot like blueberry juice. An anvil and hammer sat next to the fire on which cooled something flat and metallic. Between the smoke, the lack of windows, and the oil lamps flickering, it was hard to tell what anything was. Not the most customer-friendly shop in the artisan quarter by far.

Snooping over the counter, Fiona noticed blankets, a pillow, and a smattering of hay tucked into the bottom shelf. It looked like a hastily unmade pallet. Fiona frowned but said nothing. If Gaili was living here, that explained why it was so jam-packed. Possibly everything she owned was here. An unexpected tug of sympathy pulled on Fiona's senses, and she watched the faun working so hard to recover the potion in thoughtful silence.

Finished with saving as much as she could of the brew, Gaili turned her attention back to Fiona with a bright smile.

"There, settled. So sorry for delaying you. I'm sure you have somewhere important to be. What can I do for you?"

There was an oily smudge above her eyebrow, and Fiona wondered where it came from. Shaking her head back to the matter at hand, Fiona glanced around the small room and rapped her knuckles on the counter. In here wouldn't do. "It might be better if I showed you." She walked outside, the door jingling behind her, and called out, "Soots."

Feeling a bit warm, she loosened her scarf as Soots came flying down toward her and Gaili.

:Fiona,: said Soots, emanating happiness upon her return.

"Soots, I'd like you to meet Gaili. She's going to be helping us out today. Hopefully."

Gaili moved past and looked at the creature. She took out a pair of spectacles, perched them on her nose, and got a bit closer. "Oh goodness! Look at you. You're a flame sprite, aren't you? Well, you know what you are. Why am I telling you? Amazing. I'd love to help. Any way I can."

"I need to be able to travel around Spine with Soots and not have them...sort of...burst things on fire," said Fiona, waving her hands as if they were exploding.

"Burst things?"

"When Soots gets happy or excited, easily flammable things tend to combust."

"That's magnificent," Gaili said, clapping her hands together.

"Yes, it's a lot of things," Fiona said delicately, not wanting to hurt Soots's feelings again, "and although Soots isn't a turner, I'd like to be able to take them a few places."

"Hmm, so whatever they're using will need to survive many pages."

"Not too many. There's no taking them to Depths, of course."

"Yes, yes, certainly." Gaili stroked her cheek.

Gaili and Soots eyed each other in a sort of circular dance. As Gaili watched and looked over Soots, they spun in a circle around her a few times before coming back to where they had stood.

Gaili divested herself of her glasses and nodded. "There's nothing I have on hand that might work, but that does not mean I can't make something." She grinned brightly. In impeccable Claire, she said, "Do you like to be this shape, or are there others?" The words sounded like crackles and pops as she spoke.

Soots danced, shifting from a ball of flame to a thin scorching line and finally into a small humanoid figure.

"Marvelous!" Gaili marched back into the shop without a backward glance.

Fiona could hear the clank of metal, pots, and tongs. "Soots, give me one more moment, okay? And then we'll be heading back to Blaze. I want to get started on the Ashborn's request today."

Soots twirled and bobbed toward the smoke coming from Gaili's chimney. Fiona supposed they could be comfortable on the brick and not burn anything, and she headed back inside.

"Do you sell Blaze breathing potions here?" Fiona called out.

Gaili snapped her head up, hitting the counter. Wincing, she nodded and rubbed her head. "Of a sort. I think potions are a little mundane really. Why, you could do so much more and make them easier to transport!" She smiled sheepishly. Opening a jar, she pulled out a wiggly cube that shimmered with gold dust. "This uses the same ingredients but it's more delicious and you can carry more in a box, jar, or bag than a bunch of small clunky glass vials."

Fiona raised an eyebrow at the odd cube but said, "I do dislike the bandoliers most turners wear to carry potions. I'll give it a try."

"Really? Oh great!" Gaili put the small cube in a pouch and handed it to Fiona. "I call them jelly breaths, but I'm still working on the name. I'm sorry that it's the only one I have left. A lot of turners taking to Blaze these days. I even had an earth elemental asking for some."

"I suppose that's one side effect of being able to access more of it now. Anyone else interesting buying up your stock?" If she could get a sense of the people going to Blaze, it might help in her investigation. "What about Petronia?"

"Oh, no. No, not her. But I had a couple of elephas in here yesterday, a bunch of humans, but that's about it."

"Hmm." Fiona nodded, rubbing a thumb on the counter.

"If this keeps up, I might have to go in myself to visit, although I wouldn't want to leave the shop while I did it. And then where exactly would I go? And I'll have to make equipment, of course." Gaili went on moving clutter from one side of the shop to the other.

"Yes, I wondered about your sign. You are quite multi-talented."

Gaili moved to a side shelf, starting to rearrange bottles. "I only do what everyone else does."

Fiona could sense the faun's mood shift and wondered why the bubbly woman suddenly closed off. "Most alchemist focus on potion making. Did you take a variety of lessons or simply have a natural gift for inventing?"

"I studied a bit," Gaili said, rotating a bottle and then absentmindedly moving it up a shelf.

"Well, your signboard certainly worked for me," Fiona said, seeing she was making her uncomfortable. To close the subject, she pulled papers from her scarf and handed them out to Gaili.

"No, no need. The jelly breath is yours for free. You've done more than enough to earn it. In fact, if you want to make any paper, I am always looking for ingredients for my experiments."

"What kind of things do you need?"

"Small items from the pages. Plants, seeds, that sort of thing. If you're not squeamish, animal droppings would be great."

Fiona wrinkled her nose. "Animal droppings?"

"You wouldn't believe what you can make with elemental animal droppings," said Gaili, eyes shining.

"No, I bet I wouldn't." She thought of the jiggly square she had just received. "Alright then, if I come across anything, I'll get them."

"Excellent."

"Feel free to drop by when you've gotten an idea for Soots," Fiona said, taking out a small card with her house address on it.

Gaili took the card and nodded, a faraway look in her eyes at the reminder.

Fiona shrugged; she never did understand inventors much, but they were certainly useful. "Well then, welcome to Spine. Nice to have met you."

"You as well, Fiona."

With a quick nod she left Gaili scribbling behind her.

NOW THAT THE MATTER of Soots's clothing—if that was the right word—was settled, Fiona made her way to the official Blaze pagemark outside of the artisan district. The Ashborn had shoehorned a deadline into their laborious speeches, she had noted. Why they needed the stone retrieved by the end of the week was beyond her, but the sooner she started, the better. Her first step was to talk to the salamander clan council. There were four large sets of salamanders in Blaze, and the clan council held representatives from each area. She hoped she could get a sense of what they knew about the theft and what they thought of the Ashborn.

Soots and Fiona followed the signs directing their way to the pagemark. Pagemarks could be as massive as a mountain plateau, as small as a clearing in the woods, or even the size of a city street. It depended on where they were going. Travel was typically dangerous to another page, not from. Official pagemarks of the Guild had jacketed stations to pay the fee and were marked off by the Travel Guild insignia: an open book with various species footprints above it. It was a messy metaphor of a symbol, but people got the gist.

This pagemark was at the entrance of Fire Bowl, where most of the fire denizens, even the handful that were turners, lived in Spine. It lined up directly to what used to be a flaming forest on the edge of the salamander realm.

Fiona sized up the jacket, a small green salamander with a snug-fitting vest sitting in a blocky stone stall bearing the insignia of the Travel Guild. Above the stall was a sign with the fire rune, a wavy upturned fork, burned into it, signaling the destination. The salamander was eating what looked like a frog, if the legs were any indication, and appeared to be completely oblivious to the world around him. Approaching, Fiona cleared her throat, but the salamander barely glanced an oversized side eye at her.

"Where, who, and why?" he said, nodding to the open bound register in front of him. It too was surrounded by stone.

Fiona paused at this new addition to the process. "Since when does the Travel Guild do anything besides taking money?"

"New regulations to better the access to the great Book for everyone," the jacket said in a rote voice. The frog legs quivered in his mouth as he spoke. "Just a few questions and you can be on your way."

Unnecessary paperwork, that's what this was. Fiona grabbed the grubby quill, placed her name, *Blaze*, and *none of your business* in the register. To be spiteful, she wrote it in her human language. Taking out the required cost, she deposited the papers in an ironbound box as usual and started to walk off.

"What about the sprite?" the jacket said, looking up at Soots. "If you're taking on skimmers, you'll need to add them too."

"They're not a skimmer. They're a friend."

The jacket looked slowly at the flame sprite as he licked his eyeball with his tongue. "Either way, write it. Pulp has to be accounted for on trips now."

Unused to taking others with her, Fiona felt uneasy jotting down the flame sprite's details. Paying without all this talk had been customary, and there something irked at the back of her mind about being tracked. But since almost all the official pagemarks were under Travel Guild control, they went by their rules. Whether she liked it or not.

Looking back at the stall, she wondered who was even interested in the information being collected. What was it all for? Rippers and skips weren't going to fill out paperwork placing their name and where they were going to commit a crime. They found and protected their own pagemarks, like the elemental smuggler had.

:Friend?: Soots said loudly.

Fiona shook her head as Soots commanded her attention. "Sorry. You can come closer. That's it. Let me pop my gear on and we'll be right off. I figured since I was going to Blaze you might enjoy the trip." She didn't say that she wondered if Soots would even come back with her once she needed to leave. She had enjoyed the flame sprite's company even if it was mostly full of burning events.

:Flames!: said Soots.

Fiona laughed and put on her Blaze-proof clothing. She tucked her scarf deep into the cloak so that no part of it would be accidentally scorched. She would be absolutely sick if something happened to it. After spraying herself down with her atomizer, she noted the liquid had about one more trip left before it needed to be replenished. She set her thin glasses for the darkness she would need in Blaze and put them on, pushing them above her brow for now. She checked that Soots was sufficiently wrapped around her arm.

Gathering the folds of her cloak to use it as a bookmark, she felt the thrum that connected her to Blaze. She took a step, the world shimmering around her. Another sure-footed step, and she was on rough blackened stone, the crunch of the gravel under her feet and the smell of the brimstone and ash in the air. She clutched her burning throat. After rummaging deep into her cloak, she pulled out the jelly breath of shimmering gold and swallowed it in one gulp. An almost sugary taste touched the back of her tongue before it was gone.

Soots slipped off her wrist to hover in front of her, confusion and concern washing over her in a palpable wave.

Fiona gave them a thumbs-up for reassurance. After a moment of holding her breath, she inhaled through her nostrils slightly. When she didn't gasp for air, she let out a deep sigh. Why had she absolutely forgotten about the concoction? She tsked herself. "Acting like some unread turner, Fi. A half a minute more and you would've been unconscious, you blotter."

She sighed, patting herself to make sure her equipment was working fine, pulled down her glasses, and surveyed the pagemark she had turned to.

A smoky haze wafted through the blackened skeletal trees of obsidian spikes. The fire forest. It was called the fire forest, of course, by turners not native to the page. It had looked like trees and so they had called it so, but now...now it was nothing. Where once it was writhing in fiery limbs and wisps of flame and smoke, it was now empty and still. To the denizens it had been La'mior. Fiona was quite sure she was butchering Claire every time she said it, so she didn't say it out loud much.

She was surprised at how sad she felt. Tears were coursing down her cheeks and...it wasn't just sadness. It was an undeniable sense of loss and heartbreak. It ran deep. Realizing that the feelings weren't coming from within her, she looked around for Soots, who was bobbing on the edge of the forest, looking out away from it into a rocky formation.

"Soots, I'm sorry. I didn't mean to upset you by bringing you back here."

:Gone.:

"I know, little one. It's all gone. But it'll come back. They're working on it, I'm sure," she said, trying to keep her voice bright.

:Broken.:

Fiona reached out to the flame sprite, the heat even with protective gear a little uncomfortable on her hand. She wanted to comfort them. Make everything right. "In due time, Blaze will be alive and well again. I just know it."

Raspy voices speaking in Claire broke into the moment. "Trespassers! Trespassers!"

Specks of red and green salamanders made a quick clip toward them, wildly swinging weapons that glowed crimson in the darkened forest. Fiona idly wondered what they were made of. Magma? Iron? As they got closer, their dramatics increased for their newfound audience. One salamander had to jump back from another to avoid getting hit.

Fiona arched an eyebrow. Sighing, she slowly put up her hands and waited on the approaching army. She had always heard that salamanders could be exhausting and a bit idiotic if they put their mind to it. Between their loud thumping and shouting, she figured it was better to play along.

Slithering quickly on the ground, the salamanders stopped inches from Fiona and Soots. The smell of burning metal was prevalent as they aimed their weapons. Two held small swords and one wielded an axe. No heat from them pushed through her protections, and for that she was thankful. Now that they were closer, Fiona towered over them, their weapons barely up to her shoulder. The difference in stature did not seem to bother the salamanders in the slightest.

The smaller red one pointed. "Trespassers! Trespassers!"

"You don't have to shout, we're right here," Fiona said, moving her tongue rapidly to accommodate the language. Larrakane help her if her inability to communicate bungled everything up now.

"Trespassers found on the northwestern forest edge. Trespassers!"

"Are you telling that to someone else or just letting me know? I believe the rest of your militia are right beside you as well." She looked for any sort of communication device but just saw the salamanders.

The salamanders looked at each other and then back at Fiona.

She groaned and tried again, saying slowly in Claire, "Please quit pointing at me. It's very rude."

The green one put his sword down and smiled up at Fiona. Finally, someone understood her.

"You will be arraigned and eaten," said the smaller one, ignoring everyone else.

"I hope that's not true. I'll be very vexed to be eaten. I've just come here on a matter of business, which isn't illegal as far as I know."

"Not you, human," said the larger red salamander beside the one who was still pointing and shouting in Fiona's face. It seems her words were finally being noticed. "The flarion is a trespasser. A spy."

Fiona raised an eyebrow in mock concern. "Oh dear. A spy? I didn't know that at all. You have to believe me. I never realized a flame sprite that can barely speak and is no more than the size of my head could've been a spy. A spy from..." She trailed off.

"Iasheoxus, obviously," the green one said happily. "Where all flarion are from."

"Trespassers! Trespassers!" said the small red one again.

"Would you please stop shouting in my face? I get it. You think they're trespassing," Fiona said. *Larrakane give me strength.*

The salamander shut up. Fiona took that brief moment of quiet to say slowly, "I've come to talk with your clan council on a matter of importance. Will you please escort me to them?"

"You want us to take a flarion into our inner chambers? What do we look like to you?" said the larger red salamander.

Absolute blotters. "Absolute champions who recognize that capturing a spy and showing them off to your leaders would probably be worthy of some sort of reward. A bigger rock hut or more food?"

The salamanders looked at each other, their side eyes flickering quickly. The calm green one held up a digit. "Let us discuss." And the three huddled together.

Fiona turned to Soots and whispered in her human tongue, "Perhaps you should take a moment to escape into the forest. I'll whistle when I make my way back."

:Alone?:

"I know. I don't want to leave you alone or be alone myself. But they will absolutely do something dumb if you go in, and then I'll have to do something I'll regret."

Soots bobbed and then disappeared behind Fiona's back. She felt the sadness emanating off the flame sprite. *They're from here. They'll be alright in the meantime.* The thought didn't make her feel any less terrible.

The salamanders ungrouped and spun around. The smaller red one declared, "We have discussed the matter, and we will take you to our jail. Then once the council has found you guilty, we'll get to eat you."

Fiona dropped her hands and huffed. "Oh, for all the paper in the Book, listen—"

"Where did the flarion go?" said the larger red one.

"What flarion?" Fiona said, widening her eyes in mock confusion.

The salamanders looked at each other. The green one said, "The flarion that was right here. It was as big as my head."

Fiona looked from side to side with all the gumption she could muster and said, "I have absolutely no idea what you're talking about. Now, what were you saying about taking me to your clan council?"

The salamanders stopped. "Did we say council?"

"Yes," Fiona started off slowly, as if surprised by their short attention span, "you said you would be honored to take me to your council. I said that wasn't necessary, I was just visiting, but you said that taking a turner such as myself to your council would give you some prestige, and perhaps they would honor you with a bigger *rock hut* and more *food*." She couldn't keep a bit of annoyance from eking out as she repeated the last phrase, but she was sure their skulls were too thick to catch on.

"Oh. That was a good idea I had," said the green salamander. "Next time listen to me, Eastrun Stoneroller."

"It was a very good idea from me," said the larger red. "You said we should eat her, Westtree Axeholder."

"Best idea today!" said the smaller shouting one. "I'm glad I thought of it!"

"Excellent." Fiona smiled. "I'm glad that I could honor you with my presence. Now which way to the council?"

"Right this way, turner."

"Yes, follow me, turner."

"No, follow me."

Fiona followed the salamanders away from the edge of the deadened fire forest. She glanced back, hoping for a sign of Soots, but the flame sprite was nowhere to be seen. She sighed and turned, walking toward the salamander realm.

AREDIN'S ROCK, THE REALM of the salamanders, was an absolute dream—*if* you were a salamander. There were four cities within the large realm of Northhill, Eastrun, Southburn, and Westtree, which housed the pagemark Fiona had used.

The protrusions of rock that dug into the ground and stood towering in Westtree clearly inspired the architectural design for the whole region. Smaller clones of the big buildings were scattered throughout the city as dwellings. They were made of gray pumice with enough space for living inside and little else, it seemed. Presumably made well enough to stand against the meteors of ash and flakes of fire that rained from the volcano looming over the realm, the homes were small like the salamanders themselves and Fiona felt like she towered above all as they paraded her through the city streets to a large building on the opposite of the town.

The city itself seemed protected from all manner of hostile creatures that could be looking to invade, nestled as it was between the forest and the volcano, but there were plenty of hostiles inside. Some salamanders argued and fought off the side of the main pathway. Over what, Fiona wasn't quite sure, but it sounded like it mostly revolved around food and who owed who what. It didn't help that salamanders had a short attention span. The only salamanders she had met who seemed to be a bit smarter than their peers were the turners forced to reside on Spine. Living alongside other beings and people from different pages would do that to a creature, she supposed.

Other salamanders slithered around pulling stones, grinding them, or working on more hut-like structures. The rocky jut they were approaching was tall and full of alcoves on the outside. There was no entrance to the building, at least not one that would fit Fiona. In the alcoves sat a variety of salamanders staring out toward the forest and beyond. There didn't seem to be stairs as far as Fiona could see, and she was immediately concerned with the salamanders' plan. She decided to take hold of the situation before it got out of hand.

"Thank you ever so much for escorting me. I shall wait outside here while you convene your council."

The salamanders looked at her as if confused. "Who are you again?" said the larger red one.

Fiona pinched the bridge of her nose. "I am a page turner here to meet with your clan council."

"The council is at the fire," said the small red one. He nodded once and, swinging his sword, slithered off toward one of the indistinguishable huts.

"Well, I think it best if I wait here, as I'm not fireproof."

"Yeah, we don't want you to burn up," said the green one, smiling.

"Although then it would be easier to eat you," said the larger red one, patting his belly.

"No one is eating me," Fiona said, losing her patience. Her shoulders slumped, and she breathed a heavy sigh. *Just try to take control of the situation, Fi.* "Is there someone else I can talk to?"

"Yes," said the green one.

"Great. Excellent. I'll wait here," she said, motioning to the outside of the building.

The salamanders glided away, tails thumping on the ground. They began to crawl up the wall of the building. One went straight into an alcove, seemingly forgetting the assignment altogether.

Fiona waited, stamping a line in the dirt as she paced back and forth. No one acknowledged her. She didn't have a lot of time on the jelly breath she had gotten from Gaili and would need to get a move on soon. She could taste the acidity in the air just slightly and knew it would wear off within an hour or so.

The green salamander crawled down the wall towards Fiona. Finally, she could start getting somewhere. As he approached, alone she noted, she said, "Did you not find them?"

The green salamander stopped looking up at her quizzically. "Find who?"

Fiona palmed her face and stalked away from the creature without a backwards glance. She would figure it out herself. Hang diplomacy.

She strode down the road looking at the buildings and salamanders she passed by. A few turned toward her quizzically, but she avoided their gaze, and they seemed to lose interest. The streets were basically well-worn paths of stubbly pumice rock, and Fiona stumbled a bit.

Fiona wondered just how any of them told anything apart here. Everything looked exactly the same. The salamanders even looked similar except for coloring: short, stumpy, and reptilian.

She saw quite a lot of salamanders coming from a street ahead. Guessing that it must lead to a communal spot of some kind, she hurried her footsteps and turned down the street. It was a dead end. She shook her head. What had they even been doing here? Sighing, she glanced up at the darkened sky. She was trying to put reason and logic to creatures who, for the most part, had shown very little of either. Perhaps she needed to think a little less with her brain and more with blinding confidence like them.

Fiona trudged out of the dead end and stopped the first salamander she saw. "Clan council?" she said, staring at them to keep their focus.

The salamander pointed, and Fiona walked away without another word. She could be salamander-ish too. She went a few feet and then stopped another. "Clan council?" They too motioned the way she was going.

She did this every few feet until she came to a building that looked like all the others but was larger with smoke pouring from it. A crackle and hiss of fire drifted from the open archway. A red salamander stood at the entrance, and before Fiona could ask the direction of the council, the salamander said haltingly in her human tongue, "Greetings. I heard of a human intruder looking for the council. Figured you'd find your way."

Fiona's eyes narrowed. "Are you on the clan council?"

"No, no. A jacket. Like you."

Fiona relaxed but said quickly, "I'm not a jacket." She switched to Claire. "But glad to see you either way." With a page turner at the very least, she might get somewhere.

"Oh," he said dejectedly.

"You wanted me to be from the Guild?" she pressed.

"Yes. I've sent in many requests to the bosses. No one has come by. I don't know what else to do."

Fiona frowned. Blaze dying was huge. It impacted everyone here and everyone who relied on Blaze's fire. Trying to be delicate, she said, "I understand the flames receding must be hard."

"Food has dwindled with the forest gone. It's getting worse. I work at this outpost as much as I can before having to go back to Spine. I don't know everyone back at headquarters. When I heard a human was looking for the council..." He trailed off. "Well, you didn't come to chat about Blaze. I'm Spine Rockcruncher. I can get you into the council."

She paused and then said hesitantly, "You know, I do know someone higher up at the Guild who isn't completely worthless. I could gather some information on why they aren't looking in on this as fast as you'd like. See where your requests have gone." It would also allow her to do a fair bit of pushing herself as to exactly what the Guild was occupied with if not solving this.

"You would do that for us?"

"Of course."

"I can't pay you."

Fiona shook her head. "What are we turners with no pages? The death of Blaze affects everyone."

Rockcruncher's smile was a small thin line. "Thank you."

She nodded. "Of course. And the name's Fiona. Fiona Thorne."

"Well met. This is council fire. Their food chambers. They are..." He paused and laid a digited palm on his belly. "...ornery when they are hungry. Be careful."

"Understood."

The building was nothing more than a small, hot chamber. Even with the suit on, Fiona could feel a light heat from the fire in the middle of the room. A stone circle crowded around it, and around the stone crater lay a group of four salamanders: red, green, yellow, and black.

"Greetings, children of Aredin, leaders of Aredin's Rock, and most perfect salamanders," Rockcruncher boomed. "I have come to introduce you to a traveler of great importance."

A tail flicked. Another tail flicked toward the heat. The salamanders didn't stir, but that didn't deter Rockcruncher. He continued, "The turner Thorne has a few questions for the clan council of Aredin's Rock. Private questions."

Four sets of beady eyes riveted on Fiona, and she slid a glance to Rockcruncher. He didn't seem the type to lull her into a trap, so she assumed he knew what he was doing.

"Greetings, most perfect salamanders," Fiona said, copying Rockcruncher but trying to keep any sarcasm out of her voice. She moved closer so she could see the creatures.

Eyes shut and opened, tails flicked, but not being a great study in salamander behaviors, Fiona wasn't sure if that was acknowledgment. She put herself into an illogical mindset and blurted out, "Ashborn?"

No changes. Were the salamanders ignoring her, or was her Claire just that bad? She decided to push a little with her remaining time. "The Ashborn rules around here, yes?"

The yellow salamander sat up abruptly. The red fat one pointed a digit at Fiona. "Don't talk to us about silly phoenix, human. We are the rulers here."

"Oh, oh, of course here, in Aredin's realm. But what about elsewhere?"

"Elsewhere we are rulers there too," the yellow one said.

"What about the flarions and the ragnis? Where do they rule?" she said, poking at the names to hopefully bring about some sort of reaction.

"Nowhere soon," the green salamander said, smiling up at her.

"And why is that?" Fiona replied. There was silence. If Blaze died out, the flarions and ragnis would have nowhere to go. They needed the flames and the lava the most, she'd heard. The salamanders could find other hot places in a few mortal pages. Larrakane help the ones they moved to.

The salamanders didn't so much look at each other as stared at each other, gesturing and flicking their tongues. Fiona suspected they were communicating in a way she couldn't grasp. She broke in, "What do you know about the Ashborn's Blackstone?"

"Don't talk to us about Blackstone, human. We didn't take it from the silly phoenix," the red one said.

"Go look at the elementals. They're much closer to Obsidian's Tooth," said the yellow.

The name didn't sound familiar. It definitely wasn't where the Ashborn lived in Radiance Peak. "Oh, Obsidian's Tooth," she said, smiling to cover her lie. "Yes, yes, the Ashborn's sanctum."

"It's not the silly phoenix's sanctum," the green one said, indignant. "They're ours too."

The red salamander hissed, and the others fell silent. They were clearly covering something up. Fiona pressed her lips together. "I see. And you don't know anything about the Blackstone?"

"No. It's rude to come in and accuse the most perfect salamanders," the red one hissed.

"Very mean," said the yellow.

"Trespasser!" said the red.

"Not this again," she mumbled. She had stayed a bit too long with the hotheads and had stoked their fire.

"Trespasser!" the red rasped out again.

"Wait," Fiona said, putting up her hands. She didn't want them to do something foolish, but she could tell that was the direction they were heading. She just needed a moment of distraction. "Before you kick me out, allow me to present the gift I've brought you."

The salamanders looked at each other, and Fiona could see them wavering. The lie was a start, but she needed something to clinch it. She waved her hands, keeping their attention. "It's a nice gift. A spy flarion."

There was a collective gasp. Well, a hiss of air that Fiona took as a gasp. They rapidly looked at each other, gesturing and talking. Even the black salamander, small and quiet until then, got up and pushed into the discussion. Distracted indeed.

Fiona took this moment to whisper to Rockcruncher in her human tongue, "It was very nice meeting you. Sorry about this bit." She ran out of the building and into the dusty, crowded streets.

Fiona heard a quick shout from the building but didn't turn back to see if anyone was coming after her. Through the worn paths and foothills she jogged, searching for the entrance out of the city. Cresting over a small ridge, she spied the opening as she heard tails thumping behind her.

"Trespasser! Trespasser, slow down so we can catch you," came a voice from far behind her.

"No thank you!" Fiona yelled over her shoulder. Making her way across the threshold, she whistled long and loud, hoping that Soots would hear her.

She raced into the dead forest, the shouts of salamanders closing in. A branch caught on her cloak as she dashed around the trees, struggling to keep firm footing on the barren rocky ground. She ripped her cloak away and much of the branch as well. She ran. If she could lose them in La'mior, she could double back to the pagemark when safe. She wished fervently that the forest actually was alive and thick with flames so it would be easier to hide.

She zigged and then zagged. Thinking quickly, she stripped off a fireproof glove and tossed it on the ground. Heat arched across her skin, blistering immediately. She thrust her naked hand into her suit pocket and hoped it would hold until she could get back to Spine. Her breathing was harsh, the effects of the jelly breath wearing off from her exertions.

She whistled once more and moved in the opposite direction of the glove. Pressing tight against the remains of a large obsidian tree, she tried to remain still. With her dark garb and the obvious evidence somewhere else, she hoped she could blend in with the tree. She took shallow breaths and tried to mete out her air intake.

A salamander mumbled something too far away for her to hear clearly. More shouts of "Trespasser!" came at intervals.

"She probably went this way."

"You go to the left and I go to the right?"

"Why am I right?"

They were pressing closer as they argued, not moving farther away. Darn their inability to focus on clues set out for them. Should've waved it from a branch apparently.

As they closed in, Fiona held her breath. She didn't want to pull out her scarf and risk it getting damaged. But the salamanders wouldn't understand her imminent asphyxiation as she argued with them. She'd just have to wing it and maybe try to fight.

"We've already caught her. She's back in the city," Rockcruncher's voice rang out through the trees. The sounds of the salamanders' movement stopped. "Come on now. We've got to question her about the spy."

Fiona smiled at his words, surprised by his lying. She wasn't quite sure why he was doing it, but she was thankful. *Blessed by Larrakane himself, that one.*

The salamanders grumbled about their rewards of warm rock and food. Their sounds faded away. Fiona counted to three and stepped away from the tree to find the area empty. An immense sense of relief washed over her, and she turned to find Soots bobbing toward her at lightning speed.

Fiona held out her arm for Soots to alight on. "I missed you too."

Soots danced on her arm as Fiona detangled herself from the branch caught on her cloak. Ah well, at least she had something to give to Gaili for her troubles. Sliding it into her scarf, she made her way gingerly back to the pagemark.

She was out of time here, but there was so much to consider. She'd need to figure out what Obsidian's Tooth was and why the salamander clan council were acting so dodgy about it. It sounded as if the Blackstone had been somewhere around there, but that's not what the Ashborn had said. And she needed to speak with the elementals who lived close to this Tooth. They doubled back to the pagemark as quietly as possible to turn the page back to Spine.

10

THE CITY WAS IN the beginning stages of dusk when they returned. Fiona found herself closer to the booth with the salamander jacket. He was poring over a green paper leaflet and ignoring a geared-up human turner in front of him. The *Card* was a free leaflet produced out of the Travel Guild for all pages to enjoy. Not made quite the same as their currency, there was an element to its durability that was woven into its fabric. A trade secret that she was sure someone somewhere was probably trying to figure out. She grabbed one for herself from the fresh stack by the ledger, nodded to the other turner, and made her way out as she glanced over the daily news.

NEW GUILDHALL PUT ON HOLD FOR LACK OF MATERIALS. "IT WILL BE COMPLETED," BINDER SAYS, MATERIALS AND PROTESTS NOTWITHSTANDING.

AIRSHIP STOLEN WHOLE FROM RISE. WHO WOULD CAPER BENEATH THE QUIVERING EYE OF THE BRILLIANT QUEEN?

Someone stole an airship from Rise? Bless Larrakane, how in the world did they turn the page with that behemoth? Fiona's native page, Restless Rise, was home to many airships, and while a few had made their way piecemeal to other pages, taking one wholly intact was astounding. There was a limit to what a turner could take with them. Fiona never fathomed something so bulky could make the turn.

Scanning the rest of the bulletins, she noted that there wasn't one line about the impending doom of Blaze. It was as if the Travel Guild was completely ignoring the catastrophe.

She ran her hand across her bundles of coiled dark tresses, smoothing out flyaways. "Soots," she called out, "I'm going to take a breather."

:Hungry.:

"Aye, me too. I'm surprised you didn't eat something back on Blaze."

:Broken.:

"Oh, I guess in its state there's nothing nutritious there for you to eat... Well, let's get you back home first then."

They traversed the busy streets of the turner district. A few heads swiveled in their direction. Fiona guessed it was a bit of an unusual sight to see a flame sprite so deep into the district. Or maybe just weird to see anyone with her. A couple of friendly faces—previous clients who'd come to her for a lost dog, stolen jewelry, and a derailed book shipment—waved at her in greeting.

The last of them flagged her down. "Mistress Thorne, I just wanted to say hello." The old human woman with dark skin that matched Fiona's stared more at the flame sprite than at Fiona. She was largest in the middle and wore the tucked and puffed-up gowns of Fiona's native home, though an older style than what was currently in fashion. Her wavy gray hair was pulled into a bun, and her round glasses were pressed tight against her face.

"Ah yes, Mistress Didia, this is Soots. Soots, this is Mistress Didia."

Soots flew toward the woman but cautiously hovered above them both.

"Oh, such an interesting creature," the older lady said, adjusting her glasses. "Don't let them too close to those books I gave you now."

Fiona bit back a grimace, thinking of Soots's earlier mishaps. "Of course not."

"Did you get a chance to talk to the Elder?"

"Yes, Mistress Didia," Fiona said. "Took on a case for them."

"Excellent. Excellent," she said, shading her eyes as she stared distractedly at Soots. "Couldn't have gotten my books back without you. Hope the introduction is proving useful."

"How long have you known the Elder again?"

"Oh, a bit. I was about your age when they found me wandering the woods of Spine. Took me in. But druidry wasn't for me. Too much sitting."

Fiona laughed. Didia must be pushing close to ninety at the rate of her movements and looks. For the Elder to be even half of that pushed the part-faekin, part-human theory firmly in the forefront.

"Well, it's very good they did. Couldn't imagine not having you for a neighbor."

"Aye, you too, Mistress Thorne. Don't tread too far from my doorstep, you hear?"

Fiona smiled, warmed by the platitude. It was nice to think that at least once in her life she had made a bit of an impression. She nodded and said bye, then made her way to her manor house.

Fiona got Soots settled in the stove, happily burning what was left of her wood stockpile. She'd have to stock up for as much as they seemed to eat. Saying goodbye to the indulging sprite, Fiona made her way in the twilight to the large way station a short distance from her home.

The Thread was four stories tall with circular peaks at each corner like towers. The first floor held the public house, the second the showroom, and the rest guest rooms and private quarters. Glass windows set into the towers gave each its own unblinking eye. Its wooden exterior was robin's-egg blue with thin cream lines of crisscrossing wood making delicate, intricate hatched lines on the roof and along the eaves. These hatched patterns covered much of the upper portion of the dwelling and gave the appearance that a gentle handkerchief of lace had been draped over the entire affair. Although it had been around for most of Fiona's fifteen years in Spine, it seemed to be the only thing here that didn't feel like it came from somewhere else. There was nothing else like it in the whole Book.

Fiona strode inside the warm room filled with boisterous laughter and ripples of chatter. The smell of citrus clung to the air, and she could almost taste the sweet treats she had come for. All eyes turned to her, searching for something. Gossip more than likely. That's what they wanted. Gossip ran faster than water through the aqueducts high above the city. If anything of value was being whispered about her cases, she'd hear it here.

Fiona liked that she could learn something new every time she surrounded herself with a bunch of page turners. And the Thread was almost always packed to the brim with them. Most were old-timers, but a few Guild jackets were sprinkled in as well. No matter who you worked for or what you did, a turner could always feel at home at the Thread. It was a sanctuary of sorts where no clashes outside could be settled inside. That was thanks to Mac, an enigma of a woman who was currently filling orders behind the low bar.

"Fi!" Mac called out in greeting. She raised a golden tattooed hand in her direction and kept filling drinks with the other. Mac was faekin but unlike the fauns, fairies, and pixies that were the usual turners from the Court of Copper, Mac seemed to be one of a kind, much like her place. She was taller than all, even the fauns and centaurs. Her long sunglow-gold hair was haphazardly pulled back behind large, wilting, downy ears. Some faekin had one, maybe two tattoos, but Mac seemed to have them all over. She never talked about them much, but they told a story nonetheless in cream, olive, and indigo.

Fiona glanced around the Thread catching a smile from Dodger, who was seated in the back with some other jackets. She gave a nod but stopped short when she noticed a familiar tigress not too far from where Dodger sat. Petronia. Fiona smiled bright lest she give a hint that she had been thrown off. Petronia raised her glass in a mock salute, but there was no smile on her face. Fiona would need to warn someone about her before she caused any trouble.

Fiona sat at the bar and settled her focus on Mac in her ethereal flowing azure robe. It was her signature outfit. The threads on the garment were delicate, but she never snagged in her all running around. Fiona often wondered, if she wore that to sling drinks, what did she wear in her downtime or to go out? Not that she had ever seen Mac out in the city. Come to think of it, she had never seen her outside the Thread.

Fiona grabbed a fistful of puffy white miniature clouds set out in a bowl. They were soft and squishy, and she popped one in her mouth. She had expected them to be sweet the first time she tried one. They reminded her of the marshmallows from her native page in looks, but they were incredibly tart.

"Good to see you," said Mac when she got a minute and could focus on her new patron. "Haven't been in for a while. Was worried you were going to work yourself to death if you didn't stop for a moment."

Accustomed to Mac's forwardness, Fiona grinned. "Sitting on my behind in here won't pay the bills unfortunately."

"It could if you learned how to clean a glass or two," Mac said, corners of her mouth crinkling into a smile. "But you're here now, so I'll let it be. I missed your face."

"I missed your face too, Mac." Fiona paused and made a small nod in Petronia's direction. "What's the format on her, eh?"

Mac didn't even slide a glance in the direction. "She's unread, that's for sure. Maybe been in Spine a couple of weeks. Why you asking?"

"She's trouble. Just wanted to give you the dry in case she binds something from you."

"You're sweet," Mac said, signaling that she understood.

Fiona trudged through the first reason she had come here. Information. "You know a few different languages right?"

Mac laughed, a hearty sound coming from someone so delicately dressed. "More like twenty."

Fiona pulled out a torn sheet of stationery from her scarf. She scrawled out a few phrases she'd memorized from the ledger and showed it to Mac. "Have you ever seen this phrase before?"

Mac took her glasses from some unseen pocket in her robe and placed them on her face. She squinted at Fiona's handwriting before shaking her head. "That's not a language."

"You mean it's not a language you know?"

Mac looked at Fiona with the sort of face that told her in no short terms she said what she said.

"Okay then, so it's not a language. But it's clearly different words of Schiflan," Fiona said, pointing to her native tongue.

"Yeah and different words of Claire, Aer, and a little Court of Copper mixed in. It's someone using the languages to make a cypher."

"A cypher?"

"A secret code," Mac said plainly. She took off her glasses and pocketed them. "I've used them before with my research."

Mac rarely talked about the time before she was a turner. Fiona played with her scarf, raising an eyebrow. "What sort of research did you need to create a secret code for?"

Mac laughed, turning away to refill a mug. "A valuable one. Nuts to bolts, Fiona, if you didn't hide your research someone was going to come along and steal it. Practically guaranteed in the Court."

"Do you miss the Court?" Just because she didn't miss her pre-inking home didn't mean everyone hated their existence before becoming a turner.

"Most days." Mac shrugged, grabbed another wet glass, and started drying it. "I know someone you can talk to about that cypher. Floats out there in Airmire. Captain Henrietta on the *Big Betty*. You tell her Mac sent you. And that I'm still waiting on my blasted cocoa." Airmire was in Mistral, the page of air.

Fiona smiled and grabbed Mac's warm rag-laden hand, squeezing it. Whatever ups or downs she had, it was nice to know a person who always felt safe to her. "Thank you, Mac."

"You keep coming to see me," Mac said, pointing with the rag.

Fiona nodded. Her eyes burned, but she blinked to clear them. "Mind fixing me a Fallen Bubble?"

Mac tipped her head to the side but nodded, working to get started on the drink. The back wall was covered in silver tubes that connected in crisscrossed lace patterns across the ceiling. Where they started was a mystery, but Mac's own concoctions flowed out of each one and into the goblets and glasses she left underneath them. Valves and levers with labeling in faekin language could be used to divert the cocktails to each individual table in the place, should Mac be too busy to wait on patrons one by one. It was a system that only she knew how to work. Fiona had tried to sub in once in her earlier days in Spine and poured a valuable amount of liquor on waiting patrons instead of glasses at the bar. She knew better than to lend a hand again.

She swiveled around to survey the room. Sitting across the room opposite from the jackets and Dodger was Fali, the Follower of Larrakane elephas she'd met the day before. Catching his eye, she nodded her head and smiled. Interesting that he would be here. He stood out in his full church regalia, but perhaps that was what he wanted. Did the Followers have someone scoping out the jackets, or was it the other way around?

She walked toward Fali, easing her attention across the variety of conversations happening in the room.

"Do gnomes even go on vacation?" said a human man. "They can't even see if there's more than a candle's breadth of light I thought."

"Everyone deserves a break now and again," said their smilodon companion.

He nodded his agreement. "You heard about the new pagemark to Kerus? Supposed to take you to this giant abacus thing."

"No, but I'm not surprised. The Guild has been hot to create a new outpost there. They're basically giving away paper to get more pagemarks set up in hostile areas. Blaze was high on the request list before the fire went out."

Intrigued by their discussion, Fiona failed to notice she had hovered closer to Petronia's table.

"What do you want?" the tigress grumbled.

Pivoting to the glaring woman, Fiona crossed her arms and said, "Nothing at all. Walking around freely, minding my own business."

"So you know how to do that now, huh?" Petronia scoffed. "Thought it would've taken a few more knocks for you to learn." She leaned back into the leather-and-wood chair, slinging an arm off the side, and glanced away.

Fiona took a breath, unlocking her arms and relaxing. She would not let this woman get to her. "Some of us have more sense than others."

"Whatever you have to tell yourself, meddler," she said and took a loud gulp from her mug, eyebrows raised over the rim.

"I was not meddling. You were accosting that poor faun just because you couldn't be patient."

Petronia snorted. "Some of us can't sit around and get kickbacks doing the nicey-nicey work." She pointed at Fiona. "Some of us have to do whatever it takes to survive."

"Excuses. That's a choice you're making. That has nothing to do with other people or how you should treat them."

"Like you would know." Petronia bared her teeth, tiny white knives. Her eyes were tight, but her tail swung to the side, twitching.

"Well, if I don't know, why don't you tell me?" Fiona said. They were staring eye to eye. Fiona recognized the signs of determination and grit in Petronia. There was something there, but what?

Petronia blinked. She seemed about to say something when Mac slid over to them, the scent of citrus like a cleaver between the two.

"Everything swell over here?" she said in her breezy voice.

"Just finishing my drink," Petronia said gruffly. She threw paper down on the table and drained her mug in one gulp.

Any chance to continue talking with the tigress was lost. Everyone's eyes were on them, and Fiona realized they must've been making quite the scene for Mac to come over. She pushed down the reaction to palm her face and smiled at Mac. "Just having a nice chat."

"Well, good. Next time, you two might want to do it at a lower octave."

Petronia pushed past the two ladies, bumping into Fiona and knocking her off balance. Fiona scowled inwardly, angry that for a brief moment she had actually wanted to understand this bully.

"Be seeing you," Petronia said under her breath.

Before Fiona could reply, the tigress was already making her way through the door, tail high, head held even higher.

Fiona shrugged, pulling her scarf a little tighter around her neck and shoulders. What dark-edge nightmare had that been? She looked over for Fali, but in the midst of her conversation with Petronia he had vanished. Sighing, she made her way back to the wooden bar, avoiding the watching eyes and whispering mouths.

"Here you go, Thorne." Mac placed a large fishbowl of a drink in front of Fiona. It was a shocking bright blue and had tiny puffy clouds floating in it. "Suppose you want to tell me why you're drowning yourself in this drink and starting arguments in my house? What's going on with you?"

"It's just been a very long day, Mac. A very long day." Fiona drank from the fishbowl and then sighed. Its smell was cloying but in a familiar way that she liked. The tartness of the puffy clouds mixed with the sweet liquor on her tongue, causing small bursts of delight within her. It gave her a small rush of energy and a feeling of weightlessness that she couldn't seem to find for herself today.

"All the paper in the Book if you tell me what's got you looking so far away." Dodger's voice came up behind her.

Spinning around, Fiona laughed nervously, caught in a moment of vulnerability. "It's me unfortunately. But let's forget about that. I believe I owe you a whiskey."

"What in the dark edge did I do to deserve such an expensive drink from you?" Dodger said, sitting down on a stool next to her.

Fiona waved to Mac, who got out a mug. "Well, for one, you actually listened when I talked to you about the elemental smuggler instead of shoving me off like some of your cohorts."

"I've learned that you're stubborn. I was just trying to head you off from relentlessly going after me."

"Mm-hmm," Fiona said. She knew Dodger wouldn't give in to his wanting to actually help her. She let it drop. "Did the rest of the creatures get to their pages safe?"

Dodger nodded and sipped at the whiskey Mac placed in front of him. He wrapped his paw around it and glanced at Fiona. "I saw you earlier leaving the district with a familiar-looking flame sprite." He stated slowly, "Care to explain yourself?"

Blast. Of course Dodger would pick up on the flame sprite being connected to the ambush on the smugglers. Well, she was doing nothing wrong. Fiona shrugged. "What's there to explain? Soots wanted to stay with me, so I said they could."

"Soots?" Dodger pushed the whiskey away, saying, "C'mon, Fi, you know you can't name the thing."

Fiona leaned back, crossing her arms. "They're not a thing, Dodger, they're a creature. A creature with a will of their own, mind you. They asked to stay. I couldn't say no. You know Blaze isn't doing well."

"Spine isn't where it belongs. It could be a danger to itself and others. Turners have training to acclimate to life outside their pages. Elemental creatures should visit, not stay, unless they go through the Guild process."

"Oh, it's been fine," Fiona lied lightly, pulling on the metal straw. "Hasn't been an issue at all."

"Look." He turned to face Fiona directly. "I was told that everything from the elemental smuggler had to go back to where they lived. That includes the flame sprite."

"The Guild can't decide against the creature's wishes. That would be ridiculous," Fiona scoffed. Even the Guild wouldn't try to impose their will on every page. Did they learn nothing from the Court of Copper fiasco?

"I don't have a say in what the Guild decides," said Dodger quietly.

"Don't you?" Fiona reached out and placed a hand on his cloak-clad shoulder. "I'm not going to argue with you. It'll get us both nowhere. We both think we're right. Besides"—Fiona tried to lighten her tone in light of his anxiousness—"what I really want to know is, is there a Guild investigation into Blaze dying?"

"You know I can't discuss Guild business with you," he said rotely.

"True, but you can discuss lack of Guild business." Fiona dropped her hand and rubbed it against the condensation on the fishbowl. "I know there hasn't been a regulatory jacket in Blaze for weeks now. What gives?"

Dodger glanced around, a motion that gave Fiona a small amount of alarm. If Dodger was worried about being overheard, perhaps there was something going on besides lack of oversight. "I asked Gilded Evenhell about that, actually, before the elemental smuggler business. There are other higher pressing matters."

Unbelievable. "Higher than an entire page possibly dying out?"

"It's not Travel Guild business," Dodger said and pursed his lips. His tail twitched.

Fiona pushed through, heedless of his discomfort. "It should be! We're the only ones with the ability to go to these places. What happens if the entire page is cooled? What about the things living there?"

"I agree. I worry about it too. But I trust the Binder and the Gilded leaders are doing what they know is best. They're better than my old page leaders by a mile." He tried to smile.

"You're a good person, Dodger, but your trust is misplaced. The Guild doesn't do anything that doesn't benefit them."

"This is the problem with you, Fi," he said, agitated. "You only believe in yourself. You don't see that other people try hard too, you know. We're all just trying to do the best we can."

Fiona stammered, surprised by Dodger's outburst, "Look, I didn't mean to imply—"

"But you did mean it. You did. I get that you don't want to be part of the Guild, or choose not to be. Whatever you tell yourself about them. But that's me too. I'm part of the Guild, Fi. I'm a jacket. Maybe figure out how to believe in something other than yourself. Or keep working alone with no one to back you up. It's up to you." He got up and moved away from her, then put some paper on the bar. "For the whiskey."

Her stomach tightened in a knot. He didn't understand, she didn't have the luxury of putting her faith—her future—in untrustworthy organizations like the Guild. "Dodger—"

"There's no sense arguing. It'll get us both nowhere, right?" he said, raising a brow, and walked away from her out the door.

Fiona watched him leave feeling like she wanted to hide. She turned around to the eyes staring at her and said in a shaky voice, "Oh, mind your own business for once."

She tossed her scarf over her shoulder and stormed out into the windy street of Spine, winding her way home. She'd taken enough punches today. If she'd wanted to feel awful about herself, she would've visited her mother.

11

"I JUST NEED ONE day where I'm not gasping for my life," said Fiona as she looked over the materials for her turn to Mistral. Putting off dealing with the fire elementals had been an easy choice when she woke up. She'd have to get more supplies and she was already tapping into what the druids had given. "Breathing potions don't just show up on your doorstep for free every day," she muttered.

So Fiona decided to start with Mac's lead. She hadn't been to Mistral in a couple of months and was looking forward to it. It would give her a chance to catch her breath, ignore the inkling of guilt she felt for upsetting Dodger, and get some minor movement on the smuggling case at the same time. She pulled out her ornithopter, its intricately folded wings and crinkled brown leather over shoulder straps dusty from being stuffed in the back of the closet. Cleaning it off, she coughed as the motes rose into the air. A sense of profound joy came from

Soots, who was watching her from a lamp on her night table near her bed.

"Ha ha, yes, very funny that I got dust up my nose."

Soots danced around in the lamp. :Leave!:

Fiona bent to look at the flame sprite. "I'm sorry, but I can't take you. I don't think you'd do well. The winds can get pretty high there. But I promise once we figure out something to protect you, you can go."

Sadness emanated from Soots and they flew out to Fiona. She put out the palm of her hand, feeling Soots's warmth hovering above it. They were doing much better at controlling their temperature. Soots still couldn't land on her without protection, but the heat wasn't searing.

Fiona sighed. "I'll make it a short trip, promise. And I found another stack of papers for you to chomp through."

A faint noise like a thump on wood caught her attention. Fiona stopped what she was doing and listened intently. The sound came through the window again. Peering out past her small porch, she didn't see anyone. Was someone throwing pebbles at her house?

Still holding the ornithopter, she strode down the stairs two at a time, through the office, and threw open the front door, hoping to catch whoever it was off guard. There stood Gaili, hand raised and eyes wide.

"Oh, I didn't mean to disturb you," she said, glancing down and away. Her small black horns were barely peeking above her bright rosy-pink hair, this time curled to perfection all over her head. Her clothing, a vibrant emerald-green satin bodice decorated with a warm cream brocade in a floral vignette, was tightened over a cream satin dress that puddled silkily toward her golden hooves. The Gaili of today was a bit softer in appearance, no oily smudges on her face or leather apron dusted with who knew what.

Fiona took a step back taking in the faun's gorgeous appearance and smiled lightheartedly. "You're hardly disturbing anyone with that knock. Next time feel free to give it a big bang. Come on in."

"Oh, I didn't want to bother you. Just wanted to drop this off." She motioned to a small chest on Fiona's doorstep.

"Nonsense, in, in." Fiona opened the door wide, waving for Gaili to enter.

Slowly, the faun did with a small smile, her head held low. "I just finished up the sprite's suit and thought I would drop it off. I'm sorry."

Fiona closed the door and moved to the stove. "You finished it in one night? Whatever are you apologizing for?"

"For dropping by unannounced, of course. I know it's rude. I just got so excited, and—" She stopped, wringing her hands. "I can just leave it here. Or..."

Fiona handed her a cup of warm coffee. Just like an inventor to work all night. She grinned up at her. "You're here now, and I'm not the least put out. I can also give you the pitiful token I got from Blaze yesterday." Fiona grabbed the branch from the shelf she had placed it on. "It's really not much, but hopefully it'll help you make some more of those jelly breaths."

"This is excellent!" Gaili said, rubbing her fingers across it. "Still warm even. I'm sure I can crush this up and use it."

"Excellent. I'll probably need more in the coming days. But let's move on to more entertaining matters. Show me what you have. We'd love to see. Soots!"

Soots bobbed down the stairs and toward Gaili. Happiness radiated from the sprite, and Fiona tried to ascertain Gaili's reaction. She didn't seem to notice the sentiment coming from them at all. *Odd.*

Gaili placed the chest on the desk and shrugged off her pack. She pulled a small flat swatch of a slinky metal material from the chest. "It's flexible so you can move into any position you want. It opens here but clasps on the outside, so there are no entry points." She opened one side of it to show how it expanded like a pocket. "You'll need help putting it on. But it's made out of a new material I helped to create, so you shouldn't worry about burning yourself by touching it. Though it will get very warm of course. I couldn't help that part. It's probably not right anyway. I should take it back and try again. I'm sorry to…"

Fiona took it gently from the faun's hand and put her fingers inside of it. It was incredibly light, almost like chain mail but so very different. It was intricately made, and she was eager to see it work.

Gaili watched, her rambling ceasing for the moment as Soots flew into the opening. Fiona latched it with the small clasps. She could see the flicker of flames burning inside in small movements but no heat. A grin spread across her face. "Gaili, this is absolutely perfect. I can feel their heat but it's not burning. And they are so happy about it."

When Fiona let go of the suit, Soots flew up into the air. It bobbed once, twice, then landed on Gaili's shoulder. :Friend!:

Gaili gasped. "You can talk?"

"I guess you haven't been around a lot of elementals?" Fiona said, sitting back down.

"No, not as much," Gaili said, trying to stand still.

Soots took off into the air again, shifting into different shapes inside the suit. It conformed to and outlined each one, and the delight from Soots was overwhelming.

Fiona couldn't tell if Gaili noticed or not but kept her thoughts to herself. "Well, I think they like it. We'll take it."

Gaili clapped her hands. "Oh, I'm so glad it worked out. I was worried, but I really wanted to get it done. I'm very glad you came to my shop. I wanted to find a way to thank you too for what you did, so I made this as well." Gaili pulled out a small crystal jar. Flecks of milk white shone throughout the stormy blue liquid inside.

Fiona was taken aback. She took the jar slowly, not sure what to say. Why would Gaili give her another thing for free? "You didn't have to do that. You already gave me the jelly breath, which worked rather well actually. A bit nuttier than expected but…" She trailed off, realizing Gaili wasn't listening to her but was instead staring at the forgotten ornithopter. "Do you like it? It's an older model I brought with me when I moved to Spine."

"Oh yes, I think it's just great. I've…I've never gotten to use one before. I've seen them, certainly, but I've always wanted to fly." She gently fingered the leather straps.

"You've *never* flown?"

"No, I mean, there's really nothing like it in the Court of Copper, and I've only been inked for a few months. I needed to get my business set up if I wanted to make it out here, so I've been focused on that."

Fiona put down the jar. This was exactly the distraction she wanted, and she wouldn't shoo it away. "Well, we absolutely have to change that. You're coming with me. Today. I've got to go to Airmire on some business."

"Oh no, I don't want to put you out," Gaili said, taking her eyes off the ornithopter. "I should get back to the shop."

"No, no. You must come with me. The shop can wait. It can always wait." Fiona moved to the stairs with a brief burst of adrenaline and excitement. "Drink your coffee and grab your things. I'll be back in two moments."

Wide eyed but smiling, Gaili did as instructed, popping the cup to her mouth.

Fiona raced back upstairs, taking the steps two by two. Getting to show an unread turner the beauty of Mistral was the first thing in a long while she was actually looking forward to.

AFTER LOADING HERSELF AND Gaili down with fur lined cloaks, they walked a short distance to the edge of the turner district. Pagemarks to Mistral were abundant in Spine. It was by far the easiest page to turn to and the safest. Not that there weren't dangers. An errant lightning storm or a territorial air elemental could spell disaster for a skimmer without a guide. But, using an official pagemark would get you there with little trouble. She rented an ornithopter for Gaili, who tried refusing but was quickly shut down with a plea from Fiona. "Larrakane's love, let me do something for you!" Gaili acquiesced and put the newer model on. It was a bit snug on Gaili's tall frame, but Fiona was glad it fit.

Since Fiona's ornithopter was from her native page, she couldn't use it as a bookmark for Mistral. Instead she reached into her scarf and felt for a padded pocket with thick stiches on the side. The fabric was soft and cool, and inside she grabbed a pressed feather she had gotten her first time in Mistral from a vendor selling tokens and trinkets.

She focused on the elemental chapter of the Book, directing her consciousness from Spine to that first chapter. Then she focused on the page itself. Fiona felt in the center of her being the flip of pages until she hit the thrum of the right one. Satisfied, she tuned to the specific pagemark that lined up with their place in Spine. The air shimmered around them and the world folded away to reveal wide-open sky. Grasping Gaili's hand tight and with Soots wrapped in the crook of her arm, Fiona stepped from Spine to Mistral.

The air grew cold as the page turned and the light grew brighter. Their feet sank into fluffy pure-white clouds. Bright blue bounteous skies surrounded them.

"Mistral is mostly air and clouds but with some bits of rock imported from Cobbles," Fiona explained as she adjusted her ornithopter, settling it tighter on her shoulders. "There's no night here, just day. No sun, just sky. Traveling in the page isn't natural, but if you're not a blotter and you've got enough paper to rent an ornithopter or passage on a ship, it's as easy as anywhere else."

"It's absolutely beautiful," breathed Gaili, head turning to and fro as she looked off into the distance.

Soots agreed with a small prance in their new suit. Fiona reached out to grab them. "Don't take off without me holding you. I'm still worried about the winds blowing you away, protected or not."

"Format has it the winds could be deadly if caught in one," said Gaili with furrowed brows.

"That's quite right. You have to know where you're going and pick a pagemark closest to it. And when you do get here, take it easy. Slow and steady keeps you safe."

Gaili nodded. "Where are we off to first?"

"There." She pointed to a dot in the distance. "Airmire. There's a ship I want to stop at for a quick chat." She pulled out a heavy egg-shaped pocket clock from her doublet and checked it. "It usually takes about thirty minutes or so. In a place like this, it's best to travel using time you can check. There's not a lot of...landmarks, as it were. It's easy to get lost."

"I vaguely remember that from training," Gaili said quietly, "but to be honest, I was more interested in learning how to get back home than anywhere else at the time."

"Hmm," Fiona said, not commenting. She had been delighted to be in training. To soak up the knowledge and information. Instead of the required year or so that unread turners had to take part in to transition from living in their page to living on Spine, Fiona had stayed at the academy for three years. She learned as much as she could away from home and only traveled back when expected. And she learned how much had been withheld from her too.

Shaking her head to beat away the ugly thoughts, she thrust the clock back into its pocket and tucked the scarf into her cloak. "Anything that falls will keep falling forever until it hits the dark edge or some floating land. Keep anything you like close on you."

Gaili clasped her pack straps tighter. After a hesitant nod, she pulled the rip cord on her ornithopter. The alchemical components that helped power it combined, burst into a smokeless friction, and she had flight. Fiona kept hold of Soots tightly.

They flew then, through the blue sky, ornithopter wings flapping to keep them aloft. A constant breeze buffeted against them. Fiona dived lower trying to shake the current and settle into a calm area where she could speed ahead. She had always liked to fly. In Restless Rise, her native page, she had loved to travel to the central peak from their home on one of the floating islands that revolved around it. Her father would take her on trips when he had to trade or sell things there. He always told her she was a natural in the sky and dived and twisted almost as well as any Mistral native.

Gaili's eyes started off glued to Fiona but eventually, with a little courage, she began to maneuver and test things out. Moving up was easy. Moving down, not too difficult, and of course forward was the way the ornithopter was built to go. Moving backward was a no go.

"I think I could tinker with this and add a little more power to it!" Gaili shouted over the wind.

"I was wondering when your mind would turn to tinkering. You're so clever," Fiona shouted back.

Gaili blushed, a crimson shade of pink on her golden face. Fiona was happy to see her new friend enjoy flying almost as much as she did.

Soon the speck in the distance became various winged ships bobbing in the sky. Masts stood with colorful sails flapping in the wind like carnival dancers clapping and twirling. Big iron anchors thrust into rocky pieces of floating earth. The ships were slotted next to each other in a row, various distances from the floating earth to give each other some space. They surrounded a voluminous cloudy city. Tall towers of pure white were set against the backdrop of creamy wisps and various creatures flying in and out of the city.

Fiona flew to the closest earth isle, pulled her rip cord to stop the blades, and landed gently on the rock. She tucked the wings in, pushing them down with a click, and covered them under her cloak. Gaili followed suit. Soots, happy to be free a bit, whizzed above their heads, metallic suit softly clinking.

"One of these ships belongs to a Captain Henrietta," Fiona said, walking swiftly to the next rocky isle. "A *Big Betty*."

"There's so many of them," breathed Gaili.

"Yes," Fiona said, squinting at ship names, "but I think I can spot which one would be a friend of Mac's."

She pointed to a hulking ship of polished mismatched wood. Though it gleamed, you could tell work had been done to it over the years, patching it up from various other ships. The sails were slightly tattered but strung up high. It wasn't new like some of the others or as lean as the ships back home. On the side of it was etched *Big Betty*.

They made their way to the rocky isle the ship was anchored in. A few of the crew—a mix of humans, bird creatures of the same stature, and a smilodon—looked over the railing.

Fiona waved in greeting, saying. "Hello there! Looking for a Captain Henrietta? Is this her ship, or have I blundered?"

"And who would be asking?" came a gravelly voice hidden from sight.

Fiona frowned. "My name's Fiona. Fiona Thorne. Mac sent me. She said you may be able to help me. She also asked about her blasted cocoa."

A red head and bright peach face popped up over the side of the railing. A large, mischievous grin beamed out. The voice didn't match the look at all. "Oh, that blighter of a woman." She raised a bushy eyebrow. "Don't tell her I said that though. Well, nice to meet you, Fiona Thorne. Come on up!"

Fiona snorted in incredulity but walked up the footbridge along with Gaili and Soots. The boards creaked beneath their feet, and a hint of polish and soap smells swirled about them in the cold wind.

Fiona took the captain's waiting hand, shaking it in greeting, her rough calluses warm. Though human like herself, Captain Henrietta was much brighter in skin and style. Pear-green baggy trousers that cut off after the knees, butter-yellow shirt, and a bright rosy cone-shaped hat to top it off. It was a bit shocking to her senses. While she'd grown up with tales of sky pirates of old, before all the floating island nations had been combined into one, she didn't think they were real.

Captain Henrietta must've seen the look often, for she said, "Ah, you like my flair?" She cupped her mouth, whispering as if it was a highly valued secret just for them. "It helps entice the skimmers, makes me stand out from all the other humans that come traipsing through here giving tours." She glanced at Gaili. "And who would this lovely be?" She bowed down to her. "I am enchanted to meet you."

Gaili, cheeks crimson again, nodded and said her name quietly.

"Beautiful name for a beautiful lass. Come, let us discuss in the captain's office, shall we? You can partake of some of Mac's blasted cocoa." She bellowed a laugh and led them down a step into a wooden office that fit them all well enough amid a massive desk and a couple of deep-seated chairs. The walls held various maps of Mistral pinpointing pagemarks and blockades. There were also paintings of Henrietta with her crew and landscapes of scenic spots within Restless Rise and Mistral. Seemed as if she spent most of her time between the two. Captain Henrietta settled herself behind the desk and began to brew a pot of milk.

Fiona took Soots out from the cranny of her arm and said, "Soots, are you okay? You've been awfully quiet."

:Hungry,: said Soots sadly. They were curled in a ball. Fiona could barely feel any warmth from them.

"Does that slim metal talk?" Captain Henrietta said, brushing her strawberry hair out of her face and peering at Fiona's hands.

"They're a flame sprite friend. Gaili made this suit for them as some protection when we cross pages. It's their first trip to Mistral." Fiona frowned. "I assume."

Captain Henrietta clapped her hands. "My dear, that is an ingenious contraption. Never seen anything like it."

"Well, I made the materials myself using an old human technique combined with a Court approach. Melting the metal and then combining it with iococom powder makes them strong. Setting the metal mixture into tiny links that interlock makes it flexible. Stitching the links together creating a pocket helps displace the heat Soots outputs and feeds it back to them so they never really lose it in environments not made for them. It could work the same for other things, but..." She trailed off as the two looked at her with wide eyes.

"I think that is the most I've ever heard you say," Fiona said. She pressed her lips together at her rude comment. "Sorry."

"No, no, it's okay. I could go on and on about this sort of work. I try not to."

"You know, we could use something like that on the ship. Not being from here, sometimes it gets awfully cold during a good sail. Perhaps we can commission something or other from you."

Gaili's eyes lit up. "I'd like that very much."

:Hungry,: said Soots, interrupting the conversation.

"Yes, apologies, Soots. I've gotten distracted." Fiona turned to Captain Henrietta. "Do you mind if Soots borrows your little stove there?"

"Oh no, help yourself. Help yourself."

They watched as Fiona placed a stack of wood chips on the stove and Soots flew to it. A small fire leapt up from Soots, engulfing the bits.

Captain Henrietta jumped out of her chair and backed up. "Oh, quite right. Yes, well now, that's a bit of a blaze. Let's be careful. Ship's still wooden."

She gingerly moved the pot of cocoa off the stove next to Soots and poured it out in three mugs. Pulling out a flask, she topped one of them off and then rattled it toward the ladies.

Fiona smiled but shook her head. "On business. But thank you all the same." She sat down in one of the chairs.

"Oh yes, quite right. Quite right." She looked at the flask for a moment and then poured a little more into her mug before putting it away. "You said you had questions for me?"

Fiona pulled the stationery she had scribbled on with Mac out of her scarf. "Yes, do you know what sort of cypher this is? I had Mac translate some of the words, but nothing lines up."

Captain Henrietta pulled out a pair of spectacles, shook them out, and placed them on the bridge of her nose. She picked up the paper, peering at it closely while sipping her drink. "This here is cant."

"Cant?" Fiona asked.

"Yes, thieves cant. A few ruffians and rippers use it back on Rise. But it's been through a bit of an improvement. Let me see here." She got out a pencil and licked the tip of it, then translated onto the document.

Blaze - Firetail | One | LM
Depths - Handfish | Five | DI
Mistral - Harmina | Ten | QE
Cobbles - Rockworm | Three | DI

"And so on," she said.

Fiona stared at it trying to work out what Henrietta obviously could tell. "I suppose it's relating what was taken and from where."

"It's a bit of work, but I see how it's maybe been done. The language written should indicate what page, but that would be too easy. Most cant has a value on where it's placed. So see this word written in Aer. Well, in Aer that would be *fire*. So you know to read the rest of it as it pertains to Blaze. Not to Mistral. And then it's lined up by page."

"So you mean the way the order of the pages line up in the elemental chapter of the Book is the way this ledger has them grouped. Blaze, Depths, Mistral, and Cobbles," said Gaili, chin in hand listening.

"Yes, that about sums it. Easy enough if you know what you're reading but not so easy that anyone can just pick it up."

Fiona pursed her lips. She tried to choose her words carefully but wanted to understand just where Henrietta sat. "And this cant is new to you? You picked it up fairly easy."

Captain Henrietta sat back and sipped her mug. "Smugglers deal with all sorts of ways of talking. If I couldn't pick things up, I couldn't be in business." Fiona's eyebrow raised. Henrietta laughed, at ease. "That Mac. Direct about some things but not about what others might think is important to know. I only deal with mild things. Cocoa, for instance. And coffee. Things that are taxed too high by the Queen and the cursed Guild."

"And how do you know we aren't with the Guild?" Fiona said. It felt like the third time this week someone was saying it was clear she wasn't a jacket. It didn't feel like a compliment though.

"Well, for one thing, Mac sent you. And another, you're too nice! Jacket would've asked to see my storage hold by now. No, you ain't no Guild, lass. But you've got the eye of 'em."

Fiona nodded. "You're pretty astute. I'll give you that."

"Well, what's more, I can tell you something about those letters at the end."

"And that would be?"

"Those are Gilded initials."

"What?" said Gaili.

All mirth flew from Fiona and she sat up straight. "How can you be sure?"

"Easy as blueberry pie. Got a request to bring back harmonas from the Flurris colony a few months ago. You know those tiny birds always flitting around? Turned it down for sure. Don't deal in that kind of work. Ain't right. But the request came from a jacket who said they were acting on behalf of their boss. A Gilded leader, they said. Of course I didn't want to be trussed up for my regular work, so I didn't say anything. Who was I gonna say it to?" Henrietta put her mug down on the desk and brushed hair out of her face. "I've felt keenly bad about it ever since. If this is something you're into, I want to help. Least I can do. I can say no, but some others can't afford to."

Fiona let out a deep breath. Gilded leaders were not people she wanted to trifle with. She met a few when she worked for the Guild as a tour guide. They had been nice enough, but she was a trivial worker in the cog of the Travel Guild then. They had no reason to care about what she did, and she them. But there were only six of them in total, and besides their leader, the Binder, they had the most power in the Book.

She ran her hand through her curls. "I appreciate the information, Henrietta. I do. If this ledger links to the Gilded, to the Travel Guild at all...well, that's a bit more than I expected. I'll need to talk to my client about it. But keep your ear to the ground."

"Aye, that I can do. And the air as well."

Fiona smiled halfheartedly, mind buzzing. So much for her easy next step on the smuggling case. "It was nice to meet you. I hope to see you again soon. Do you often stay near Airmire?"

"Aye, it's the best city in all of Mistral, if I do say so myself. And I can move around as easy as a bird when I want to. You ever need to go somewhere in the blue sky, you come see Captain Henrietta now."

"I absolutely will," Fiona said, rising. "But first I promised Gaili I'd show her around Airmire. If you have any information for me, you can find me in the turner district. Thorne Investigations."

She nodded. "And don't be a stranger yourself, lass." Captain Henrietta said to Gaili, "I'd love to see you again."

Gaili nodded softly, glancing at Fiona before saying, "Maybe when she comes back I can join her."

"Soots, we're leaving," Fiona called out to them.

Soots moved from the stove, ashes and tiny bits of wood the only remains of their meal, and flew into Fiona's arms, warming her. She didn't realize how cold she was until they were nestled there.

THE BLADES WHIRRED ABOVE their heads as they made their way down to the entrance of Airmire. Densely surrounded by clouds, they could hardly see. Once they broke through the wet barrier, Fiona shouted to Gaili, wicking moisture from her face, "Now you'll see what it's really like."

The majestic city was sprawling. Peaks of thick cloud-like structures overwhelmed the horizon. Although the appearance was floaty and bright, the docks, buildings, and rails were solid and dense. A sweetness hung on the air, like the tarts from the Thread, mixing in with the scents of travelers, humidity, and something crisp and clean. Travelers swarmed in and out like ants from the main entrance. Some wore different variations of the ornithopter, but a few walked with striking turquoise amorphous creatures leading them.

"So you can enter the city and walk on the lower level. That one is more accommodating for land dwellers—us—than the higher levels. I suggest you always keep a hand on your rip cord. You could fall through the floor in some parts of the city."

Gaili's eyes widened and she clutched at her cord handle. "Are we allowed in all parts?"

"Mostly, yes. Airmire is a bit more touristy than other spots in Mistral. Those places, land dwellers don't go over so well. But we should be safe here." Fiona adjusted her scarf around her neck and tucked the ends of it into her collar. She didn't want anyone ripping it from her. "Soots, want to sit on my shoulder?"

Soots pushed out of the crook of her arm so quickly she suspected they were just being polite by staying there. They landed on her shoulder and radiated a happy sort of contentment. Fiona enjoyed the minute warmth from the small creature in the midst of the chilly air.

They got in the short line to the city's entrance. "Mistral natives can fly into the city, so this is just for us. Guild run, of course," Fiona said.

"An outpost?"

Fiona nodded. "Feels like they have more and more every day."

They got to the front of the line where a human jacket was writing in his book. "Pleasure or business?"

"Pleasure," Fiona said, letting her natural musical accent shine through. She moved closer, curious to see if anything else was being noted down. She could make out a brief scrawl of names above hers with a *P* or a *T* next to it.

"From?" he said, sounding bored.

If they were tracking turners, she wanted to see if little inconsistencies would be caught. "Rise," she said.

"Name?"

"Fiona Thorne."

He nodded his head, never looking up, and she walked on through. Gaili caught up with her in a moment, and they strode into the busy rush of various pulp. A strikingly tall birdfolk in little more than a thick leather belt below their gray-plumaged breast pushed past them, cuffing Fiona with their wing. They didn't bother to look back or apologize. Whirls of stark white air in tight curls passed by them speaking in Aer, and Fiona strained to understand what they were saying. She had only studied enough of the language to be passable when she first started training.

The whirls of air moved on, and Gaili whispered excitedly to Fiona, "Sylphs! I've never seen them up close before. I think I stared too hard. One of them called me nosy." She pouted.

"Can you understand what they're saying?" While Fiona had been actively listening, she didn't think Gaili had even focused on them, much less anything else, for more than a few seconds.

"Oh yes. It's important in the Court to be able to speak as many languages as possible. My mentor taught me all the elemental languages, your language, and even the difficult purr of the smilodon..." Gaili trailed off lips pressed together in a grimace. The faun's expression seemed conflicted.

Fiona laid a hand on Gaili's arm to comfort her. "Your mentor?"

She bit her lip, nodding and shifting her eyes away from Fiona.

Seeing that her friend was clearly anxious when talking about her, Fiona grew hot. Whoever this person was had to be the cause of Gaili's timidity and excessive apologizing. No doubt someone with more power than sense. The faun was clearly warm, sweet, and clever. Fiona squeezed her arm gently. "Dear Gaili, I don't want to make you uncomfortable but if you ever want to talk about her, I'm here to listen." She dropped her hand and smiled brightly to chase away Gaili's sadness. Going back to their previous subject, she said, "Well, your understanding of languages is quite brilliant. And sure to come in handy. If you hear anyone say anything about the Travel Guild, or elemental smugglers, or a giant black stone, do let me know."

Gaili nodded, giving only a brief sidelong glance of curiosity. Fiona felt she probably deserved a rundown but not while they were out in the open. Linking her arm in the faun's, she said, "Let's shop a bit, shall we?" and led her off to the next level of the city through an open entrance.

Doors weren't truly a thing here. For one, they were seen as an unnecessary barrier for most of the natural citizens. And the amount of material that would need to be imported to make enough doors for all the shops, abodes, and more would be enough to feed everyone in this page for a solid decade.

It was much less busy and crowded on the upper level. Their feet sank into the cloudy floor with each step. The streets turned into a maze of corridors, runoffs, and dead ends. The city hadn't originally been made for land dwellers but adapted after the Blessing of Larrakane. It was easy to get lost or turned around. Having a guide or a way to fly up to get a view from above made it much easier to tell directions, but Fiona knew exactly where she was headed.

She strode into the craft district that was wide open with loads of space for people to move. A sky-top clearing. A small fire was lit to one side, and a handful of crafters were working a forge of conflicting visuals. The stone and brickwork containing the fire, all very much imported, floated on a cloud that had tendrils to keep it tethered to the city floor.

The handful of individuals working the forge never looked up as the trio approached. They were air that whirred like tiny cyclones in one spot. Vaguely visible and faintly humanoid, but that could've just been a biased view. Small flicks of rapid, piercing wind came off them as they worked. One was holding long tongs with a large rain cloud, its gray coloring stark against the brick. Another was blowing air directly into the fire in a thin stream, keeping it going while the third held a glass in tongs to catch the resulting steam. Soots flew off Fiona's shoulder to the forge and broke into the group rapidly before she could reach out and grab them. She quickly trotted forward lest there be a repeat of the loom incident.

"Good heavens," one exclaimed, whistling.

They peered at Soots as a brief burst of flame flared in the forge, and then Soots came back to sit on Fiona's shoulder.

The one blowing air into the forge sat back. "Thanks there. I could use a break."

:Fire!:

"Yes, that was rather well done, Soots," Fiona said, proud of them for helping, though she had a sinking suspicion they'd merely taken the chance to get warm when they saw it. She was glad Gaili's suit passed the unexpected test.

Fiona noticed Gaili wasn't beside her and found her slowly walking through the area looking in workshops and chambers. Her hand covered her face, but there was a large grin on it.

"Find anything you like?" Fiona called out. One typically did in Airmire, unless they hated lovely things.

"Oh, it's just amazing. All these delicate items, and these clouds. Look how they use them." Gaili motioned to a blue-skinned creature with lines of white crisscrossing their skin. They held a small cloud, like handfuls of dyed cotton, and tucked it into a golden-handled azure paper fan with a large luminescent feather. It was like watching a watercolor come to life, the hues playing against one another. They kept tucking until the cloud completely disappeared into the folds of the fan.

"Wind fan?" they said in Aer.

"I can buy it?" said Gaili.

"Well, you can't take it for free," they said, nonplussed, and dropped the fan on the table in front of them to begin working on the next.

Gaili's golden face tinged a blushing pink. "No, certainly not. What does it do?"

"Fans the wind," they said, face crinkling.

"Sorry, yes please," Gaili said. She paid for the wind fan, more papers than Fiona would've advised, and a small cloud as well. There was a tendril connected to it, and she gripped to it tightly. "I wish I could live here. It's so gorgeous. The fire makes the sky behind it somewhat blush and violet doesn't it?"

"Hmm, yes it does," said Fiona, noticing for the first time how the small forge changed the atmosphere around it. The clean smell was gone, replaced by whiffs of earth and smoke coming from the forge. It unexpectedly reminded her of home.

"It's hard knowing you can never live anywhere else again," Gaili said, running her fingers over the fan.

"Is it?" Fiona said, rubbing her scarf. "I didn't want to stay at home, so it was a relief when I was inked."

"Really? Why?"

"My mother was terrible," Fiona said, her voice throaty. For some reason she wanted Gaili to understand her. Dodger's comments poked at the back of her mind. "She demanded a level of perfection that I could never match. My actions reflected on her, and they had to be very good actions indeed."

"Who was she trying to impress?"

"The Queen. Our leader. Unfortunately it never quite worked out under her terms. She got everything she wanted when I was inked though, oddly enough. Land, title, notoriety. And I got to escape to Spine." Even after almost two decades, it still felt like an escape.

Gaili clasped her hands together, nodding. "It is sort of an escape, isn't it? Having to live there forever and get distance from people's previous expectations. I guess that's why they call it the Blessing of Larrakane instead of a curse."

Fiona shook her head to remove the thoughts she had shoved down years ago and laughed, forcing some gaiety back into her voice. "Only a curse if you had a good home life, I suppose."

Gaili inclined her head in agreement, her look as far away as her own. A small bit of heaviness released from Fiona. It was nice knowing someone else understood what she meant, especially when it was an awful thing to say.

14

AFTER ESCORTING GAILI BACK home from Airmire, all Fiona wanted to do was relax. It had been a long but enjoyable day. The oil lamps flickered in the dark as she meandered down the street. She stretched her arms walking the lane that led to her home. She should practice with the ornithopter more often. They were not light, and she didn't want to get caught in the big blue sky with an arm cramp just because she was out of shape.

Soots flew above her not too far out of reach, lighting up the path ahead. They seemed content with the silence as they walked. Fiona was glad of the company even as her mind wandered.

That the Gilded were somehow potentially involved in the smuggling and theft of elemental beasts confounded her. The Travel Guild had more paper than any other organization in the Book. They should—they printed it. And heaps of power too. To get involved in something as lowly and icky as smuggling—no, snatching at this point—elemental creatures, what could they possibly be doing it for? She knew they were corrupt; all big organizations were in some way even if you couldn't see it. But this was something she wouldn't have placed on their doorstep.

Buying the creatures didn't make them more money, did it? Even if it did, the ledger only contained something like thirty or forty trades. Not really what one would call a large enterprise. What could they be doing with them? She couldn't see the whole organization taking a part in it. Too hard to keep something like this a secret if everyone down to the administration office knew about it. Perhaps an individual or small group under a particular leader in the Guild.

"Mistress Thorne," Mistress Didia called from across the way, waving her arm frantically. "Yoo-hoo!"

Fiona smiled brightly, thoughts of the Guild pushed aside for the moment. "Good evening. Is everything alright?"

"Oh yes." She nodded, adjusting her glasses. She glanced up and down the street before saying, "I just wanted to let you know you missed a visitor. They were out there for about an hour or so on your doorstep, but they didn't leave a note."

Fiona fought off the habit of raising her eyebrow. She didn't know Mistress Didia was paying that much attention to her home. Perhaps it was for the good? "What did they look like?"

"Oh," Mistress Didia said, glancing away as if she had trouble remembering, "tall elephas man. Broad shoulders. No tusks, not on that one."

"Any particular clothing?" Fiona prompted the amusing woman.

"Oh yes, yes. Larrakane regalia on his tunic. Maybe a librarian from the temple?" she said, voice bright and hopeful.

"Perhaps." Fiona shrugged lightly. She didn't want to give Mistress Didia too much info to work with. Though she was a client and a good neighbor, Fiona could see the telltale signs of a gossip. "Thank you for letting me know." So Fali had come to visit her. Interesting. Perhaps she would seek him out at the temple tomorrow and figure out what he wanted.

"Of course." She nodded, slowly walking back to her porch. "If you figure it out, let me know."

It sounded like a tiny demand but not meanly meant. Fiona laughed lightly. "Good night, Mistress Didia." She headed toward her home but stopped when she realized the office door was slightly ajar. Frowning, she motioned for Soots to come closer and whispered, "Stay here and don't say anything."

Walking quietly up her front porch, she listened for any noise coming from the house. Silence except for the background chatter of the city itself. She peered through the open door, the lock busted, the wood cracked, but saw no movement, no flicker of shadows. Reaching into her scarf, she pulled out her whip slowly. If someone was still here, she wanted to surprise them. She threw open the door and advanced into the office.

It was empty.

She moved lithely to the living room, keeping an ear out for sounds.

It was empty as well.

Taking the stairs two at a time in her practiced manner, she barely heard the floorboards creak under her feet. Checking all the rooms on the second floor, she was dismayed to find they were empty as well. Everything seemed to be in order. She strode back downstairs to check her books, her collectibles, and her essentials. It was all there.

Her stomach tightened, and she made her way to the desk where she had locked the ledger. The drawer was empty. Everything was gone. How they had even known it was there bothered her. Without it she had no evidence to back up the Guild connection besides hearsay. Not that it had been much at all, but it could've helped authenticate the lead with the smugglers.

Had Fali, a Follower of Larrakane, stolen the ledger? Perhaps that wasn't the right question. Fali had undoubtedly stolen it. He seemed like a person who could do such a thing, and he had been here at the right time. Why did the Followers want it? She didn't want to confront him before she figured out the connection. She wasn't on her best footing when surprised and lacking information.

Fiona shouted out Soots's name. They came barreling into the house, more white hot than their usual amber glow.

"It's okay, it's okay. Everything's fine," Fiona whispered. "I just wanted to check things out. Seems someone's helped themselves to my evidence."

:Home,: said Soots, emanating displeasure.

"Yes, I'm not happy about someone being in here either. I'll figure it out. Don't worry."

Soots bobbed to the stove and dived into the fresh wood Fiona had placed there this morning. Seeming to take their feelings out on the wood, there was a loud pop as they hunkered in.

Fiona rushed to the stove to see if Soots had been hurt, but was surprised that the smell of melting metal wasn't coming from the stove but the front door. Throwing it open, she found the Ashborn with their wing on her door knocker. Or what was left of it.

"Perhaps you should discover a new way to allow guests to alert you of their arrival," the Ashborn said. Instead of lighting up the night, the darkness seemed to surround them, shadows clinging to their fiery flickers of light where the daylight soaked and reflected them. It somehow made them more formidable.

Bowing her head to give herself a moment to switch tracks from the theft to their arrival, Fiona said, "Yes, Your Eminence, I do believe some upgrades are necessary." She didn't want any further damage to her home, nor did she want people to see them talking on the front porch. She sighed. "Please, come in."

The Ashborn entered, their golden plumage tinged with red on the tips. They didn't move to sit on the stove or even farther away from the door. The wood around them creaked. "Time is dwindling and, lo, I have come here directly on important business with you, young one. Have you found my Blackstone?"

So much for privacy. She moved from the open door, hoping the Ashborn would follow. "As of right now, no," Fiona said, eyebrows furrowed. It had only been a day since she had gotten the job in the first place. "I have talked with the salamanders. They directed me to the elementals. I am working to find who stole it so I can—"

"I am not looking for who stole it," said the Ashborn, flipping their wing, a blur of rust and copper flickering together as they spoke. "They can be dealt with later. But the Blackstone must be reclaimed as soon as possible."

That had to mean they already knew who the thief was. It must've been a salamander, flarion, or ragnis then. "What is this Blackstone for?" Fiona said shortly. It had sounded like a valuable trinket yesterday, but their reappearing so soon made it feel like much more.

"For? It is a relic of our page. Nothing more needs to be said upon the subject." The Ashborn fluffed their feathers, making themself bigger. "And furthermore, you have not attained sufficient rank or favor to be questioning me. You are to find out where it is at all due cost and with the utmost urgency and bring it back to me. Focus on that."

Fiona raised an eyebrow at the Ashborn's ruffled feathers and irritated tone. *Struck a nerve, did I?* "Of course, Your Eminence. Please forgive my questioning you. It is appropriate in my line of work."

"Find others to question then, I do suggest."

"As you say," said Fiona and then immediately, "but why do you need the Blackstone back so soon? You gave me a week's time."

"The sooner it is in its rightful place, the sooner I can begin to put Blaze in order so we can, as one, face our catastrophe."

"And what would be its rightful place?"

"With me. I am responsible for—" the Ashborn stopped. While the light from the phoenix stilled, their shadow did not.

Fiona focused on the shadows. They danced around them as if they were a part of the creature, illuminating some internal struggle of theirs. "You're responsible for the Blackstone?" she prodded.

"And   more,"   the   Ashborn   finished   their uncharacteristically short sentence.

The Elder's words clambered up from the back of her mind. She watched the Ashborn carefully. "And you are the rightful owner?"

The phoenix narrowed its beady copper eyes. "Are you questioning the domain of my power?"

The room warmed but Fiona didn't wince. She wouldn't be intimidated by a show of fire. "Of course not, Your Eminence. Merely wondering where the artifact's ownership lies so that I can physically assess the site for clues. But only by your permission, naturally." She could gain a lot from being around the Ashborn at the site of the theft.

"Naturally," the Ashborn nodded. "Come to me on the morrow and you can search for your clues in the sanctuary of my people at Radiance Peak. I take my leave of you now."

Before Fiona could reply, they exited the house toward a lone floating shapeless fire elemental waiting for them on the street again. Mistress Didia waved from across the street, eyes round like saucers. Fiona sighed and gave a small wave back before closing the door and leaning against it. She'd really have to invest in somewhere less flammable to entertain guests.

The Ashborn was clearly hiding something. If getting the Blackstone back was such a pressing matter to them that they would show up twice in Spine in a matter of days, there must be some sort of countdown that they need it for. If the Blackstone could somehow help them face the dying of Blaze, it must be powerful indeed. She palmed her face and trudged to the desk, thinking.

"Soots," she called out.

They came bobbing out of the candle :Friend.: They stopped in front of the window, the glass reflecting the little sprite's glow.

"Yes, though I'm curious why they're not telling us everything about the Blackstone." She looked at Soots, watching the floating fire elemental closely. "Are you a flarion? The salamanders called you such, but I've only seen your kind from a distance."

:Soots,: they said adamantly.

"Okay, okay, you're Soots. I am sorry to have questioned you." Fiona threw up her hands, muttering under her breath about hot headed elementals, and made her way upstairs. She needed to talk to the elementals to see if it was a waste of time, a diversion, or a true lead.

She thought she might as well prepare for a full day in Blaze tomorrow. She could do some research at the library before making her way. Getting lost in the hot page was not her idea of a fun day. She would need quite a few breathing potions for the time. She wished, not for the first time, she could find a source that allowed her to breathe in all of the pages.

Fiona stopped on the stairs, placing her hand on the wall. Of course, that was it. The Blackstone had to be a source for Blaze. Something that kept the fire going. Otherwise why would the Ashborn be so focused on it in the midst of their page dying? But why wouldn't they go to the Guild, who certainly had more resources to find it than she did?

She had been too distracted by the break-in to coax more information out of the Ashborn. She needed to find someone who she could trust from Blaze to tell her what was really going on so she could poke her nose in the right direction.

Fiona smiled realizing she had at least one ally there. Perhaps her new friend Rockcruncher had a little more knowledge about the dynamics of the denizens and could give her a better picture. She would focus on the bigger issue of the Blackstone and deal with skulking priests later.

THE NEXT MORNING FIONA and Soots quickly stopped at Gaili's for more jelly breaths. Prepared to be disappointed by low stock, Fiona was pleasantly surprised that Gaili not only had a batch just for her but also wanted her to try a new concoction. The faun had stayed up all night making it from her Mistral purchases and was practically asleep on her feet.

Fiona didn't know why the faun overworked herself so, but she made a note to invite her over for dinner later and poke her about it. Not out of judgment of course—who was she to judge someone who worked as much as herself—but she was interested if it had something to do with her previous mentor.

Leaving the artisan district, Fiona and Soots made their way to Fire Bowl. It was a fortified area next to the artisans. There were no fences that guarded it or hills that shielded it. The entire district was located within obsidian rock that resembled an upside-down bowl from a distance. The crust of

Spine was too dense for the digging required to place a hot top, as the salamanders called the heavy flat rock they preferred. Though they did give it a good try. So instead they crafted a sphere of obsidian and placed their homes within it.

It was almost impossible to get to the top entrance without flying or crawling up the side. Only the citizens of the district used that entrance.

A small trail of lava had poured out of the top entrance of Fire Bowl for decades now. It was why the artisan district was built so close to it. Now, that was dried up as much as Blaze.

When they arrived, Fiona took a moment to prepare herself. She put on her fireproof equipment, sprayed herself down with her remaining mist, and popped on her thin, snug glasses. She hoped to catch Rockcruncher at a good time of day. Once her gear was on, she went to the ebony rock entrance of the bowl that faced the artisan district. From a distance it was impossible to see if there even was an at-ground entrance. Up close the outline of the inset door was barely visible. Without experience one could miss it entirely. Fiona pulled on the warm, heavy iron door knocker, the sound hammering against the stone door. She heard no reply.

Soots bobbed beside her in their metallic suit, softly clinking, the rays from within making dappled amber lines on the volcanic rock. Soots swirled around her, and she turned about to tell them not to run off when she noticed a dark shadow move from one of the buildings toward them. She couldn't tell if it was humanoid, the morning light making it hard to pinpoint features. She squinted and took a step forward to get a better look.

A thud sounded behind her and she whirled around to see a rectangular slit open in the door. Two beady gray smoke-filled eyes pierced the dark slot. A waft of noxious gas eked out as a raspy voice said in Claire, "Who you?"

She turned her attention to the door, momentarily forgetting the shadow. "I'm a visitor."

"You don't look like a visitor."

Fiona bit back a sigh and tried to speak clearer in the crackling language. "I'm a friend of a salamander who lives here." Fiona covered her nose with her scarf to talk through it as a filter. Jelly breath didn't do anything to oppose the fumes coming off of this creature.

The stone slit shut, and Fiona waited a minute as the keeper of the door opened it. She looked back across the way, but the shadow was gone. She shook her head, feeling muddled in the brain, and rocked on her slippers impatiently.

The stone gate slid to the side and a wave of heat escaped out the door as Fiona and Soots made their way inside. A miasmit sat on a stool within the gate, seemingly in charge of the door. The smell wafting off it combined with the heat was almost enough to make Fiona rethink looking for Rockcruncher near his home instead of sending a message asking him to visit her. But thoughts of her manor house catching fire seemed worse, so she pressed on.

"Thank you," said Fiona, ever pleasant. Her eyes pricked with tears at the noxious stench, and instead of asking for directions, she hurried on deeper into the darkened district. The fact that the glasses didn't protect from the miasmit was duly noted.

There was some order to Fire Bowl in that there appeared to be cleared lanes for foot travel. But that was pretty much it. A flarion, their amorphous shape only outlined by the inky ichor flowing through their body, darted in the dark down the path.

Fiona hurriedly called out in Claire, "Excuse me. I'm looking for a Spine Rockcruncher. Salamander?"

The elemental stopped, their flickering flames casting soft burnt orange light on their initial surroundings. "Hot rocks. Two paths down, hang a left at the pool of lava. Number six. Ya can't miss it."

Fiona nodded her thanks and turned to move on, but the elemental addressed Soots: "You're a tiny bit, aren't you? You come here often?"

:No,: they said, fire crackling as they spoke.

The elemental stopped. Fiona tried to understand what they could possibly be thinking. Having no expressions to go off of, she said, "The flame sprite is with me. They're alright."

"Yes, well..." The elemental trailed off, hesitating. "Um...be seeing ya." And they floated away.

Fiona bit back a smile. "Soots, I do believe you're a conundrum to everyone we meet. I'm not sure if that's because you're hanging out with me or something else."

:Friend,: said Soots, amusement spilling out with the word.

"Oh, so you're blaming me. Very well. I have a thick skin either way," Fiona said with a small laugh.

They came upon a street filled with flat rock homes similar to those found in Westtree. Fiona looked for number six and knocked on the stone arch outside it. Seeing that she made absolutely no noise, she said loudly into the arch, "Rockcruncher? It's me, Fiona. Sorry to show up so abruptly."

Fiona heard a bumping in the house. A wide-eyed Rockcruncher popped his head out of an open window. He licked one of his eyes with his long purple tongue. "Fiona?"

"Yes, sorry to bash right in, but I wanted to ask you some questions about Blaze. Thought maybe you could help."

"Oh, right. Come on in."

She had to bend to get all the way through the open archway. The ceiling of the hut was lower than she was. Soots bobbed in behind her and settled down on a stone table in the middle of the room. A few rock stools low to the ground surrounded it. On the opposite side was another open archway, but the dwelling was sparse. How often did Rockcruncher stay here really? He probably spent as much time as he could in his pre-inking city, by the looks of things.

Fiona perched on one delicately, making sure to keep the fireproof cloak between any of her fleshy parts and the warm stone.

Rockcruncher padded over from the window and sat opposite Fiona. He eyed the flame sprite. "Is this a flarion?"

"This is Soots. A friend of mine," Fiona said, avoiding the questions.

The salamander nodded and then ignored them. "You said you need help?"

"Well, I need a few answers about Blaze from someone who is direct. You seem very direct. And you clearly know when to hustle someone."

Rockcruncher licked his eye. "Hustle?"

Fiona tried again trying to be clearer in her translations. "Yes, you covered my escape the other day. Why did you do that?"

"The council can be a bit shortsighted. I didn't think putting you in jail was the best outcome for any of us."

"Well, you definitely helped save my life. I couldn't breathe there much longer. I owe you for that," she said, rubbing her gloved hand on the warm stone table. Her options had been rather limited, and she was grateful for him being there.

"It was nothing." Rockcruncher shrugged.

"It was most definitely *not* nothing," Fiona said firmly. If there was a moment Fiona didn't mince words, it was when she believed something to be true and needed others to believe it as well.

There was a brief pause before Rockcruncher broke eye contact from Fiona. He nodded. "What questions do you have?"

"What is Obsidian's Tooth?" Fiona rocked back on her stool.

"Skinny twin spires. They pierce through all the layers."

"Hmm," Fiona murmured. So there were towers in Blaze. She tried to remember if she had ever seen anything like them there, but they must've been on the other side of the volcano. "Can you sketch me a map? Of where Obsidian's Tooth sits? And its relation to Radiance Peak?"

Crunchers tail thumped on the ground. "Well, sure. But I wouldn't go there."

"Why's that?"

"The towers"—he started outlining them with his hands—"they're full of fire."

"I should be a bit protected." Fiona motioned to her apparel. "But I'll keep my time there short. I'm curious about the relationships in Blaze. I know some of the salamanders often fight with the elementals. How far does that go?"

"There's almost never any actual fighting."

"What?" Fiona said a little too loudly, causing Soots to jump. She was fairly certain she had heard of battles from history lessons. Of many, many fights. "What do you mean?"

"Well, we prepare for fighting. And we build things for the fights. The council tells us what to do and we do it. We travel and scout and generally insult the elementals. But more often than not, attacking each other never actually happens. Maybe it did before the inking, but it hasn't since. Other things occupy us." Rockcruncher said, "Between Arden's Rock and their realm, Iasheoxus…" He shrugged his shoulders "There's not a good translation for it in your tongue. But there are things that distract salamanders from arriving."

"Such as the forest?" said Fiona.

"For one. Food for always. The forest used to hold an abundance of food for the salamanders."

"And now the food is all dying out with Blaze."

"And we may actually have to fight the elementals. The council is excited, but the feeling is split among the rest of us. Some of us don't want to fight in a real battle. You can see why it's an issue that the Guild hasn't stepped in."

Fiona nodded. No wonder the council was giddy about the flarions and ragnis being no more. It wasn't Blaze dying they were thinking of but fighting them. Absolute blotters, the four of them. She sighed. "Speaking of the Travel Guild, I did talk to my contact, but—"

"But they don't care that the page is dying out," Rockcruncher said, looking away from Fiona.

She reached out and placed her gloved hand on his, hoping he understood. "To a point, yes. Have you considered that they might be the cause of it?"

He shook his head. "Why would the Guild kill Blaze?"

"If it becomes more inhabitable, the Guild can profit from increased travel, set up cities, take over."

He sat there, head lowered. Fiona moved her hand back, unsure of what to say. She didn't want the Guild to be the enemy, maybe. But with the news that they were part of a smuggling ring and hadn't moved to help out Blaze, they seemed destined to be. All signs pointed to it.

Standing up, Rockcruncher thumped the table with his hand. "Drown the Guild in lava. We'll figure this out for ourselves." His eyes met Fiona's, and he said quickly with a little less surety, "If you'll help us?"

"Absolutely." Fiona grinned. "And on that topic, I might have a lead. Or a suspicion. Do you know much about the Blackstone that I was speaking to your clan council about?"

"Not more than I heard in the chambers."

"I've been hired to retrieve it, but the Ashborn is holding back information. What can you tell me about them? Not the stories but from a native's perspective?"

"Well," Rockcruncher started, "the Ashborn has always been more of an idea than a being we see a lot. They stay above in the A'shar layer for the most part. Some salamanders do make a journey to the Ashborn, though, and stay there."

"Why would that be?" It was a bit unimaginable that any of the salamanders she had met the other day would think beyond where they lived.

"Peace," Rockcruncher said simply. "They promise them peace. The elementals fight among themselves over land. We fight over food. The Ashborn has a whole realm far away from all that. So they can offer peace that you can't find living on the cap."

"Does this peace sound good to you?" She wondered if Rockcruncher wished he could also go and live with the Ashborn, still in Blaze but not under the thumb of the clan council.

He nodded his head vigorously. "Honestly, yes. Before I was inked I only cared about food, shelter. It's pretty easy to remain in that mindset. Focused only on what I wanted. But now that I'm forced to live here, I find there are other wants."

"Hmm, I can understand that feeling." Fiona glanced at Soots. Since they had come into her life, her home felt less lonely. She hadn't known how much she really wanted that until things had changed.

"So if you're not inked and you can't get out of Blaze to live someplace like this"—he waved his digits around—"then yeah, I can understand the thought of peace and plentiful food and no fighting sounding like paradise. I don't know if the Ashborn can give it to anyone. But I haven't heard any complaints yet."

"Yes, well, I think the Ashborn feels if the Blackstone can be retrieved, then it could happen for more people."

"I'm not sure why."

"Which leads to my suspicion. I think the Blackstone has something to do with Blaze dying out," she said slowly, watching him. If he didn't seem surprised, she'd know the part about being ignorant earlier was untrue.

Rockcruncher scratched his face with a digit. "What makes you sure?"

"I'm not sure," Fiona murmured. "It's just a suspicion. The Ashborn said the Blackstone went missing last week. They're clearly lying about that though. If it was missing longer than that, it might have coincided with the cooling of Blaze. I may be completely wrong, but if I can get it back, we'll know whether it's true or not."

"I'll help however I can," Rockcruncher said, leaning forward, black eyes flaring up amber.

"For now just keep what I said to yourself. If the page is valuable unlit, then there may be others who want the stone to remain missing."

"If the Blackstone does control Blaze, why wouldn't the Ashborn tell you?"

Fiona had wondered the same thing. Rockcruncher was quicker than she had been. "Would you want to be the one who has been guarding an artifact that important, only to have it disappear?"

"You think they made a mistake and someone took advantage of it?"

Fiona nodded. "It's one of the reasons I think they're so impatient for me to find it." She could see the Ashborn's visits in a new light now. They had been scared, anxious. Not arrogant. Their haughty commands were what they thought would produce the quickest result. What must it be like to be the only one of your kind and have no one who understands everything you've seen and done over lifetimes? "Can you find out what your clan council knows about the Blackstone? I think it's interesting that they mentioned it was missing and Obsidian's Tooth when I didn't."

Rockcruncher smiled his thin-lipped smile. "Can do."

She patted his hand and then rose gingerly, stretching her legs and being careful not to hit the ceiling with her head. "Well then, if you don't mind, I'll be taking my leave. I want to get through talking to the elementals in a few hours. See if they have anything valuable to add to my suspicions."

"Good luck."

She said her thanks as Soots climbed into the air. They flew ahead of her, only lingering in the archway a moment before lighting up her path back out of Fire Bowl. Fiona left

Rockcruncher to his morning and walked back to the stone entrance. There was so much to consider, so much left to answer: whether the Blackstone had to do with Blaze cooling, what Obsidian's Tooth really was, and why the Ashborn wasn't raising the alarm about the stone to the Travel Guild. She knew why she wouldn't—she didn't trust them, as Dodger had reminded her. But why didn't the Ashborn?

Thinking of Dodger gave her pause and her chest tightened. She hadn't tried to reach out to him since the other day. What would she say? *Dodger, you're being a blotter, of course I know you're not evil.* He knew that, of course he did. But until she could figure out where the Guild lay in all of this and the smuggling, she didn't wish to hear him defending them. And she didn't want to argue with him. If she could prove that they took the stone, then she could show him that they were very different from him. That would settle it and he would forgive her blunders. With an uncomfortable mixture of drive and despair, Fiona prepared to turn back to Blaze.

16

"I'm telling you, we haven't seen any Blackstone," said the flarion sitting lazily in a small pool of boiling lava. *Sitting* was a generous way to put it. There was no telling where the elemental started and the pool ended. The inky crimson ichor running through their bodies seemed to be feeding into the lava and then back into them.

Fiona tried not to stare as she wondered what the back-and-forth flow between the lava and their body meant. Was it eating? Digesting? "Yes, that's what the ragnis said too." She waved her hand. "But then they pointed to you lot as possible suspects." She didn't even have to lie to get them mad enough to spill something. The ragnis accused the flarions the very minute Fiona had started to ask questions. She suspected that she could've asked to borrow sugar and the ragnis would've shouted that the flarions stole all the sugar. The tribe of metallic-boned quasi-flame creatures had not wanted to be bothered by Fiona in the least. They insisted that they had no knowledge of the Blackstone, that they had other things to worry about like becoming extinct, that they wanted nothing to do with anything the flarions were cooking up, and then they asked, nicely actually, for her to go very far away.

She suspected they didn't trust Soots, but she wasn't going to send them away again. So she had, with Soots in tow, made her way to the other half of Iasheoxus to see if she could get anything useful from the flarions. She kept to the outskirts of the crowded pools of magma and fire that, while dangerous to her, seemed small for the number of bright red and orange creatures within. As bubbles popped from the wine-red lake of lava, the air filled with an acrid smell Fiona was thankful didn't literally burn her nostrils with the jelly breath in her system. The area outside of the pools was dark, crumbly, and flameless. It seemed miserable.

"Right," the creature said, shifting in the lava pool moving away from Fiona, "those ragnis are a bunch of lava worms. Always accusing us of things. If I had a vapor rat for every time one of them came over to our side to complain, I'd have enough to eat for a solid month." They rose from the lava, dredges of it dripping back into the pool, to shift to another pool only a few steps away. Fiona saw quite a few of them moving from pool to pool. They never stayed out for too long and they rarely shared. A singular society.

"Be that as it may," Fiona started, unsure of what steamy rats had to do with eating, "if you do think of anything, let me know. I'm on Spine, of course, but give a message to any turner and I'll get it."

The flarion melted to the ground and poured itself back down into the lava pool. Fiona wasn't sure if they heard or were dismissing her. Fiona pinched the bridge of her nose, headache forming. It had been quite the waste of her morning.

"I will say," came a disembodied voice from the lava. Fiona stared down to see it ripple but no features. "I'd take a look at the salamanders. Those blundering lava worms would do just about anything to get rid of us so they can take our land. They send us messages constantly demanding we surrender or they'll fight us. It's as if they don't even realize there's a whole volcano in between us. What are they going to do with pools of lava?" The pool bubbled with a loud hissing and a pop. "Lava worms," the creature muttered.

Fiona figured it must be their favorite, or only, insult. She wondered if they knew about the salamanders' re-enthused plan to actually arrive and fight. "But without food to distract them, they just may reach here and fight you."

A tennis ball–shaped blob emerged from the pool. "Come here? Really? The Ashborn wouldn't let them."

This was surprising. It was the first time she had heard anyone other than Rockcruncher speak of the phoenix with any sort of authority. "Why not?"

"They're the ones who gave us these lands. They purposely said the elementals could live between the volcano and the spires traveling the great lava lakes. Or previously great," the creature said sadly. "They wouldn't go back on that and let the salamanders take it over."

"Do you believe the Ashborn has the power to stop them?"

"Obviously," the creature said in a tone Fiona was fairly sure was mocking. "They're the hottest thing in this place."

"Obviously," Fiona repeated slowly. Apparently the level of scorching someone was meant everything here. That probably put salamanders low on the list. Probably made them, at least their council, angry as well.

"Now if you don't mind, I'd like to eat in private."

"Oh, of course," said Fiona, averting her eyes. If they were eating now, what were they doing earlier? She whistled for Soots, who had been flying around in the vicinity watching some of the flarions as they chattered. The flarions had regarded Soots with open pleasantness, making the sprite's time here a little easier than with the ragnis. They seemed as a whole less disturbed by the cooling of Blaze, but perhaps they put their faith in its restoration with the Ashborn?

Fiona rested far away from the elementals and their settlements of primordial fire and blackened islands. She needed to get to Radiance Peak before the jelly breath or her resistance spritz wore off.

"Oh, Soots, I wish for a moment I could be like you. It would make traveling higher in this place much easier." She sighed. "If I could just turn it off and on again, that would be brilliant."

:Up?:

"Yes, we'll have to go up, although..." Fiona consulted the map of Blaze that Rockcruncher had sketched for her. Radiance Peak was the farthest the page went up and to what she would consider east. High above the cap where the realms of salamanders and elementals lay. Rockcruncher assured her there was nothing much in between, but it would take some time. It was also past the spindly twin towers known as Obsidian's Tooth. "I'm curious what's at the spires. Let's take a gander there first." The place had been mentioned several times, but the Ashborn had never brought it up. Her curiosity nagging at her once more, there she would go.

Since the ornithopter relied on the flapping of wings, a thing hard to do in a place like Blaze where the air was so thin, Fiona had to use chemical means to achieve flight. "Hopefully this concoction of Gaili's will help." The faun had assured her the potion would last for hours. Still, Fiona took precautions, putting on the ornithopter as a backup. She also dug out a small grappling hook, a gift from Dodger she hadn't yet had the chance to use, and held it tight in her hands. She tied a length of leather, made from a type of bat native to this page, to it and then around herself. Once she was sure it was secure, she knocked back the potion and grimaced. It tasted like bitter burnt toffee. "I do hope that was just cloud and not mixed with sylph excrement."

She waited. She had never tried to fly without a contraption before. But she had never spent so much time in Blaze before either.

:Friend?: said Soots, concern emanating from the small creature.

"Hmm? Oh yes," said Fiona, looking about. She realized she had floated about a foot in the air. Laughing, she said, "Well, that's a bit unnerving, but at least we know it works!"

A mixture of amusement and joy emanated from Soots and the heat around them sizzled hotter for a moment. Fiona shook her head, astounded once again at Soots's ability to transform the temperature around them. She had felt the Ashborn do it too, but Soots seemed to manage it much faster.

She watched the ground move away from her as she continued rising up. The pools of lava where the flarions lived were visible along with some of the trickles that divided them from the ragnis. Soots flew right along beside her, shaping themself in a thin line. They curled and twirled as Fiona rose and rose.

Fiona waved her arms trying to change directions but found that she couldn't manipulate her flight in any way. "Excellent. I can float but no controls. Honestly, if it's not one thing, it's another." She gripped her cloak and grappling hook tight, looking for something solid she could throw it onto. That's when she noticed the ashes.

Ashes in Blaze were nothing new. They'd landed on Fiona the whole while she had been interviewing the elementals. But she had never considered before just where they were coming from. The volcano a distance away bellowed fire, lava, smoke, and ashes into the sky. The air was thick with plumes of midnight-black smoke and particles of ash. Above her it gathered in a roiling froth like sheared wool. She was making a steady and quick ascent into the thick of it.

She didn't see anything to connect the grappling hook to and slow down. Hoping to make some sort of hole, she waved her hands above her head as she entered the cloud. She grabbed the ash, powdery like fistfuls of ground spices. It swirled around her, getting into her cloak, brushing against her cheeks, and pushing in where it could.

Even with the glasses and jelly breath, her eyes were irritated. She could barely see a thing through the darkness. She had even lost sight of Soots's amber glow. She kept her mouth closed, not wanting it to fill with ash, and frantically searched for a way out of this predicament.

A shot of light erupted from in front of her, followed by a sizzle and pop. Lightning.

She clenched her fists and started to breathe shallowly through her nose. Choking seized her and she could feel herself growing faint. She folded in on herself to be smaller, hoping the lightning would miss her until she could rise out of the ash. She tried to feel for where Soots had gone, but her hands only found more airborne grit. She closed her eyes, too dry now to be anything but painful. She was scared. Terrified. She let that feeling wash over her, hoping that somewhere Soots would understand. They seemed to catch on when she was sad or scared before. She wanted to believe she hadn't been reading too much into the flame sprite's connection with her. She let herself hope as she continued floating upward through the storm.

A warm force encircled her. She heard another pop of lightning close by and startled. The force propelled her upward, away from the lightning. She felt herself heating up, as if she was inside a fire like the ones that used to rage in Blaze. But she was moving. Faster and faster until she emerged from the ash cloud storm, the air around her finally free from powder and smoke. She took a breath and was immensely relieved that it wasn't filled with grit. She let out a heavy sigh, tears pricking her irritated eyes. *Soots.*

Fiona peeked one open eye and saw that she was moving away from the ash cloud, no longer floating among it. Soots was encircled tightly around her, pulling her up and away. She didn't know they had the force to lift her, but considering they could still fly when they were wearing their suit, she was surprised she hadn't thought about it before.

"I was sure that was the end of my shenanigans," Fiona said, throat dry and thoughts jumbled. "Thank you."

:Friend,: Soots said, the crackle light and simple.

"Friend," Fiona said and then fell silent. She had needed them, and they had been there for her. It was more than she could've asked for. She thought back to what Dodger said about having backup and sighed again. She didn't want to think of what would have happened if she had been here alone.

The heat from Soots interrupted her thoughts as she began to sweat. While their surrounding her was working to move her, she might roast by the time they got to Obsidian's Tooth.

"Why don't I hang on to you and let you direct, eh?" She reached deep beneath her cloak and into her scarf to pull out a set of manacles. Though she didn't enjoy the things she did believe they came in handy every once in a while. She slapped one side on her wrist and closed the other for Soots to loop through. Until she took them off she wouldn't be able to turn the page, but she didn't think she'd be doing that midair anyhow.

Soots wrapped themself around one of the manacles and propelled her quickly up through the atmosphere and toward the darkened spires in the distance.

Fiona tried to brush the ash off her face and out of her irritated eyes as best as possible. Jagged cliffs with small studded fires dispersed throughout them came closer into view. They looked sharp and dangerous to her squishy bits. She shouted up to Soots to propel her around to the middle of Obsidian's Tooth.

Soots swung her around and drove her floating body in that direction. They moved around one spire and descended between them. The peaks were darkened shapes looming among a smoky haze, the only light the glow coming from a wide waterfall of magma that cascaded into a fast-moving stream of amber and bone-white fire below. Like cooking oil bubbling and ready. Here it was like nothing was wrong with Blaze at all. Molten crimson liquid like cherry juice gushed out of a cave in the second spire. Fiona shuddered at the thought of falling into it should her potion wear off.

Looking around for a good place to land, she spied small arched windows set inside the spire. Where there was a window, there was definitely a way in.

"A bit higher. Over to that opening," Fiona shouted over the raging lavafall below.

Soots flew her through a window. The light from the flame sprite flickered on the walls to show an empty area that continued upward. Fiona could see no bottom in the darkness.

"At least it's not filled with fire," she muttered to herself. "Thank you, Soots, I can float up from here." Unsure of what they could handle, she wanted to keep their exertion low in case she needed them again. "Let's keep an eye out. We're probably not the only ones who use those as ways in."

:Trouble?: said Soots. Worry emanated from them.

"It is the only thing one can truly count on in life," Fiona said.

Soots bobbed closer to her as they began floating up into the spire of Obsidian's Tooth.

SOOTS'S LIGHT DIDN'T REACH far. The crags that formed the gently sloped walls looked crumbly and rough. Fiona reached out a hand, straining to touch it. Breaking off a piece, she examined it. Pumiced lava rock filled with tiny holes that smelled of dry dirt. Different than the cap, where the cities had been built. She tucked it away into a pocket of her scarf quickly as she continued to float up.

The higher they went, the narrower the hollowed peak became. "This space could fit inside the house, it's so narrow," Fiona mused.

Outside she could see the ash storm rage below. Tendrils of smoke wafted into the tunnel but didn't encapsulate them. Above the windows, the space within the spire was only big enough for three people or so. Fiona could just make out above them a flat surface instead of the empty peak she was expecting.

"Soots, please come and shine a little higher."

They cast a warm golden glow across the ceiling, revealing a black stone circle. Mottled gray flecks twinkled throughout its surface and thin lines of crimson like the lava outside swirled within it. They pulsed, slowly fading in and out as Fiona watched the ceiling in concentration. It looked like some sort of mechanism. Not specifically mechanical but unnatural either way. She saw nothing that connected to it from the wall, and with only a moment of hesitation, she reached out her hand to caress it. Smooth and solid. Cool to the touch.

The air vibrated with a grinding noise as the ceiling rotated in a full circle. Soft rosy light shone down on Fiona, and she heard a sizzle, smelled the burning of stone as three runes in Claire appeared around the edge. It wasn't just a ceiling. It was a gate.

Fiona sighed deeply once again wishing she had learned a bit more of the language than the required basics.

"Soots, can you read this? I'm not good at the ancient version of your language." They always seemed to know what people were saying. Perhaps they'd have better luck.

:Fire?:

"Yes, that makes sense for one of them." Fiona traced her fingers over the runes trying to remember what she had learned in training. The first one was *fire*, its wavy fork pattern familiar. That much she was certain for how often she had seen it on Guild signs in the past. The third one was harder. Perhaps *wave*? Why would that be on a gate in the fire page? Before she could puzzle it out, a scorching clawed hand grabbed her ankle from the dark wall.

She shrieked and kicked trying to remove the claws from her leg, but its grip was tight. It pulled her from the air and slammed her against the wall. Fiona managed to get her arms up in the nick of time to protect her head, but she felt the impact on her arms and ribs as she made a human-sized dent in the brittle wall.

A growl, low and crackling, echoed through the spire. Wisps of wings made of curled bright blue fire flew out from the darkened creature's spiked back, lighting up the area. It was about the size of a salamander with none of their softness or smoothness. Its jaw jutted out from its face and there was a flash of sharp iron-colored teeth. It pulled Fiona down away from the gate. She dug one hand into the crumbling rock to slow herself from being dragged into the darkness. With the other she swung the grapple she had been clutching and threw it against another wall. It clicked on the wall and dug in. She held on for dear life between the two walls as the creature pulled with all its might. Bits of the rock began to crumble beneath her fingernails as she slipped.

A bolt of scarlet shot past her from above. Soots barreled into the creature, causing it to drop Fiona's leg. Flying back through the creature's wings, Soots transformed from scarlet to a fiery indigo slamming into the creature's chest. In the middle of the tunnel the two struggled, the creature dwarfing Soots. It grabbed Soots and tried to shove the flame sprite toward its mouth. Soots quickly shifted into a thin line, moving out of the creature's claws.

Fiona reached past her cloak and dug around for her scarf. Holding on to the leather of the grappling hook, she pulled out her whip with her other hand. She lashed out at the creature, aiming for its mouth. She prayed to Larrakane that her whip could withstand a few blows from its heated skin.

It howled in pain and turned its attention to Fiona. Soots shot like a slender burning arrow through the creature toward Fiona, creating a crack in its rocky exterior. Fiona could see now that whatever this was, it was just like the walls of the spire. She lashed at it again, targeting its chest where Soots had injured it. Pieces of it tumbled away.

The creature lunged at them growling and snarling and knocked Fiona into the cool stone gate ceiling. She swung her arm trying to hit it with the manacle; perhaps the metal would do some damage. Its sharp teeth grazed Fiona's arm and she grimaced, bracing at the pain.

Then there was a yelp. Deep and pitiful. The creature released her, backing away, heat retreating from Fiona. One of its claws was ashen and gray. It cradled it near its broken chest, wings flapping to keep it aloft.

Fiona threw her curiosity out the window and turned toward the gate. The gray flecks within were now lit up as well. "Soots, watch my back." She focused on the runes in Claire. The creature had been hurt, but it would attack again. They couldn't outfly it. They had to get through the door.

Fire. Wave. And something in between. She pinched the bridge of her nose, mumbling the various runes she could remember. Nothing fit.

The warmth of Soots left her back as she heard the creature howl again. Glancing over her shoulder, she saw it grab the flame sprite, but Soots was shifting too quickly for it to keep hold of them. They flickered like a tiny flame from side to side.

Flickering. Fire flickered all the time. Why did that sound familiar? "Fire flickering?" she said to the gate. Nothing happened.

A grasping claw raked across her back, the pain worse than the heat. She arched and spun around kicking, hoping to connect in some meaningful way. She heard a crunch and sent the creature back a few feet. Soots moved in between the two to protect her.

The gate probably protected something. Something old enough to be covered in runes, a language from long before the inking. Perhaps this was where the Blackstone had been held.

Fiona thought through her conversation with the salamanders, the elementals, and the Ashborn for clues. Fire flickered in her vision, blinding her for a moment.

She turned away but something caught in her mind. "Like the light..." Fiona murmured, working it out, "...of a thousand flames." She remembered what the Ashborn had said about the stone. "Flames of a Thousand Lights! Flames of a Thousand Lights!" she shouted toward the gate in Claire.

The pulsing crimson lines on the gate flowed into each other as the gray flecks became muted. The gate dissolved to reveal a dark interior. Fiona pulled herself up into it quickly. She turned back, looking down at the creature and Soots. She lashed out with her whip and yelled, "Soots, hurry!"

They flew faster than she had ever seen, directly toward Fiona. The creature gave chase in the small space. As Soots flew past her, Fiona kept striking out to discourage the creature from following them. The creature pressed as close as it could toward the small opening, trying to fit its body within. As Fiona cracked the whip once more for it to get back, the gate congealed back into solid material as the creature rushed it again. There was a loud bang and then a terrible howl of pain from below.

Fiona winced. The gate had not been kind to the creature, it seemed. She reached out a hand and pressed it against the gated floor. It was still cool. Curious, she slipped her hand free of her glove and touched it again. It was ice cold. The chamber was cool as well. How was that even possible?

"Soots, are you feeling the cold?" she said, watching the flame sprite.

:Cold,: they said simply.

"Oh, little one, come here." Fiona put out a gloved hand for them. She reached into her scarf with the other, pulled out their suit, and opened it up for them to dive in. "There, that should keep you warm until we can get out of here."

The area was almost tall enough for her to stand up all the way. She watched her head as she began investigating the small cavern. Soots's shrouded glow brushed against the top of the chamber, and Fiona saw the peak she had been looking for. Within the wall of the chamber near the peak was an oddly shaped inset, about the size of her stove but not as deep. It was short, sort of round, and not meant to seat a creature by the looks of it. A crumbled pile of rocks was lumped to one side of it.

Fiona ran a gloved hand around the inset, Soots's light showing all the nooks. It looked far more natural than the gate had. She sifted her hand through the dark black rocks and debris that looked as though it had been chipped from the wall. Had someone made the hole here bigger? To pry out the stone?

The light reflecting off glass caught her eye, and she pulled from the pile of rock a chipped piece of obsidian the size of an apple. She dropped it immediately, scorching heat piercing through her glove into her fingers like pinpricks.

She narrowed her eyes as she waved her hand trying to get the feeling to stop. "Probably part of the Blackstone," she murmured to Soots. It had circumvented all her fire protection in the blink of an eye.

Stooping to get a closer look, she saw its wicked sharp edges. It had been broken off. Probably when whoever had taken the stone dug it out of the wall. She wanted to bring it with her, but she wouldn't be able to hold on to it. Certainly didn't trust it anywhere near her scarf. "This must've been where it was originally from. Why was it here?"

Soots hovered above Fiona's head and then bobbed down away from the inset to the rest of the chamber. Fiona watched them, head tilted and smiling. They were becoming quite nosy themself. She loved it.

:One,: they said closer to the floor behind Fiona.

Fiona looked down to inspect what they had found. She had assumed she was trudging over rock and debris but saw there were a few piles of powder on the floor. Picking up a handful, she let it sift through her hands back into the pile, its gritty texture smearing her glove gray. "Ash. I think we have an appointment to get to, Soots."

FIONA WAS RELIEVED THAT the same command opened the gate for them to get back out. She had never seen anything like it before and wondered who had made it. Anything that seemed a little advanced or miraculous was either from the Court of Copper or Larrakane herself. Considering that it had seemed unnatural and no one had seen or heard from Larrakane since the inking, Fiona assumed it must've been the former.

She watched for any signs of the winged creature that had attacked them. They'd been in the chamber for a good while. Maybe it had run off to get reinforcements. She grimaced at her own thoughts and pulled herself back down into the spire. "Soots, perhaps you pull me out of here? It'll be quicker that way."

They encircled themselves in the manacles still attached to Fiona and pulled her back down toward the window. Fiona was surprised her grappling hook was still stuck in the wall and yanked it out as they went down. Through the highest window they moved out of the spire and away from Obsidian's Tooth.

"Let's make haste before I plummet to the basin and get boiled."

Fiona directed Soots as best as she could in the direction of Radiance Peak. The map had put it on the other side of Obsidian's Tooth and high above. Rubbing the back of her neck, she let out a deep sigh as the darkness continued. Besides Soots there was little light here. Fiona ached. Her back hurt from being slashed, her arm from being bit, and her brain from being overused. She wasn't sure if she was livid at the Ashborn or herself or anyone at all. All she knew was that she was tired.

The smoke began to dissipate around them, and Fiona saw a small dot of light in the distance. As they continued flying up, milky and golden beams of light shone vibrantly in the far corner of the page like a beckoning sun. It broke through the darkness like cream poured lovingly into a cup of coffee.

Radiance Peak lived up to its name. It was a gorgeous summit of glow, heat, and thirsting flames. Here Blaze raged on, though in a different hue and warmth.

She removed her glasses and shielded her eyes lest she go blind. "Soots, if you see land, go for it. I've pushed my luck enough for one day."

They stopped on a small inlet of what looked like white-hot metal. It was smooth as glass and too shiny and bright to look directly at. Soots set Fiona down on the condensed fire that flared up around her. It was like walking on the muddy bottom of a lake. Her boots felt suctioned as she moved farther in, but with it came the assurance that she wouldn't float off quickly. Why didn't alchemists make potions that could be controlled?

She trudged, back aching, to the bright light of the peak. Eyes half-closed, she made her way as quickly as she could until they broke through the piercing light. Before them stood an immense, luminous structure of sculpted silver. Perhaps not the metal itself but definitely the sheen and glint of it. As tall as a castle from her human page but not the same shape at all. Natural or molded—she couldn't tell—it rose up from the ground high above them, but instead of coming to a point, it opened up like a flower blooming at its top. She saw specks in the distance. Elementals perhaps. Hopefully friendly ones.

"Soots, have you ever been here before?" She never knew what to expect when she asked them questions. What had their life been like before they were with her? She was worried about upsetting them.

:No,: they said, a wave of wonderment washing from them.

"Well then, I won't be the only one new here. That's comforting." Fiona tightened her cloak, readjusted her scarf, and kicked off toward the tower.

The entrance was overly formal with a short barrier on either side of a direct path toward the structure. Beyond the railing the pathway dropped on either side. The glass-like condensed fire that she walked on gave way to rocky terrain more like the cap below. Did the Ashborn have this place constructed, or was it always here? She could see it was a well-worn path, much like the salamander streets in Arden Rock. This layer of the page went far above them, a mixture of burnt orange and stark white beams immolating beyond the tower.

On the edge Fiona could just make out an abrupt jut of void. Not inky darkness like the rest of the page. Nothingness. The dark edge. She frowned at the oblivion. Too close for her comfort. She had never been this close to the edge of a page in all of her days as a page turner.

Her attention was pulled away as they crested over the threshold of the opening and were stopped by a flarion, its oozy and flickering shape barely outlined by the inky ichor flowing through it.

"And how may I help you today?" they said brightly, crackle and hisses, toward Soots.

Soots bobbed in the air. :One?:

"We have an appointment with their eminence," Fiona cut in, smiling.

"Ah." The flame creature rolled in place; the only evidence of it shifting was the veins of fluid within moving. They began moving off. "If you please, you may wait for the Ashborn this way."

They moved farther into the silvery structure. The walls dripped with thin rivers of undulating liquid. Fiona had never heard of anything like it. She rubbed her finger across it, the liquid giving way and pooling into her hand warm. She'd hate to think what would happen if she wasn't wearing protective equipment.

The elemental took them to a small chamber. There were no seats that looked comfortable for Fiona to sit on. She guessed they didn't have many human guests. There was a brazier of indigo fire in the center of the room and some flat rock benches surrounding it. It was very reminiscent of the salamander clan council chamber. Did they steal the setup from the Ashborn, or the other way around?

"Fiona," the Ashborn boomed, entering the small chamber. They seemed to shrink themself down to not take up any more space than necessary. "Welcome to our radiance." They glanced at Soots but quickly swiveled their piercing gaze back to Fiona.

Now that the Ashborn was in her presence, all her aches and pains flared up. Narrowing her eyes, Fiona ignored the pleasantry. "You didn't tell me this would be such a difficult place to access. I don't like being tested."

The Ashborn, instead of huffing with anger as she'd expected, bowed their birdlike head. "I assure you, no test of your fine mettle was conducted. An oversight on my part, merely forgetting to give you the required instructions, was all. I keep the pagemark to my realm a secret from all who are outside."

Prepared to duel with words, Fiona was surprised at how apologetic they were. She tilted her head and watched them, trying to understand their intentions. "Be that as it may, I ran into a bit of trouble making my way here. I expect my favor at the end of this to live up to my experience."

"As you wish." The Ashborn looked to say more but seemed to stop themselves. "Shall we adjourn to the location the relic was stolen from?"

Fiona nodded, holding her tongue. This interrogation would be difficult enough without riling the Ashborn up at the start of it.

They flew out of the chamber and down the long, wide hall. Fiona let out an exasperated sigh and followed with Soots behind her. Other elementals, salamanders, and one particularly tall black-and-red-mottled humanoid were going about their business. All stopped to throw out greetings and what bordered on merriment as the Ashborn approached or flew by them. No one bowed—well, none of the salamanders—and no one spoke formally. It was as if they were saying hi to a beloved neighbor. A bit unexpected to Fiona.

The phoenix led the way through a wide archway into another chamber. This one was open at the top, and radiant light from outside cascaded into the room. The walls went all the way up with alcoves only someone flying could get to. The Ashborn's chamber. The central area within the tower.

The large ground room held another brazier, stone benches, and a brass statue in the likeness of the phoenix. Soots went straight to the brazier, but Fiona walked toward the statue. The carving was softer than the Ashborn looked in real life. There was an arch to the neck, a curvature of the wings, a gentle flow to it that was beautiful. Ethereal even. Whoever saw the Ashborn in this way had admired them, that much was evident.

On the back silvery wall was an empty hole the size of a wood stove. Fiona examined the area. It was perfectly rectangular. There was no dust or crumbly rocks out of place. It looked more like it was waiting to be filled than like it was missing something.

"Did someone clean up the area?" Fiona said, running a finger around the edge. There was nothing remotely dusty about the space.

"No, no one may enter this chamber besides myself. I have on occasion had others help me move a few things, but this is my private sanctum."

"I see," Fiona said, nodding. How could she dive into the lies and untangle the truth from the Ashborn? She knew they were scared. Of not retrieving the Blackstone, of failing perhaps. But of what else? She decided to start slow. "Where did you obtain this relic?"

"How is that relevant to its disappearance?" the Ashborn said, pacing across the room toward the statue.

"If I know where it came from, I may be able to understand how it left and where it is," she said, giving them an avenue for honesty.

"I've always had it," they said, staring at the statue.

"Always?"

"Since my third rebirth, yes." They flapped their wings a bit.

"And before that?" Fiona pressed.

"And before that it was here. It's always been here."

"I see." Fiona walked to the brazier, giving the Ashborn a moment. "Had you ever tried to remove it?"

"Absolutely not," they practically shouted.

The temperature in the room grew warm enough for Fiona to notice even with her protection, and she was again grateful for it.

"Why call it a relic if you've never touched it, don't know what it does, and didn't make it in the first place? Why care about it at all?" She said quietly, "You hired me to find it, but I can't without the truth."

The heat in the room shifted from warm to scorching in a moment. The phoenix seemed to take in a deep breath, their chest expanding as they lifted into the air. It was hot, much hotter than before. It almost burned, and she knew the Ashborn had the power to make her protections useless. She licked her lips, gazing up at the brilliant white-hot creature before her. This was what the sculptor had seen: the phoenix barely contained. Softly, she said, "I know you're scared.

Whatever you've done or not done, Your Eminence, it doesn't matter. The only thing that matters is how you move forward to correct it. To save Blaze."

The Ashborn, in their eternal beauty, dimmed. Fiona waited, pressing down the urge to flee before she crumbled into ashes. They flew down and landed in front of her, shrinking back to their size and returning to their burnt orange hue.

"How did you come upon this information?"

Fiona smiled. "No one cares about a stone that much unless they're a gnome. It must've been more than that. Tell me, what happened?"

"It is my fault, my arrogance that brought us here. I am the leader who is intended to bring calm in the fire. Instead I have let everyone down." The Ashborn pulled their wings across their body, folding into themself. "I had kept watch over the Blackstone since I stumbled upon it. I was getting ready to transport the relic to its new location here. I thought something so majestic should sit with other singular majestic things. I likened it to myself. Only the one. In that foolish vein I sought a way to have it removed. I attempted it once myself, but I immediately immolated. I knew then I couldn't touch it."

So the ash in the chamber *had* been from them. Fiona rubbed her jaw. "No fire being can touch it?"

"I have never attempted it with anyone else, but I would suppose not. I requested a barrier for this space be constructed from a reputable alchemist in the Court of Copper. But once it was completed, I went to retrieve the artifact, and it was gone."

"And this person didn't remove it?"

"No, no, they wouldn't have known about it. I requested the basics and skimmed on any particular details. I trust them."

"Did they create the gate in Obsidian's Tooth?" Fiona said, laying out her cards.

They glanced quickly at Fiona, a flush of scarlet waving through their features. "How did you know to go there?"

She smiled. "It is sort of my job to figure things out."

They nodded. "Yes, they did. I didn't want other fire natives to be able to interact with the relic. They assured me it would dissuade any who touched it."

"That it does indeed." She didn't feel like rehashing the battle, so she quickly moved on. "Who took it then? You seemed to not be as worried about that part. You know, don't you?"

"I can't be sure but the only ones who may have known of its location were the salamanders. In my mindless youth, before I separated from the others, I told that fool Aredin about the stone. It was, and still is, the only thing I have ever seen in the fire that was more in tune with the flames than I was. Hotter than I was. It glowed brighter than anything I had ever seen." Their voice grew heavy.

They must feel so alone all the time, being the only of their kind. No wonder they tried to keep it to themselves. Fiona understood the sentiment. "And so you deemed it important."

"Oh yes." They sighed and moved slowly back to the statue. "It wasn't until it was gone and the page started dying that I realized how important it actually was. The spires used to be filled with unbridled flames. An unquenchable fire. It was a beautiful sight."

Fiona ached a little for the phoenix's loss. She loved Spine and couldn't imagine what it would be like if it was slowly being ripped from her, especially if it may have been her fault.

"This information. It helps immensely. I can focus on finding it with the right direction now."

The Ashborn nodded. "And now all will realize that I am not the protector I believed I could be. The Guild will certainly take over."

She frowned. "What does any of this have to do with the Travel Guild?"

"I have been delaying and stalling them against having another outpost in the page for quite some time. The last century at least. Blaze belongs to us. If we want to allow skimmers to tour here or travel to flow in, we should lead the charge." They reclaimed the proud tone Fiona had become used to.

Fiona rubbed her face, pacing the room. This was bad. Very bad. "If Blaze cools, they could push their way in?"

"There won't be many of us left to defend against it. I am able to withstand the shift, but not many are. We were invincible with our fire. Now, we are not."

How in the world was she going to figure out who was responsible for this? There were so many people in the Guild, even Gilded leaders, it would take time to find out exactly who was pulling the strings. Time Blaze didn't have. Regardless, she wanted to assure the Ashborn of one thing. "I'm not here to report on you, Ashborn. I will find the Blackstone. That's all that matters."

The phoenix cleared their throat. Fiona couldn't tell, but she thought for a second she saw their features shift back into the face of the statue. "You were well recommended, and I see why now. I am in your debt, Fiona Thorne."

Fiona stopped pacing. "Recommended by who?" Who even knew of her well enough to tell the Ashborn she could help?

"I was worried about taking this to the Guild, but I had nowhere else to turn. I spoke with one of their jackets, a smilodon. Only the parts I told you as well, mind you. They seemed to think on it for a moment before denying my request. They said the Guild was too preoccupied with other matters to chase after some lost rock, but they did recommend me to you. Said that you were well versed in deducing what others found trivial."

Tears pricked at Fiona's eyes, but they evaporated as soon as they appeared. "That's good to know." It had to have been Dodger. Dodger, who knew her well, who was cleverer than she was by a mile, and who knew what kind of connection having the Ashborn as a client would make for her.

The phoenix stared unabashedly. "If you'd like to turn the page from here, you may. Naturally it won't get you directly to Spine, but I believe traveling through Rise may be a bit more comfortable for you."

Fiona laughed, all seriousness gone at the absurdity of the large phoenix appearing in the human page's sky. "You travel through Rise?"

"Mistral may be secure for you, but Rise is undoubtedly safer for me. Pesky windstorms," the Ashborn muttered.

Bowing to hide her amusement, Fiona said, "I'll take my leave of you then, Your Eminence."

The Ashborn bowed in return. "Fare you well, Fiona Thorne."

KNOWING A NEW SPOT in Rise that made a safe pagemark
to the Blaze was valuable information but Fiona didn't want
to risk testing the spot out by herself. What a phoenix could
survive was not the same as a human. She made a mental note
to canvas the pagemark at a later date.

The view didn't shift much from Blaze as Fiona made her
way back to Spine. The city was dark—close to midnight, she
reckoned. She filled out the obligatory paperwork at the turner
booth before making her way back home with Soots.

Fiona decided to walk with so much on her mind. That the
salamanders had taken the Blackstone she was more uncertain
of than the Ashborn. Yes, the salamanders had threatened
her, but she got the sense they threatened a bunch of people.
They had known about Obsidian's Tooth as the location. Their
motives could've been a range of things, from trying to kill
off the elementals to just taking whatever power they thought

it might bring for themselves. But how had they carried it through the gate, and where did they smuggle it to?

The elementals had known nothing about the Blackstone, but that doesn't mean they didn't have a hand in its disappearance. They were awfully against the salamanders and each other. But that amount of power would help them, not hinder them, right?

She walked slowly, chewing on her thoughts as Soots flew beside her, guiding her back home. All signs pointed to the Guild, or someone working at the Guild. It benefited them to not have it replaced, and if they kept hold of it, they could press their advantage to get the Ashborn on their side and in their pocket. And if not, once Blaze cooled down enough, they could go and come as they pleased in the wasteland. If the Guild was also behind the smuggling, it would make even more sense. They could take more and more creatures, and no one would be the wiser. It all fit hand in hand very neatly. But then where was it?

Fiona bit her lip thinking about Dodger. He worked for and believed in the Guild. If they really were behind this, it was unlikely that people like him even had an inkling about it. He believed in her abilities to help the Ashborn, but did he know what he was signing her up for?

She rubbed her face, tired, but she needed to rule something out so she could get somewhere with all this. "I put it off yesterday, but I think we should make a stop at the temple," she called to Soots. Fali had stolen the smuggling ledger. She needed to understand why. If Gilded leaders were behind the smuggling and the Followers knew something, then she should know it too. Maybe it would pinpoint what the Guild was doing with the stolen creatures and give her a location for the Blackstone at the same time. It was a thin connection but safer than accusing the Guild outright with no proof.

They changed directions and made their way to the temple district. Where her district was a hodgepodge of homes and dwellings from cultures all over the Book, the temple district was singular in its looks and color. It was beautiful and quiet, carpeted by lush green grass. Foot traffic was routed around it unless one was specifically coming to pay their respects or work within the holy place at its center or the shrine nearest the market.

Her feet hit the grass, the fragrance of wet earth rising up with each muffled step. Other pages held temples to Larrakane cobbled from the deities they'd worshiped before her appearance; each was unique and slightly apologetic for praising false gods when they discovered there was one true one. But the temple on Spine had no such history. It was crafted solely for Larrakane. It had always belonged to her and would remain hers. It was three stories tall and as large as a manor house, though round in shape. Central open archways dotted every few feet of its wall framed by thick forest-green vines of ivy. They flowed up over the sides of the building to create a knotted and twisting roof, shielding the interior from light and water that sprinkled down from the aqueducts.

Fiona stepped into an archway and found herself in a darkened room, soft amber candlelight flowing from several tall tables in the center. Benches surrounded the tables, some wooden, some flat stone, others padded with soft cushions of dark-gray fabric, and there was room in the middle for a few people or one large creature, like an elephas or ursidon, to stand. A couple of worshippers sat on the benches, none looking up as she entered.

"Stay low and near me," Fiona whispered to Soots. It hadn't occurred to her to be too worried about them being in here with their suit on and all. But a little niggle of caution was working its way to the forefront of her mind. "Why don't you sit on my shoulder, hmm?"

Soots followed her suggestion promptly. :One.:

"You do know how to say the most with the barest of words, little one."

She walked quietly around the benches, incense drifting from all around, as she scanned the seats for Fali's familiar face. Not seeing him, she made her way toward the stairs that led to the temple keepers' offices. Taking the carpeted steps, the thread worn down and smooth wood peeking through, she got to the second floor and the open window on the side wall.

An older woman, human with an olive complexion and sable hair, grinned at her. She was dressed in much the same way Fali had been with a large black circle emblem on her flowing cream robes over a broad lavender dress of human make. Her hair was loose and swayed silkily with her minute movements. Setting down the hot cup of coffee in her clasped hands, she asked, "May I help you?"

Fiona straightened up a bit, smoothing out her doublet and scarf. She should've made herself more presentable before barging into the temple. "I'm looking for Fali of Spine. I believe he resides here." She gave a somewhat apologetic smile.

The woman tilted her head, letting her dark, shiny hair fall across her face. "Yes. One moment while I see if he is available." The woman departed, disappearing through a door Fiona hadn't noticed. She had only been to this floor a few times before, and always on a case. In her own worship of Larrakane that, she grimaced, was few and far between these days, she stayed to the main floor or the green outside. The thing about Larrakane, Fiona assumed, was that it didn't matter where you praised her; she'd take the reverence anywhere in the Book. It was all hers after all.

The olive-skinned woman came back, barely making a sound as she picked her cup back up. "On the green at the market entrance," she said simply.

"Thank you," Fiona said quietly. The way the woman moved, the way she talked, something about her was comforting to Fiona. Warm even. She wondered who she was but pushed the curiosity aside. She had other things to worry about now, and she was practically dead on her feet. She left with Soots in tow and made her way to stand in the cool air of the open night.

Fiona wasn't acquainted with Fali well enough to know exactly how to approach him about the ledger. She figured her best bet was to ask why he'd visited yesterday, letting him know he had been spotted. She could read him from there and direct the conversation accordingly until she got what she needed.

Soots hovered in the air above Fiona but seemed listless, not bobbing or moving with any of their usual speed. Perhaps they were tired as well? "Why don't you take a rest in that oil lamp?" Fiona pointed to the lantern by the archway. "When it's time to go, I won't forget you."

:Tired,: Soots said before moving over to the lamp and settling within.

Fali came out of the archway striding to Fiona with a wide smile and leather gray trunk waving. For a thief he seemed pretty happy to see her.

"Well met, Ms. Thorne," he said with his booming voice. "The Priestess said you wanted to speak with me?"

So that had been the Priestess, leader of the entire temple. Larrakane be blessed. She had assumed the woman was nothing more than a clerk. She threw away her embarrassment of having looked so ramshackle in front of one of Spine's most respected leaders and focused on Fali. He seemed in good spirits, which froze her thoughts for a brief second.

"That is right, yes? Or did your neighbor let you know I came calling yesterday?"

"You spoke to Mistress Didia?" Fiona said, out of sorts. Blast, she didn't mean to give him information. She was off on the wrong foot. She tried to pivot. "Yes, why did you come to see me yesterday?"

Fali glanced around and moved closer to Fiona. "I heard from a good source that you helped tackle a few issues earlier this week. Of the elemental kind."

Fiona narrowed her eyes. "I suppose that depends on why that might interest you."

The elephas moved his trunk from side to side, sniffing the air. For a brief moment it looked as if he was going to say something else, but then he reconsidered. "Can we have this conversation elsewhere? I'm getting a whiff not entirely familiar to me." He switched to her native language. "Prying eyes and ears, I think."

Fiona glanced around the empty area but didn't see anyone in the dark space. An elephas's nose was not to be mistrusted, but this could be a trap. She adjusted her scarf nonchalantly to give her better access to her whip. "Sure. Perhaps we can go into the shrine?"

Fali nodded, and they made their way farther from the temple into the small shrine on the edge of the green. One could enter its smooth gray marble walls and sit in silent, solitary prayer with Larrakane. Angled windows cascaded light in a spectrum of colors across the floor and walls. No candles lit its interiors, and no more than three or four people could fit at a time.

With Fiona and Fali inside, there was barely room to do more than stand, turn around, or leave again. This wasn't the best place to take out her weapon should she need it. But then again she had a better chance of getting out of the small space quicker than the large elephas.

Fali stuck his trunk outside the opening, sniffing the air. "Better. Nothing unfamiliar here."

"What's going on?" Fiona said tartly. "Why are you interested in my work?"

"I've been tracking the smugglers myself, that's why," Fali said quietly. "I won't bother speaking cryptically, better to have you as an ally than an enemy, I think. Besides, you've done more on that front in two weeks than I've been able to in the last two months." The elephas laughed but it was choked back in frustration.

"The elemental smuggler I ambushed this week?"

"Yes, when I found out that you were the one who orchestrated the job, I wanted to connect with you. Exchange notes perhaps. There's more of them out there, and my leads have been mostly hogwash."

Fiona rubbed a finger across her scarf, frowning. If Fali wanted her information enough to steal it, why was he out here talking to her now? This didn't make sense, but maybe he knew something. "And what have you learned?"

Fali made a noise like a muffled trumpet. Was it a sigh? Elephas could be so hard to read. "That the smuggling has been centered on the elemental pages. They're using odd pagemarks, definitely unofficial ones. It's increased over the last few months from sporadic activity to somewhat of a concentrated effort. I think they're gearing up for something big, but that's as much as I've gotten. They used to burgle businesses in the area, alchemists and the like, but I think they've decided to branch out."

He was right, he had almost nothing. She had gleaned most of that before she trapped the smuggler. It wasn't valuable information to her, but there was something nagging at her about his story. "Wait a minute, you keep saying 'they.' They who? The Guild?" She was hedging her bets that Fali would either have made the connection with the ledger or not.

His eyes grew wide, and he brought his trunk back inside the shrine swiftly. "The Guild? You think the Guild is involved with them?"

"Perhaps. What do you think?"

Sighing again, he said, "They...are a singular organization. Much smaller than the Guild. They move quickly, organized, yes, but much faster than the Guild could ever accomplish. I haven't found a name yet, but nothing makes me think it's the Guild."

Fiona gauged his mannerisms, watching his eyes. He seemed genuinely surprised at her assertion. So he hadn't worked out the ledger initials or cypher at all yet. "What evidence do you have it's not the Travel Guild?"

"What evidence do you have that it is?" He folded his arms.

She could sense he was waiting for an exchange of information. He honestly seemed eager for anything. With dawning surprise, Fiona realized that Fali did not have her ledger. He was smart, yes, but no one could pretend this well to be...so earnest in his thoughts and mannerisms. "So...so," she stuttered, trying to catch up to her thoughts, "when you came to my house, how long were you there?"

"About an hour or so. I noticed your neighbor across the way but didn't want to tell her my business with you so just waved hoping she would bring it up. I probably should've left a note, but I get nervous..." He trailed off, looking at Fiona's face. "What?"

Fiona blinked rapidly. If Mistress Didia had noticed him, and Fali had waved to her, then it would be pretty foolish of him to have taken the ledger. Who could've broken into her house then? "She said you had been waiting there for an hour. Gave me a description of you. And my house had been broken into. I just assumed...I assumed it was you."

He shook his head, holding up his hands. "No, I assure you. When I was there, everything was fine. I promise on my life as a Follower."

She nodded. "I believe you. I just... This whole time I thought you were the ripper in my home. But..." Fiona tried to piece together who else could've known she had something valuable like that.

"What did they take?"

Fiona winced. "A ledger. The only evidence I have tying the Guild to the smuggling. I got it during the ambush." She had left it in her drawer the whole time, only showed it to the Elder, Mac, and Henrietta. Of the three, Henrietta seemed like the one who would come closest, but that was unlikely.

Now it was Fali's turn to freeze, mouth open. His trunk shook, and he said, "You had evidence stolen? They must've known you most likely retrieved it from your capture this week." He shifted, lifting his trunk to the wind and sniffing the night air.

"Yes, yes you're probably right." Details of who did what were not hard to come by in Spine if you knew where to ask around. Perhaps some jacket had heard her talking to Mac at the Thread. She balled up her fist. "The Guild will have to take everything I have if they think stealing from me will stop me from learning the truth."

"I don't want to tell you how to run your business, far be it from me. But I still don't think this is the Guild. Consider this: Why would an organization as powerful as the Guild, with all the paper in the Book, smuggle creatures from their pages? For what reason? Everyone would know about it." He scoffed. "It would be the gossip of the century."

"Because they are without a doubt the absolute worst thing to come out of the inking," she said loudly. She was tired of everyone defending the Guild. They were dishonest, disloyal, and uncaring. They wanted what they wanted regardless of who it hurt. How was she the only one who could see that? "If I had paper for every time they ignored people, hurt people, and made my job harder, I would be rich and living well in one of those hoity-toity castles in the center of the district."

The elephas stepped back as best as he could. The night air drifted between them, the earthy smell of grass and sweat lingering where Fali had given her some room. She closed her eyes and got a hold of herself. She didn't need to prove anything to anyone. She just needed to get on with her work. Everyone would see the truth soon enough.

"I may not agree, but that doesn't mean I don't understand," Fali said gently. "If you want to combine forces, perhaps we could make more headway. I still have one lead I'm following up with tomorrow. May I come by afterward? Share information?"

She nodded, too frustrated to trust speaking. It wouldn't hurt to have someone else tracking the smuggling case while she continued wrestling with the Blackstone's whereabouts. Although it felt a little uncomfortable to agree to, Fali seemed to be trying hard to put her at ease. Probably something the Followers taught on day one.

He patted her shoulder and strode out of the shrine, barely squeezing under the archway. He waved with his trunk and said, "If there's one thing I know, it's that Larrakane doesn't give us more than we can handle. Trust me—I asked her directly. We'll figure this out one way or another." He turned, not waiting for an answer, and walked back up the hill toward the temple and out of sight.

Fiona blew out a deep breath and unclenched her hand. Her house was being watched, her security threatened, and at the center of it all stood the Travel Guild. She just knew it. And she'd take an immediate turn to the dark edge before she let them get away with meddling in her life like this.

EARLY THE NEXT MORNING Fiona woke to a loud knock on her door. Her neck was stiff from being slumped over where she had fallen asleep at her desk making a list of possible avenues to take next. Finding the Blackstone was her priority since it impacted Blaze's rapid cooling. After that she'd pinpoint who exactly had arranged things at the Guild.

Soots was in their customary place in the lamp on her desk, casting flickering light that clashed with the morning brightness streaming through the window. They shot up out of their position and flew to the window.

So much for pretending not to be at home. The knock sounded again, louder and more frantic. Fiona got up, stretching and smoothing down her clothes. She noticed a rip in the stockings around her knee. Her doublet smelled of burnt velvet, and one of the buttons had popped out. She must have looked absolutely awful.

:Friend!: Soots shouted in their crackle voice.

Fiona raised an eyebrow wondering who could attract Soots's attention so. She opened the door to find Gaili on her porch, arm raised. Her hair was standing in the most ridiculous puffs Fiona had ever seen. Charcoal smudged her face and her dark-brown apron was covered in white powder. Her eyes were wide and glistening.

Fiona immediately grabbed her arm, ushering her inside, as all other thoughts vanished. "Good heavens, what's wrong?"

The golden faun stomped into the house unsteadily. "Oh...oh! I'm so sorry to burst in like this, but I didn't know where else to go and I needed to get out of there. Petronia came back to my shop, and...and I tried to give her the rest of the stone breathing potions, but then she said she wanted all the paper I had on hand and I said no and she was ever so angry and all I could think was to run out and then I got lost for a while and, and—"

"Okay, okay, it'll be alright," Fiona said, rubbing a hand across Gaili's back.

"Oh, Fiona, you're too kind. If she finds out I'm here, she'll be awful to deal with and you shouldn't have to do that. What was I thinking?" She drew her long fingers through her pink hair, creating more puffs. There was something jelly-like making the strands stick together, but she didn't seem to notice.

"Dear, I can handle quite a bit, you know. It'll be fine. You can stay here for as long as you like." Fiona had never seen someone so distraught before, and it took everything in her not to immediately go and track Petronia down.

With that invitation, Gaili burst out with a fresh set of tears, and Fiona led her upstairs to the empty bedchamber she used for storage and the occasional guest. She directed her to the made bed, set her down, and fetched a cool washcloth for her puffy face.

Soots, not one to be left out, bobbed along with them and settled in the lamp by Gaili's side. It was cold in the room, and Fiona whispered, "Soots, how about a little more warmth?"

Acquiescing, the room warmed up as Soots glowed brighter.

"Thank you." She placed a hand on Gaili's shoulder, pushing her to lie down. "Now, you stay here and I'll be back with coffee in a moment."

Making her way downstairs two at a time, Fiona wondered at what other run-ins with the tigress poor Gaili had to have dealt with. How had she gotten involved with the blotter of a woman?

Gathering the coffee, cups, dried fruit, and nuts she kept on hand for clients, she carried the tray back up to the room to find Gaili balled up in the center of the bed. "I don't want you to make yourself sick. Come, have some coffee and a little something to eat." Fiona placed the tray down. She poured Gaili a cup without any additions and handed it to her. "Eat, eat. Food is always the first solution to any problem."

"Is that something your mother used to say?" Gaili asked, sniffling, then immediately covered her mouth with a tattooed hand. "Oh, I'm sorry, Fiona. That's none of my business."

Fiona shrugged, used to being around blunt folks. "No, she used to say I ate like a farm boy who didn't have any manners." She waved away the memory, ignoring the rest of the terrible things her mother used to comment on. "But if a problem isn't fixed by the end of the meal, you can at least face it with a full stomach. That was something my father used to tell me."

"Are you much like your father? I'm not." Gaili scrunched up her face.

"A bit." Fiona smiled. "All the best bits really. My nosiness and curiosity. My love of flying. My ability to drink three cups of coffee and still get a good night's sleep." She sipped her cup as a point, imbibing the slightly sweetened hot liquid. Vanilla notes swam over her tongue, and she hummed in appreciation.

"What else did you get from him?"

"Well, I suppose my aversion to the Guild started with him." Fiona thought back to her early days before he passed away. "Maybe not the Guild exactly but somewhat."

"What do you mean?" Gaili grabbed a piece of dried apple and took a tentative bite.

Fiona fiddled with the handle of her cup, rubbing away a drop of coffee. She'd never really thought about it before and tried to put words to the instinct. "He always said never trust a ruler who treats their people like dirt. He was talking about the Queen, of course, but...I dislike how the Guild handles page turners. I don't think they have our best interests at heart."

Gaili munched with a thoughtful expression. "But isn't the Guild mainly run by turners?"

"Yes..." Fiona had thought about this once too. "But we're not all alike. Where you and I see freedom to explore ourselves, do some good, enjoy the life of the pages, some turners only see a way to fatten their pockets or control others after being inked."

"Pulp think that way too. It's not just turners."

"Yes, of course," Fiona said, waving away the distinction, "but most pulp don't have the power the Guild has."

Gaili nodded and picked up the coffee to sip on it. She scrunched her face at the taste. "Blech." Then tumbled in half a dozen cubes of sugar and stirred slowly.

Fiona decided to venture as delicately as she could into the heart of why Gaili had arrived. "What is this about Petronia taking all your paper?"

"She said that from now on I was to give her half of my earnings every week. And that I would be selling some new stock for her at no cost. If I didn't, she'd take over my place and I'd have nothing." Gaili's eyes filled with tears again.

"What? That's extortion." Fiona pursed her lips. "I'm proud of you for standing up for yourself."

"Well, I blurted out no. I didn't mean to say no directly to her." Gaili stopped, biting her lip and hanging her head. "My mentor was right about me."

"What do you mean?"

"I...I was inked not too long ago."

Confused Fiona tried to follow her flow of thoughts, "So you haven't been away from your training too long then? Did she say you should come back more often than you are?"

"Yes. Well, no. I mean, I thought she would be pleased I wanted to come work as much as possible after being inked. She always praised my work to others which she didn't have to do. She's a legend." Gaili said quickly, "One of the best inventors in the page. Maybe even the Book. I was lucky she made me her assistant."

"What did she say after you finished turner training and went home?"

"She told me coming back was unnecessary. That she had others more talented and worthy of her teachings than me. I should've learned turn the page home faster. If I hadn't stayed so long in training she might've kept wanting to teach me." Gaili wiped her face as she teared up.

Fiona wrapped her arms around the faun, hugging her. Her mentor had built her up and then torn her down making her doubt herself and her skills. No wonder she was so distressed. "She's an absolute blotter. And extremely undeserving of your admiration. You don't need her to tell you you're amazing. Now look at me."

Fiona stared into her eyes. "You are going to stay here, and we are going to figure this out together. To the dark edge with her and Petronia."

For the first time since she arrived, Gaili broke into a small smile.

Fiona gave a crisp nod, lightness in her chest from being able to shift her mood. She rather liked Gaili, and she would not see her upset by Petronia or anyone else any further. "As for the ill mannered tigress, did she say what sort of stock she had in mind?"

Before Gaili could answer, a knock on the door sounded throughout the house. Fiona frowned. She was getting more visitors than a carriage stand.

Gaili set her cup down, eyes frantically darting to the window. "That'll be her. It'll be for sure."

Fiona patted her leg, standing up. "If she's knocking, then she's really a blotter. I'll be back in a moment."

Stomping downstairs, she marched straight to the office door and flung it open. She wanted to use the element of surprise herself for once.

A gray elephas, small for her species and with ivory tusks, took a step back from the door. Trunk curled back, she raised her hands. "Pardon me, ma'am. I'm just coming with a summons." She gingerly held out a cream-colored envelope with her trunk.

Fiona snatched it up, her exhaustion and anxiety controlling her emotions, and ripped into the envelope. Unfolding the short letter on elegant crisp paper, Fiona noticed it smelled of ink and was still warm.

"The Travel Guild?" she said, perplexed at the header lettering. She scanned the document, running her fingers down the page. "The Travel Guild wants to see me?" What in Larrakane's blessed name could they want with her? Did they know she was on to them?

The elephas nodded. "On a matter of urgency, yes, ma'am."

Fiona looked past the young elephas to a white-and-gold chariot standing outside her home with a couple of beautiful horses. Some of her neighbors stood in the street and Mistress Didia on her porch. A summons from the Guild could be bad or good, but it would certainly give everyone a bit of gossip for the rest of the day. Movement in the alley across the way caught her eye, a large shadow she couldn't make out. The elephas cleared her throat.

"Let me get my assistant," Fiona said, not wanting to leave Gaili alone. If Petronia did show up, she would be defenseless besides Soots. A burnt manor house and a hurt Gaili would do her no good.

"Oh, just yourself ma'am."

Fiona paused, focusing on the messenger. "Really?"

The elephas nodded again.

Alone, urgently, to the Guild? Something was off, but Fiona didn't know what. She'd have to see it through, but she wasn't about to go without her guard up. Fiona sighed, showing her clear frustration. "One moment please."

She closed the door and ran back up the stairs to find the bedroom empty. Soots and Gaili were nowhere to be seen. She called out, "Gaili. Soots. The door was for me."

Happiness emanated from the closet. Fiona opened the door to find Gaili tucked away in the corner with Soots in the lamp.

"You'll never be able to hide with them. Their emotions make them easy to find."

Gaili looked at Soots with wide eyes. "Really? I didn't feel a thing."

Cocking her head, Fiona narrowed her eyes but then threw the thought away. "The Guild is summoning me."

"Oh no. What have you done?" Gaili unfolded herself and stepped out of the closet.

"Done? I've done nothing. Well, I've done many a thing, but nothing that should get me in trouble." *Yet anyways.* She couldn't go like this. She probably looked frightful.

"Then what could they want with you?"

"I suppose that will be the first thing I ask them." She moved toward her bedroom. *And more.* "There's a chariot and a jacket waiting for me outside. I tried to get you on with me but was denied."

"That's awfully sweet of you, but I'll just go and get out of your way. I—"

"Absolutely not." Fiona stopped mid hose change. She poked her head out her bedroom door. "You stay right here, make yourself at home, and don't let Soots burn the place down." Fiona smiled and ducked back into her room to finish changing. She put on her second-best velvet doublet and a wide skirt of copper silk that just barely covered her slippered feet. She tied her scarf around her waist to act as a belt but still provide access to her weapon and paper. She glanced at herself in the mirror, fluffed up her dark curls, wiped sugar from the corner of her plump brown cheeks, and shrugged. This was the best she was gonna get. She strode out of her room and pressed a reassuring hand on Gaili's shoulder. "I mean it. I'll be worried sick if you leave while I'm gone. I shall never forgive myself if something happened to you while I was off dithering with the Guild."

"Okay, Fiona," Gaili said, wiping her hands and sitting back on the bed.

:Careful,: said Soots.

"I will, and you be careful too." Fiona whizzed out of the room, through the office, and opened the door. The motion startled the poor elephas, who stumbled back. "Right, I'm ready. But I get to drive the horses." Fiona closed the door behind her. "Oh!" She darted a hand into her scarf, feeling for a soft cottony pocket. Reaching inside, she thought for a moment and then pulled out a set of soft dove-gray riding gloves. "I almost forgot."

She bounded down the steps, leaving the jacket running after her to catch up. "I've always wanted to do this," she shouted back. Stepping into the chariot, Fiona grabbed the reins, took a deep breath, and shouted, "Yah!"

FIONA DREW TO A stop outside of a massive white-and-black marble building as the elephas jacket clutched the railing of the chariot. Jumping from the chariot, Fiona walked around to the horses, patting them and talking gently to them. Though not the same as the native breeds from her page, the horses of Kerus, where the chariot had originally come from, were very similar. It was uncanny how two completely different pages could breathe life into such similar beings. If she hadn't already been a believer of Larrakane, that certainly would've swayed her. Only someone who created everything could keep all the details organized in such a way.

The immense stone columns looked stunning, especially up close. The many stairs gleamed in the light of the day as if just polished. Fiona had always found the Hinge, Travel Guild headquarters, impressive regardless of what went on inside. It was ostentatious to be sure, but the architecture was still quite well done.

The jacket came to stand beside her. She stammered, "I-I've *never* had a ride like that before."

"Thank you," Fiona said, beaming, and began to make her way up the marble staircase.

Fiona had only been to the Hinge a few times in recent years. She had avoided the place like a plague after turner training. She marveled at how high the ceiling reached as she walked through the large open doors. She had memorized every decorative mark and every angle—it was just the way her mind worked—but she still appreciated the sight of it now.

People teemed in and out of the Hinge and crowded the floor. Fiona stared up, checking to see if there had been any architectural changes since she had last been there.

The elephas cleared her throat and tucked a pocket clock back into her tight tunic folds. "Shall we?"

Fiona shrugged—she'd have time to look around more later—and followed the elephas through the rest of the grand building to a back archway. This was deeper than Fiona had ever been before within the Hinge. She noticed that it was not so new or so lovely as the front of the massive building. Dust trailed in some corners of the wall and the light from the front didn't reach here. The smell of bodies, stale coffee, and burnt paper permeated the air. This is where the majority of Travel Guild work happened. The jackets, the printing of paper, and the *Card*, everything took place in this building. No wonder they were trying to build another one.

"If you wait one minute here, Gilded Evenhell will be out for you."

"Gilded Evenhell? Is that who I'm to meet?" said Fiona. The name sounded familiar. *Dodger's director. How interesting.*

"Yes, miss." The elephas nodded—perhaps it was her favorite gesture.

Fiona leaned forward conspiratorially. "What's she like?"

Her trunk quivered before she spoke, and she clasped her hands behind her back. "She's smart and quite strong as might be expected. She's head of regulations." The elephas finished as if the title said it all. Regulations was the department in the Guild most involved in traveling the Book, doing the type of work Fiona did. Evenhell must have been responsible for overseeing quite a number of people and cases.

"Do you like her?" Fiona asked, leaning forward.

"Like her?" Her hairless eyebrows creased.

"Yes, do you enjoy her company? Do you find her fun?"

"Well, no, miss. I mean, not that I don't like her or that she's not fun. Just that we don't look at her like that. She's a Gilded."

Fiona nodded. "Of course. Of course. No one wants to like their boss. How odd that would be."

The elephas looked relieved that Fiona was understanding. "Exactly. It would be unlikely that she even does the type of things that would make one fun."

"Oh, is that unlikely? I should think I'm quite capable of being amusing," came a high-pitched voice behind them.

A short peach-skinned human woman with flowing straight brown hair stood behind the two, chin jutting out. A smirk crossed her face as she watched Fiona. Although Fiona stood at five feet nine and the elephas at seven feet towered over her, they were by no means looking down at the woman. She gave the impression that would be quite impossible. There was something off about her appearance, but Fiona couldn't place it.

"That'll be all," she said, dismissing the elephas without glancing at her. Turning her full attention to Fiona, she put out her hand. "Gilded Evenhell."

"It is nice to meet you," Fiona said politely, shaking her hand. It was clammy and uncomfortably bony.

"The pleasure is all mine. Let's speak in my office. I'm most excited to talk to you."

Fiona's pulse increased at this assertion, and she followed the small woman into a room. A few chairs and a desk took center stage, but the trappings on the walls were the stars: animal heads, weapons of all types, and artistic tapestries from across the Book. You could tell a lot about where a turner had been by the things they had collected. But you could tell even more about who they were by what they displayed from that collection.

Fiona looked over the room and put on a show of enjoyment at the vast display of death and destruction. "This is quite the diverse compilation. You must be one of the most well-traveled turners in the Book."

"I do like to be in the know and see what's out there. I'm sure you probably have quite the collection as well. You were one of the youngest to have ever been inked, I'd heard."

How much the Guild knew of Fiona, she didn't know, but she was sure they had the resources to find anything they wanted. Luckily for her, she had nothing to hide besides her casework. "Yes, I was supremely fortunate. Becoming a turner was the greatest day of my life."

"I know there are those who count being inked as a curse. Always having to live on Spine and such. But even then, we are the keepers of the Book. The power brokers of every page."

"Some would say, yes." *You. You would say that.* Fiona kept smiling, trying to appear calm and not as though she was bubbling with disgust.

Gilded Evenhell nodded with a wide smile. "As part of my job I keep a watchful eye out for those who may attempt to disrupt the word of the Book. Or who can help maintain it."

Fiona nodded back, letting her lack of response be seen as agreement to keep the woman talking.

"I think you could be helpful here. Format has it your minor work among the pulp has people recommending you. And your work curtailing one of those terrible elemental smugglers earlier this week has added to your renown."

Fiona adjusted her posture to give herself time to watch Evenhell. She brought up the elemental smuggler rather quickly in the conversation. But Fiona could detect no rush in her even voice and mannerism. The woman must either be incredibly good at hiding her knowledge or unaware.

"With all that to say," Evenhell continued, "I'm offering you a place in the Guild. A place on my team."

Fiona sat back, a bit warm. A job? Of all the places she was expecting this to go, a job offer wasn't one of them. She swallowed and said slowly, "I have my own investigations."

"Yes." Evenhell waved her hand dismissively. "With Guild resources, you would be able to do so much more than small jobs for small clients. I believe you've had a taste of those resources this week, yes?"

She knew calling in Dodger for the ambush on the elemental smuggler would come back to haunt her at some point. Fiona schooled her face so she didn't openly grimace and said, "The Guild has many offerings that make the life of a turner easier some days." *Don't agree or give too much information.*

"And those could be yours if you joined my team."

Fiona leaned in, tapping the sides of the leather chair. Perhaps she could work this new direction to her advantage and gain information about the Guild that could help her pinpoint them. "How tight knit is your team? Do you know what they all do on assignments and the like?"

Evenhell furrowed her brow. "I keep a close watch on them. Their actions reflect on me, and perception can be everything."

"Yes, it can be," Fiona murmured.

"I don't take failure or deception lightly."

Something in Evenhell's eyes at the thought of someone pulling one over on her felt like daggers to Fiona. The woman would not be trifled with if someone on her team disobeyed her. Fiona sat up and clasped her hands together. "I understand."

"You could keep doing your current cases if you choose. The rewards would go to the Guild instead, naturally, as we pay a monthly stipend. And any case you closed would be under our banner but by your name. You could also have help from the variety of jackets on the team who could be assigned to you."

"I could keep my current cases?" Even the Blackstone search and the smuggling business? How much did the Guild already know?

"Needless to say, yes. We wouldn't want to pull you from anything you're doing now. That would be a terrible way to handle clients. Powerful connections are key in our line of work." Evenhell's bony hands wrapped around each other in a tight grip.

"Connections are the lifeblood of a good investigator, you're right." Fiona nodded thoughtfully, mind churning. While the offer was unexpected, the careful setup from Gilded Evenhell was not. Manipulation was not new to Fiona. Her time before becoming a turner had made sure of that. She saw the cracks in the careful facade of the proposal. She had no intention of handing over her cases to the Guild so they could do who knew what with them. Plus she had worked hard to earn relationships with people like the Elder and the Ashborn. Deciding to drop the pretense of being interested in the job and trying to catch Evenhell off guard, she said, "What are you doing about the smuggling of elemental creatures?"

Evenhell titled her head. "Well, thanks to your efforts, we're further along in finding out who is behind the affair. The smugglers have been interviewed and are awaiting sentencing. We have leads. Leads I can't share, of course, until you're part of the team. But we know who they are, and they'll be dealt with soon." Again there was no hint of deception or duplicity in Evenhell's assertions.

Fiona shuffled her feet, crossing and uncrossing them. It didn't make sense. The ledger had Gilded initials, clear as day. Or so Henrietta had said. Right? Maybe the ledger wasn't as clear as they thought.

Evenhell could be lying, but for all of Fiona's experience, nothing was telling her she was. Nothing suggested she wasn't being upfront. Perhaps she really did have leads. But that was impossible. It had to be the Guild who was behind it. Or had Fiona just pounced on the information tangentially linking the Guild and stopped investigating from there?

"I will say," Evenhell started, motioning toward Fiona, "since you did the start of the work, perhaps we do owe you some information. The stolen airship coinciding with a rise in gossip about the Guild was not a coincidence."

Confused, Fiona racked her brain trying to line up what Evenhell was saying.

Evenhell searched her face and smiled. "You'll get there in time, no doubt. But that's all the information I can offer for now. Unless you are ready to join the Guild?"

Fiona shook her head, mind buzzing through the possibilities. "Why is the Guild not interceding on behalf of the fire denizens in the waste of Blaze?" No matter if they weren't behind the smuggling, they still weren't doing anything about Blaze.

Evenhell's unnatural smile dropped. "The Guild has many duties to concern ourselves with, and we can't be everywhere. We're handling Blaze with delicate care."

"But isn't it a duty of the Guild to make sure pages are safe for turners and skimmers alike? And in order to keep a page safe, we should be trying to keep it alive."

"I see you aren't clear on all the functions we are responsible for," Evenhell said in a clipped tone.

"Oh, I'm quite clear, thank you," Fiona said, rising. They may not be smugglers, but that didn't automatically make them good. "To turn a profit across the Book, hang who it hurts."

"Well then. I suppose we were incorrect in our assessment of you being an asset. Disappointing."

"I could never join people who valued their own business above the lives of everyone else." Fiona strode to the door without another word and slammed it behind her.

Fiona exited the Hinge without a backward glance, ignoring the architecture and the people. It was smart of the Guild to try another route to get to the Ashborn. If they really did want to own a piece of the fire page, her job for the Ashborn would have been a sure link. But that meant the Guild didn't have the Blackstone. Otherwise, they wouldn't need her to cooperate with them at all. They could just bargain with the Ashborn directly, power in exchange for the stone.

Fiona worried her lip as she made her way out into the heat of the day. She felt like she was back at square one. Her only good theory had been that the Travel Guild was sitting on the Blackstone. That they were doing the smuggling. That they were the linchpin in it all. If they weren't, then who was? And what had Evenhell meant about the airship?

She elected to walk the hour home instead of trying for a carriage to give herself some time to think. The lighted sky baked the air, and Fiona meandered under the shade of trees as best as she could outside of the travel corridor and deeper into the turner district.

She turned a corner, a back way with fewer people, toward home. She didn't want to stop or be stopped by anyone who may know her. She was sure the gossip had spread by now of the chariot outside her door and the Guild assistant to accompany her, and she wasn't ready to face it yet. It was rare for a chariot to come for someone like her. Unimportant and unconnected.

"Perception is everything," Fiona murmured, thinking of Evenhell's words.

Lost in thought, Fiona trudged down the path toward her home. She didn't see the smilodon tigress until her claws swung out and wrapped around her throat.

PULLED OFF THE GROUND, feet dangling, she grasped at the claws on her neck. Large patches of hair were missing from the tigress's arms where the bandages used to be. Fiona could still breathe for now but didn't want to count on the benevolence of Petronia.

"Hello again," the tigress growled in her ear. She squeezed and dragged Fiona from the desolate path into an alleyway.

Fiona winced, struggling at the claws, her breath caught in her chest as she tried to frantically think of a way out. They were in between districts and off the main streets, so chances of people walking past were nil. Maybe a few people who lived here or a passing carriage. What Fiona wouldn't give for nosy neighbors right now. She kept one hand pulling on the woman's paw while her other snaked down to the scarf around her waist.

Petronia relaxed her hand, allowing Fiona to breathe a tiny bit. "I'm glad I get to deal with you. Two birds with one stone." Petronia chuckled at herself. "I thought it would be a challenge. But you're terrible at noticing anything but yourself. Figures."

"Sorry, I didn't realize I was supposed to be cowering today," Fiona rasped out. Her chest tightened as the situation continued to dawn on her. Perhaps it wasn't the smartest idea to bait the person strangling you. She tried to distract her while digging for her whip. "What do you want?"

"To give you and your employer a message." She squeezed Fiona again. "And to have a little fun."

Fiona jerked out her whip and lashed at the tigress. They were too close together for her to get any strength on it. The tigress caught the whip easily and yanked it out of her hands.

"I've been wondering about that scarf. Seems valuable." Raising Fiona up against the wall, Petronia ignored her scrambling kicks and raked her paws deep across Fiona, ripping the scarf from her waist.

Pain blossomed across Fiona's torso, and a sticky liquid she suspected was blood clung to her slashed doublet. She groaned, nausea making her dizzy. Tears pressed themselves from her eyes. Her brain couldn't process this moment; this unbelievable moment surely wasn't happening to her. It was as if she was outside of her body, at the end of the alley watching.

"Now where did you pull that blasted whip from?" Petronia's voice broke through the fog.

Heat pushed through Fiona, and she began kicking again with all the energy and strength she had. "Quit getting blood on my scarf." She enunciated each word as she scratched and kicked. If she was going to die, she was not going to do it limp and pleading.

Petronia released her hand and jumped back.

Fiona dropped to the ground roughly, elbows and legs hitting the stonework, causing her to cry out in pain. She didn't understand. "Why?" was all she was able to get out as the knot in her stomach grew. She pressed back tears as the pain in her chest became more and more pronounced. It was getting hard to focus, but she tried, staring at Petronia's face.

Petronia kneeled and tucked the scarf into the neckline of her short tunic, revealing the thin blue bar tattoo on her chest. She grasped Fiona's face with one paw. Tapping it with her claws, she said, "Leave. Us. Alone. You can't win against the Guild."

Trying to parse what she was saying, Fiona stuttered, "You...you work for the Guild?"

"Of course," Petronia said simply. "The Guild is everything." She grinned, sharp teeth gleaming. Her tail twitched, catching Fiona's eye.

Discomfort, worry, or something else, she didn't know, but Fiona had been around Dodger long enough to understand smilodons a bit better than other creatures in the Book. Petronia was nervous. Taking a shaky breath, Fiona pressed, "Who put you up to this?"

Petronia shook Fiona's head. "You have enough info for now. Back off. And tell the same to your boss." She let go of Fiona and jumped away all in one swift movement. "Unless you want another visit, I'd do it soon."

"But..." Fiona started. Her chest throbbed, the pain excruciating and persistent. It wasn't just the wound. Something was pulsing through her blood like sparks from a burning log. She choked back the rest of her question as she doubled over.

Petronia scoffed, "Weakling." And bounded up the side of the wood wall next to her.

Fiona barely registered the woman leaving. She squeezed her eyes shut, trying to block out the fire and the pain inside her.

Time slowed down until she heard what sounded like hooves on the stonework some distance before her. She didn't know how long she had been there, but the pain came to her in a wave as her brain kicked into gear. "Get up, get up," she commanded herself.

Rising slowly using the wall for support, she got to her feet taking shaky breaths. She let her control slip, tears streaming down her face, as she shuffled along the wall toward the alley entrance. In the back of her mind she wondered if Petronia was watching her. If the tigress had been instructed not to kill her. Was she valuable alive?

Dragging herself from the alley, she emerged into the empty street to see a carriage far down the lane. She stumbled into the middle of the road, waving feebly. Her muscles went weak, and she collapsed.

From the carriage, a square-faced ursidon squatted above her. "Hello? Hello?" He picked her up gingerly, placing one paw to support her head, and put her into the carriage.

"Thorne Investigations, please," Fiona breathed out. She closed her eyes and then her world went dark.

"She was caked in blood. Oh, oh, I don't know what I would've done if you hadn't been here," Gaili whispered.

"Think nothing of it, lass. The winds of Larrakane brought me at the right time. You've done the best you can by her. She just needs rest now."

Fiona opened her eyes, scanning for the familiar voices. She recognized the splotches on her ceiling where water had leaked from overfull aqueducts. A glow of amber light infused the whole room with its warmth. The smell of fresh, chocolaty coffee roused her consciousness, and she breathed a sigh of relief. She was home.

She struggled to sit up but winced at the pain in her chest and stopped. It didn't feel like there were thousands of needles piercing through her veins. A good sign. Glancing down, she saw that she had been bandaged up, quite tightly actually. Her breasts hadn't been this flat since she was inked.

Gaili rushed to her side. "I'm so glad you're awake. Oh, Fiona!" The faun gripped her hand tightly in her tattooed one, crinkles etched in her face. "You looked just awful."

Fiona groaned and snorted at the same time. "Thank you for being delicate, dear."

"Oh no, I just meant you're all banged up. Not that *you* actually look awful. Well, the bandages make you look bad. I mean, what happened? Did the Guild do this?"

"No, our old friend Petronia." Fiona cringed and rushed to reassure the faun. "But it had nothing to do with you, Gaili. I promise. This one I definitely brought on myself." *My confrontational, bullheaded self.*

Eyes wide, Gaili covered her mouth with her hands. Worn hands with peach skin pulled her gently back, and Henrietta stepped up to the bed. "Aye, lass. Point me in the direction and I'll make short work of her."

"Henrietta," Fiona said, her voice rising, "what are you even doing here?"

"I came to give you some of that information you asked about. Didn't know Miss Gaili was staying with ya, and we sat down for some coffee before a carriage showed up with you in tow. You've been out for a few hours now." She rubbed her face. "Was just waiting on ya to get back to this side of the living."

Fiona pulled herself up at this new information, groaning. She grabbed the cup of coffee and took a sip for her troubles. It warmed her immensely, and she closed her eyes, inhaling the nutty scent.

"Easy now." Henrietta tsked.

"This is as easy as I get." She waved at her to sit down on the bed. She didn't have time to be modest. "Petronia, who I'm sure Gaili will fill you in on, ambushed me to give me a message."

"What was that?" Gaili said, sitting on the other side of the bed.

"To leave the Guild alone. That I couldn't win against them." Fiona bit her lip. Yes, that had been the gist of it. She pushed through the fog in her brain. "But she also wanted me to talk to my client. And quickly." A special message from the Guild. Petronia had been sent from the Guild to warn her. But it didn't add up.

"That's an awfully illustrative message," Henrietta said, motioning to the bandages. "You could've bled out before you even delivered it."

Fiona shook her head, thinking back on Petronia's actions. She had wanted to hurt her, yes, but not kill her. Or at least, she couldn't kill her. "I think the pain was a bit more Petronia than the message."

"Well, I'm just glad you're alright. I can't believe the Guild ambushed you."

"Yes," Fiona said slowly, "I can't either. Especially because they were offering me a job."

"A job?"

"Mmhmm." Fiona shook her head. "But I refused."

"Why send a chariot and make all that fuss just to ambush you? Everyone will know it was the Guild."

"Yes." Fiona rubbed her thumb across the rim of her cup. "Why indeed?" How did they know she'd take the backstreets home and not a carriage or the main road? Had Petronia been following her? There had been some odd happenings at the corner of her eye over the last couple of days, but she didn't like to think it had been the tigress stalking her all that time without her noticing.

It didn't make sense why the Guild, who could've done any number of things to stall her investigations, would've sent Petronia of all people to deal with her. Petronia, who she would've bet very good paper hadn't been working for the Guild. The Travel Guild had their own alchemists, their own weaponsmiths, their own everything. They didn't need to shake down alchemists for potions.

They all lifted their heads to a knock sounding from the door below. Fiona frowned, her mind still trying to pick its way over her day. She really didn't have time to entertain. "Gaili, will you see who that is? If it's Mistress Didia from across the street, please tell her politely that I'm busy. But no information!"

Gaili nodded and trotted down the stairs.

Fiona watched Henrietta as she left, the captain's eyes following the faun with something akin to a smile. She pushed her curiosity there aside. "What did you learn?"

"Did some digging with the—" She glanced back down the hallway. "—cloak and dagger set. I got a mighty big earful from an acquaintance of a friend in Rise."

"Rise? About what exactly?" Fiona said, brow furrowed.

"Person was very chummy and happy to tell me about the deals she's had come across her plate from the Travel Guild. Said to keep it under seal obviously. They've been asking her to bind all sorts of elemental creatures for them. She's not as particular as I was apparently, so she's done a few jobs for them. Even offered me one."

"That's terrible," Gaili broke in angrily, walking up behind them.

Fiona hadn't realized that faun had gotten back so soon. Lumbering up the steps behind her was Fali. Fiona opened her mouth but then closed it, waiting till he made his way up. Her small stairway had not been built with the gait of an elephas in mind.

"This priest said he had business with you, Fiona," Gaili said, wringing her hands, "and I thought maybe it was important enough to invite him in?"

Fiona nodded, setting the faun at ease. "Your instinct was in the right place. Hello, Fali, make yourself at home." She smiled, biting back a hysterical giggle at the ridiculous number of people in her bedroom.

He looked around the room, trunk tucked as if trying to make himself smaller. "I didn't realize you would be busy. I can come back later perhaps?"

"I think now's the right time actually," Fiona said, setting down her cup. "We are all dealing in the same business." She gestured between Henrietta and Fali. "Henrietta, Fali; Fali, Henrietta. Now, let's try to find some smugglers, hmm?"

Gaili grabbed the empty cup from the side table, her hands fumbling with it. Fiona reached out and grabbed her hand, focusing on her tattoos. There had been a tattoo on the man during the smuggling ambush, a blue strip. "This woman you talked to," Fiona said, turning to the captain, "did you happen to see a tattoo on her?"

"Well now…" She glanced back at Gaili and her cheeks reddened. "I wasn't looking on purpose or anything, but I did notice a bit of a blue streak on her…er…chest."

"Petronia has a similar one on her chest," Fiona said slowly, "and the smuggler did as well. He had to take his shirt off when Soots burned him."

"That fits with what my lead told me today," Fali said. All eyes swiveled toward him, and his face grew a few shades darker at the attention. He cleared his throat. "The groups that've been burglarizing businesses here and there have banded together. No longer operating in small disjointed groups. There's a lot more than I had suspected, and they've gotten organized. They're turners working somewhere away from the city. In the forest possibly, although I can't imagine the druids would allow that no matter how big it is."

"Could be they're operating on the move," Henrietta said, scratching her face. "Would make them harder to find."

"Yes," Fiona said, pieces clicking into place, "especially if they had an airship to work out of."

"An airship?" Henrietta frowned. "Out here?"

"Nowhere to dock or keep it maintained," Fali interjected.

"Yes, we don't have a particular need of them here with just the one city. But it would make them tougher to track in the forest if they can move around as needed." Fiona nodded. "What you said was right, Fali. It's not the Guild. But they want me to think it is."

"But why?" Gaili asked.

"To create some sort of play. Something they want the Guild blamed for."

"Well, that's mighty easy to do," Henrietta chimed in. "The Guild isn't the cream in everyone's coffee."

"Too true," Fiona said, thinking back to Evenhell's indifference to Blaze dying. "But if there's a whole league of rippers, organized and pretending to do things under the name of the Guild...then it must be pretty bad indeed."

Henrietta nodded, bluster and ruddy cheeks smoothing out. "Well, I'll continue keeping an eye on matters all the same. Can't be having honest smugglers' reputations sullied by these rippers."

"Be safe. If they're all as bad as Petronia, they won't hesitate to hurt you if they know you have a notion they aren't with the Guild."

"Lass, I've been in this big Book almost twice your lifetime, and I'm not looking to go to the dark edge anytime soon. Never you worry." Henrietta wiggled her eyebrows at her and turned to Gaili. She took her hand delicately. "And you keep yourself safe as well. You owe me a stroll out on the bluffs, don't you forget it."

Gaili blushed, her golden cheeks turning copper. "I'll keep Fiona company."

Henrietta nodded and dropped her hand. Fiona looked up to the heavens, shaking her head. Henrietta was an absolute charmer, no doubt about it. She'd have to remember to ask Mac how they became acquaintances. She suspected it was quite a story.

Henrietta nodded to the priest cordially and made her way out of the room.

"Fiona," Fali said, "I kept your name out of dealings with my contact. But this is bigger than we expected. I will be connecting with the Guild on this, to enlist their help." He coughed, his trunk shaking just a bit.

She assumed he meant the Followers of Larrakane. She nodded. "I understand you have to do what's best for you and your organization." She breathed out a sigh. After her rant the other day, she could understand how nervous he was telling her this. She sought to put him at ease. "If you speak with Gilded Evenhell, you may find an ally there. I will have to speak to my client, but I don't think that prevents you getting on with it."

Fali looked visibly relieved.

She hadn't realized that her thoughts on the matter meant that much to him. Who was this quiet elephas and what exactly did he do in the Book? She had so many questions. "Perhaps when you've gotten a direction we can share information." She smiled. "A parlay of sorts."

"That would be great," he said, raising his trunk as he smiled. "I would enjoy picking your brain, as your people often say. You've been most impressive."

Fiona's face warmed, and she was glad it was hard to tell on her dark-brown skin when she was blushing. He thought her impressive. My, that was a mood lifter.

Fali said his goodbyes to her and Gaili, then left slowly down the stairs. Fiona made a mental note to invite him to the Thread for dinner sometime. She didn't think him to be an unread turner, but it was clear he was new to being an operative of sorts. She couldn't wait to get to know him a touch better.

She sighed, leaning back in her bed as Gaili cleared away the cups and fussed over her. There was still so much to figure out, and she needed to update the Elder. She would have to—

A sudden thought hit her as she shivered with the cold of the light withdrawing outside.

"Gaili, where's Soots?"

"Oh!" Gaili said. "They're in the stove. When they saw you, they got so upset I was worried about the whole place going up in flames. I convinced them the stove would be a safe place for now. I'll go let them out so they can see you're alright."

"Thank you."

It wasn't too long before a blaze of heat rushed up and into her bedroom. Soots in their little suit flew into the room and bobbed above Fiona as close as they could get.

:Friend!: Soots emanated concern.

"I'm alright, I'm alright. I promise." She held out her arms, and they flew into the crook of them, warming Fiona's chest.

:Careful!:

"Well, I did try to be. I didn't think I'd be getting ambushed." Fiona grimaced and laid her hand on her bare neck. Her scarf was gone. Not only the thing she loved the most but with it all her essentials for living as a turner. Her tools, her page equipment, everything. She just prayed to Larrakane that stupid tigress didn't rip a hole in it.

Seeing Fiona rubbing her neck forlornly, Gaili asked Fiona what happened. Fiona recounted in light detail the ambush and her stolen scarf.

"We'll get it back, Fiona. I promise."

"I know we will." She reached out to squeeze the faun's hand.

Gaili squeezed back and then popped up from the bed. "Look at me still up here blathering on. You should rest. I'll watch the house and Soots will stand guard. If you need anything, just ring this bell." She pointed to a little engraved silver bell she had produced from nowhere.

Fiona smiled, not used to being cared for so sweetly. She wasn't sure if she had ever really let anyone try.

FIONA WOKE TO CLANKS and bangs sounding from downstairs. She pulled out her pocket watch and noted the time as entirely too early. Swinging her legs over the side of the bed, she grunted loudly as the bandages rubbed against her wounds and a flood of memories came back to her. She had almost forgotten about the state she was in.

Soots in the lamp beside her warmed the room as they saw her in distress.

Fiona winced at the brightened light. "I'm okay. Just moved too quickly for comfort." Another loud clang came from below. "But I'll never get back to sleep with all that noise, so may as well investigate."

She picked up the lamp with the flame sprite and made her way to the door and down the wooden steps. Everything hurt from her neck down to her feet. It was slow going, but as she got closer to the bottom floor she heard a small crushing sound, and the scent of something foul and fungal wafted toward her.

"Ack, Gaili, I hope that's you and not a bog spider dripping all over my rugs."

"Oh, Fi, you're up!" said Gaili. "Do you mind if I call you Fi? It's such a cute name for you. You really shouldn't be up and walking in your condition," she admonished, fussing around. She had changed into a clean taupe dress fitted at the waist that fell into a long full skirt. Lace attached sleeves trimmed in gold billowed around her arms in a new style Fiona wasn't quite sure what to call. Faekin were entirely too fashionable for her to keep up with. She wore an apron over it all, but this time it was one Fiona recognized from her kitchen.

"Yes, whatever was I thinking?" She padded to the dining table and sat down among the mess that was now her kitchen. The counters were filled with bottles and pots. Smells of fragrant lavender mingled with hints of rotting meat. Had she been out for days?

"Where in the world did all this come from? I thought I told you not to leave the house in case Petronia came snooping by."

"I didn't, I promise! After you fell asleep yesterday, a friend of yours stopped by and he seemed so nice and offered to get me whatever I needed for you and it was the sweetest thing. He brought back so much from the shop and this bottle for you and everything." Gaili grabbed a tall bottle of whiskey off the shelf behind her. "Although I don't think you should drink in your state."

Fiona's eyes widened at the sight of the brown bottle and grabbed it from Gaili. "Dodger came by?" He was the only friend she had who hadn't already seen her beaten-up form and would offer the right libations to go with it. It was thoughtful of him. The kind of thing she had taken for granted, she realized.

"I've never known a smilodon to go by a nickname." Gaili grabbed a pile of papers and vials and moved them from the table to a kitchen shelf.

Fiona pulled the cork out of the bottle with her teeth and spit it on the table. This was her home, and she was hurt, manners be thrown to the dark edge. She motioned to a pewter mug on a high shelf. Gaili retrieved it and her eyes widened as Fiona poured a hefty portion. She took a deep drink and sighed. "He didn't really have a choice with the nickname. Did he say what he wanted? Was he mad?"

"Heavens no. He was very sweet. Just enquired about you being hurt and said he would come back later. He carried everything in and set it up. He had no idea where to even go. He acted like he'd never been in here before."

Fiona took another drink. It burned nicely in her throat and eased some of her discomfort. "He hasn't really." She had never just had him over before. She always met him at the Thread or the like. She considered him a friend, but had she really treated him like one?

"Oh no. Did I invite in someone you don't like? He just seemed so...thoughtful. I'm sorry, I shouldn't act like this is my home and just let anyone wander in here. I—"

"It's fine, Gaili. Really. Besides, I'm glad you feel comfortable here." She surveyed the kitchen with its new accouterments of pots, bubblers, and apparently a saw board. "Clearly I wasn't using this space correctly." But as she joked she felt warm with the truth. It was nice to have someone she liked around asking questions and just living.

"You didn't even have a way to make bread! Oh." Gaili ducked into the corner and banged open a large iron pot Fiona had never seen before. The faun opened cabinet doors, grabbing dishes and blowing dust off them.

Fiona looked at Soots and shook her head in wonder.

:Hungry.:

"I know, I know," said Fiona. She'd have to figure out how to make sure Soots was fed when she wasn't around or able. Maybe she could set up a small place for them and have wood delivered.

In what seemed like no time, Gaili came back to the table with a loaf of bread, a bowl of olive oil, and a platter of hard cheese and roasted chicken. "I assumed you could eat these and we can figure out what to do next." She set them down and then fished a bundled of papers out of her apron and tossed them in the lamp with Soots, who quickly devoured them.

Fiona smiled, rubbing her hands together. "Keep feeding me like this and you can stay forever."

The light around them grew brighter as Soots finished their meal quickly.

"I think Soots agrees."

"I just like a good meal," Gaili said, blushing. "Baking in general. Although I promise there's no rock breathing potion in that."

"Well, that's good for me I suppose." Fiona cut into the bread, drowned it in oil and took a bite. It was absolutely delicious. The taste of olive and wheat was just right and enough to jolt some energy into her tired brain.

Gaili shoved a hunk of bread into her mouth. For being dainty, she was not a graceful eater. It made Fiona enjoy her more. There was oil smeared across the faekin's cheek, and

Fiona laughed, but it did remind her of something. "Gaili, what else did Petronia say to you yesterday?"

The faun sat down and cupped her mug. "That she had some stock I was going to unload for her."

"What do you think it was?"

"I don't know." She chewed slowly. "I keep all sorts of things in the shop. It could be anything from weapons to elixirs."

Fiona mulled that over as she took another bite of soaked bread. *Concoctions, eh.* "What else can you make from elemental excrement?"

"All sorts of things. You can infuse most mundane things with it. Say you want to go to Depths but you don't want water rusting your dagger. A clever alchemist could add the oily excretion of the kora fish to wax that you coat the dagger in to block the water from it."

Fiona stopped mid bite. "What if you used other parts? Besides excrement or clippings from nature or what have you?"

"That's not allowed," Gaili said, waving a dismissive hand.

"Says who?"

"The council of the Court of Copper."

"But we're outside of the Court."

Gaili shook her head. "No alchemist taught in the Court would be caught doing that. You'd have everything stripped from you."

Fiona pursed her lips. Those sort of rules only stopped good people from doing things they wouldn't already do. She started to ask another question but bells chimed loudly outside her home, pulling her attention. Was someone traversing the streets ringing bells? It wasn't a holiday.

Gaili grinned. "Oh! It's being used already. I hope you don't mind, the knocking was so hard to hear upstairs, so I installed a pull."

Once again Fiona was at a loss for words. Seeing Gaili's pensive face, she closed her mouth and quickly shrugged. "Far be it from me to dissuade innovation." She started to get up, but Gaili waved her back down to get the door herself. With only the smallest amount of reluctance, Fiona sat back. Why had she never thought to get someone to help out around here?

Fiona heard the door open and then a slight hiss of noise. Worried that it was Petronia, she got up quickly, wincing at her wounds threatening to reopen, and hurried into the office.

Rockcruncher stood at the door talking rapidly in Claire to Gaili. To her lesser astonishment, Gaili was talking just as rapidly back. It wasn't until then that Fiona realized just how poorly she botched the language of the fire denizens.

Gaili turned as Rockcruncher's gaze went to Fiona. "Do you know him, Fi?" she said.

"Yes, thank you," she said and then waved to Rockcruncher. "Come on in. Mind the rug please." She motioned to the floor but was surprised to see a heavy leather covering at the entrance of the office. It had definitely not been there before. She inclined her head to Gaili, and the faun smiled shyly. Fiona nodded her approval. "Although it seems Gaili is quicker to address the needs of this office than I am."

Rockcruncher slithered into the house, watching where his tail thumped, and stayed firmly on the leather covering by the door. He wore a thick brown leather duster, and his eyes were bright and animated. Although Fiona didn't understand salamanders well, she could tell he was worked up about something.

Rockcruncher looked to her and Soots. "I heard you got in a tussle with a jacket."

"A jacket? Where'd you get that gossip from?"

"Format has it you were in the Hinge and then a jacket attacked you. Everyone's talking about it. And how the Guild has no control over their regulations anymore."

"Format has it, hmm?" Of course this played well into the hidden organization's hand. "Anything else being said?"

"There's some sort of smuggling group working out of the Guild. Turners are starting to worry about what the Guild's been up to."

"Yes, and perception is everything." Fiona rubbed her neck, missing the surety of her scarf.

Rockcruncher thumped a digit across his belly and blinked rapidly. "That's not the only reason I came over. I talked to the clan council about...what we discussed." He glanced at Gaili.

"It's okay. She's quite trustworthy."

He nodded. "The council worked out a plan to retrieve the stone. They knew it was important to the Ashborn but not why. They thought if they had it the Ashborn would be forced to side with them over the elementals about the volcanic land between the two realms."

Fiona glanced at Soots for a moment. "Did they say how they got the stone?"

He shook his head. "They didn't get it. They tried on their own but couldn't, so they found someone to help them. A group of rippers called the Painted Edge. So they hired 'em, but they never got the stone."

"The blue strip tattoo." Fiona clapped her hands together. "I suppose it could stand for the edge of a book that's been painted. But why didn't the council get the stone?

"The rippers said they'd found another use for it and since they stole it was rightfully theirs. The clan council can't do anything about it because they don't know who to go to and they don't want the Ashborn to know what they've done. They've been trying to sort it out. They only told me because I said I could help."

"So the Painted Edge has the stone." She slowly rubbed her hands together. "They work out of Spine, so it has to be hidden somewhere around here. But where?"

"Aren't those the same people who have been smuggling?" said Gaili.

"Wait, are they with the Guild?" said Rockcruncher.

"No, but that's what they want everyone to believe," said Fiona. "I think they're just solving multiple problems with one Blackstone." Fiona froze. She couldn't believe it was right there. Two birds. One stone. "Thank Larrakane Petronia hates me."

"What about her?" said Gaili, moving to Fiona's side.

"It's what Petronia said to me yesterday before she stole my blasted scarf. They allowed her to deal with me because it killed two birds with one stone. They wanted me out of commission but not dead, and Petronia wanted to get back at me for causing a scene with her."

"Why would they want that?"

"Because I'm on a case that they want me to solve in a specific way. I mean, I think they want me to point to the obvious guilty party: the Guild. All the clues line up and even the Guild is playing into their hand by being so greedy." She ignored the part where her bias against the Guild had made it rather easy. She could deal with her own failings later.

"But I thought you said the Guild didn't have anything to do with the Painted Edge."

"They don't, I'm sure of it. But the Edge wants the Guild to be blamed. You said format has it that the Guild did this to me, yes?"

Rockcruncher nodded.

"So if people believe their gossip, then the Guild will look worse than it already does and whatever the Edge does with the smuggling or the Blackstone will also fall on the Guild if it fails."

"What do they want with it?" said Rockcruncher "If what you told me the other day is right, it keeps my home alive. It shouldn't even work outside of Blaze."

Fiona went to tug on her scarf but laid a hand on her naked throat. The Blackstone shouldn't work outside Blaze. But maybe it did. She thought back to the missing patches of fur on Petronia's hands and arms. "I think it still has some heat left to it. Maybe a strenuous connection to the page across the Book."

"But why keep it just for the heat if Blaze is dying out? Surely it'd stop working eventually," said Gaili.

"Well, it makes Blaze a whole lot easier to smuggle from. No one's ever had access like this before." They could do multiple things if they were smart enough. Her mind raced.

"Okay, but where would you hide a big fiery rock?" said Rockcruncher.

"The only place someone wouldn't notice one rock is where there are lots of rocks," said Fiona. It hit her like a gust of wind. She turned to Gaili. "How good is your Sod?"

Fiona watched the carriage carrying Dodger pull up in the midday light. She smoothed down her hair and waved with the bottle of whiskey. She hoped that they wouldn't fight. She didn't want to fight at all, but she certainly had a habit of starting them with him.

He moved slowly, head lowered. He wasn't wearing his customary Guild cloak, and she realized she hadn't seen Dodger without it in some time. She never made the effort anymore. The cream linen he wore draped across one shoulder and his body. A leathery rope tied it around his waist where it hung artfully past his knees. Though new for her, she thought it a natural fit for him.

"I didn't know if you'd come," she said. She'd sent a message for him to the Hinge, but there was no guarantee he would get it.

"Of course I did. I wanted to check in on you." He stood a short distance from her.

"Yes, I heard you came by this morning. Gaili was practically cover to cover about how sweet you were." She smiled trying to ease the tension.

He shrugged. "I only got a couple of things for you."

"Well, I appreciate it. Thank you." She patted the stone step next to her. "For that and for recommending me for the Ashborn's job."

He looked up then, head tilted. "I didn't know you took it."

"I know. I didn't really talk about it. Or anything for that matter."

"You're good at what you do, Fiona, but you're always so closed off." He finally sat down next to her. "It's not like I thought you would fail or anything."

"I know, Dodger, I just…I'm terrible at this, alright? I'm not good at having friends."

"But we've always been friends."

"Yes, of course, but," she said slowly, "let's be honest. I think you've been the real friend here. I've been the…" She searched for an appropriate word. "Blotter. I know you put yourself on the line for me with the smuggling job. I know it's not the first time you've supported me. And I haven't given anything back to you."

Dodger started to say something, but she held up a hand. "Let me finish. You're too nice. You'll just let me get away with it. But you deserve a friend who supports your decisions too, regardless of her hang-ups. I'm sorry I haven't been that for you." She made direct eye contact. "Truly."

He nodded and then took the bottle from her hand. He took a swig and pressed a paw to his whiskers, wiping them down. "Okay, forgiven."

Fiona relaxed and took the bottle back to take a sip herself. She didn't want to cry, she knew it would probably make him incredibly uncomfortable, so she took another sip and coughed. "Good. Come on." She nodded to the house. "There are leftover meats and bread to be had."

Fiona led him through the office and living room. Gaili was upstairs, and her hooves lightly sounded on the wood above them. Soots's light glowed in the lamp by the dining room table. She wondered if Dodger would even notice the flame sprite that way.

Dodger slowed his pace, staring at the walls of her home, at the tapestries and the busts. He glanced at the shelves bursting with books. "You've got a better collection than I do."

"I doubt it. I'm sure you've been to some exciting places." She smiled.

"You'd be surprised how much of my job is paperwork and reading reports. I hardly get past the Guild outpost in most places."

"Really? I expected that you were constantly chasing down rippers and skips from our conversations."

He rubbed his neck, furry face darkening in color. "Maybe a little drunken embellishment on my part."

She laughed. "Uh-huh. Well, the next time I have a case that pushes me to some edge of the Book, I'll make sure to bring some backup."

He smiled. "I'd enjoy that quite a bit." Glancing at her bandaged chest, he said, "I want you to know I'm clearing the Guild trying to find out where the person is who did this to you."

"Gaili told you about Petronia?" Fiona raised an eyebrow. She motioned to the table, and they both sat down.

"Yeah. I accidentally called you Fi in front of her and she sort of started telling me everything." He helped himself to the mountain of food before him.

Fiona shook her head—that faun was entirely too trusting. "I think I know how to solve this mess with Blaze and make a dent in whatever the smugglers are planning."

"They're connected?" Dodger asked.

"Not entirely, but the organization behind them is. I think they're gearing up to put concoctions in the market that aren't exactly legal. Strong-arming sellers already in the public eye to cover their tracks. And everyone would be distracted by shenanigans from the Guild." If the Painted Edge was smuggling elemental creatures, that would give them plenty of source stock. She bit her lip thinking of the poor creatures and what they must've gone through.

Dodger whistled. "That's more than I expected. We have nowhere near that much information." He looked uncomfortable at his words and rubbed a paw over his face. "What's your plan?"

Fiona nodded, happy to get the only question that mattered. "It's still formulating, but I have some ideas. I need you to hear me when I say I trust you to do what's best for Blaze. I do believe in you."

Dodger looked back at her earnestly. "I believe in you too."

Fiona smiled and then poured them each a good finger of whiskey. "Good. Because in order to set things to right, I'm going to need you to do what I say and look away a couple of times."

Dodger grinned, shaking his head. He picked up his drink. "Make it a good story at least."

She toasted him and then told him everything that had happened in the course of the last week. And she didn't mince on the details.

24

FIONA, SOOTS, AND GAILI made their way via carriage to
Little Cobbles on the edge of Spine. Soots rode in their
metallic suit cradled in Fiona's arm. Gaili and Fiona were more
liberally attired for a day of rough gardening than going out
in the city. They both wore coarse woolen tunics over sturdy
linen shirts and loose pants with padding on the knees and
outside of their thighs. Their boots were light and flexible
with metal spikes underneath. They wore thick worker gloves
and had metallic helmets in the seat next to them ready
to be donned when needed. They'd gotten the equipment
from the Travel Guild storage room itself. Thank Larrakane
for Dodger's insight on the difficulty of missing her usual
equipment.

The carriage dropped them off speedily outside the mess of
rock and hills of the district. Fiona smiled at the driver before
giving him a rather large tip to not mention their likeness or

destination to anyone they should cross. With a crinkled brow but a quick nod, he indicated he was happy to oblige and take her paper.

They headed directly to the small booth with the Cobbles emblem on its banner overhead. A lot of the earth in the district was imported from Cobbles itself. Burrowing into Spine proved impossible when the first earthly turners tried it, and the druids quickly banned it, making it a nonnegotiable.

The booth, like other Travel Guild posts, contained a small register that was more than half-empty and a jacket to watch over it. This jacket, a gray rock creature with what appeared to be boulders for a head, arms, and body, rumbled as they approached. It sounded like two rocks slowly grinding against each other, and Fiona winced at the noise. The jacket didn't greet them but the rumbling continued on. She peered in closely. "I think they're asleep."

Gaili moved closer, examining them. "Should we wake them?"

"I don't think it's necessary." Fiona scribbled, *Marcius Festinius Cervidus, Bipbipplurg, official business.* She was relieved she had a chance to talk to Dodger before going to Cobbles for the Blackstone. It helped to make this a coordinated effort. Of course the Travel Guild wouldn't know it was a coordinated effort until it was all complete, but filing paperwork could be really slow these days.

She finished filling out the register and then quietly slipped away from the booth. Soots followed, but Gaili continued examining the creature. Fiona got the sense she had never been this close to an earth elemental before and was making the most of it while she could.

Whether the Blackstone was in Cobbles Fiona wasn't hundred percent sure, but *anywhere* would be an unlikely hiding spot for something that could burn through just about any concealment, if the chip she had found in Obsidian's Tooth was any indication. There's no way it would remain unnoticed on a wooden airship or in a forest. Perhaps in the Court of Copper or the feverlands of Kerus, but no, her gut told her that the safest place, the most obvious but absolutely grueling to prove it place, was Cobbles.

Gaili joined her, scratching in a small book and grinning. Fiona wasn't quite sure where it came from, but she was glad someone was taking notes.

Fiona looked at her pocket clock, noting the time. "Alright, it should take us about thirty minutes or so once we're in to get to the gnome warren. Would you like to do the honors?" She had never seen the faun turn the page before and was curious if it would feel any different.

Gaili looked up wide eyed but nodded her head, placing her book and pencil into a pocket. She clasped Fiona's hand and allowed Soots to sit on her shoulder. Closing her eyes, she rubbed a smooth, flat oval pebble in her other hand.

Fiona found Gaili's hand warm and then grow cold as the world folded away from them. It had been years since Fiona had allowed someone else to turn the page for her. She shivered, glancing around as darkness appeared before them. Relaxing, she let her mind view the pagemark of earth for what it was: a small cavern of rock and stone. If she focused too much on getting there or the turn itself, she could accidentally pull it away from Gaili. There was no telling what would happen then. Turning the page with multiple turners trying to lead could be unpredictable in every way except that it usually ended in disaster—missed pagemarks, wrong pages, or even split destinations. So she intentionally focused on their plan as they took a step from Spine to Cobbles.

Fiona breathed a sigh of relief as the world folded back behind her. They were in a large pocket of empty space that had been created for such travel by the Guild. Surrounding them entirely was a mass of unyielding rock. It smelled earthy, and she could practically taste every mineral in the page on her tongue. Breathing felt more like sucking in sand through her nose and mouth. It took a moment for the potion she had drunk to take effect.

The pressure was intense. They immediately donned helmets and began crawling, moving close to the ground. Fiona clipped a piece of thin metal rope on Soots's suit. The flame sprite could move forward quite a bit ahead of them, but if there was a tunnel collapse, Larrakane forbid, they would be able to find each other among the rubble.

The amber glow from Soots lit up the space, bouncing light across the rocky interior. There was a small pale tubular creature in the space doing nothing more than eating a small amethyst. Without meaning to, they had turned the page close enough to reach out and touch it. Fiona put out a hand to Gaili to stop her from moving and whispered, "Let's take the long way around it. It may be preoccupied now, but I don't want it latching on anything rock- or gemlike we have."

"What is it?" Gaili whispered, moving around lightly to the other side.

"A rock worm. Pretty common here and mostly harmless unless you have any gems, paper, or earth on you." She had read it could destroy a diamond the size of a horse in a matter of minutes. She really didn't want it close to her valuables in any way.

Gaili murmured interested noises but followed Fiona out of the cavern and to a tunnel opening on the far side.

The plan was simple. Fiona and Gaili would go to the gnomes Fiona thought most likely to be holding the Blackstone for the Painted Edge and talk them into taking it back to Blaze. The gnomes had stopped working for the Guild, putting off several projects. Fiona thought that must be because of the stone. Perhaps they were under the thumb of the Painted Edge. She wasn't sure how it lined up, but if anyone knew about a stone or a gem being in Cobbles, it would be the gnomes.

If the gnomes couldn't or didn't want to part with it, Fiona planned to steal it and deal with the fallout after getting it back to Blaze. She had told Dodger to keep on Petronia and make sure he knew where she was going at all times. From the burns on her arm, Fiona guessed she had personally handled the Blackstone. Fiona wasn't any match to deal with the tigress physically. Her chest ached, and being bent over in this position wasn't helping. She was far better because of Gaili's administrations, but she was not in great shape. Not that she had ever been physically much before, but she moved on from that thought. She used all her control and focus to bear the pain so they could hurry along.

"We stick to the tunnels already made. It's the safest way to travel in this page," Fiona whispered. The sides of the hard wall pressed on her shoulders and reinforced thighs.

"Do the gnomes leave the tunnels for travelers on purpose?"

"More like a by-product of how they live. The rock and stone has to get displaced somewhere, so the Travel Guild collects it. But they also don't pay for the gnomes to mine."

"So they just take advantage of them?" Gaili said, her voice high and tight.

Fiona frowned at her friend's distress. "The gnomes made a deal directly with the Guild without any guidance from the Followers or anyone else when Cobbles was discovered." It had not readily come to light until about a century ago that it was even happening. Not until the Followers got involved investigating the large influx of imported stone to Mistral.

Gaili started to say something and then yelled out in pain.

Fiona stopped. "Are you alright back there?"

"Yes, sorry. I put my hand down, and it went through into a hole. I'm alright."

"As long as you're okay. Just be careful. You don't want to cause too many tremors. Everything in the area of this tunnel knows we're here. But if we keep small, steady movements forward, we shouldn't be of interest." She began moving forward again slowly. Cobbles was not her favorite page, but it wasn't their fault that it was a pain to travel in. As soon as a larger area was built, there was a high chance it could collapse or be filled with the natural creatures of the page. Not the best holiday spot, given all the other choices.

"What I was gonna say was...if the Guild does things like that, why are you trying to fix their reputation?"

"I'm not. If we get the Blackstone back to Blaze, then hopefully all will be well there. That's all that matters to me. The Guild can sort out their own standing." It would take more than rumors to take them down. They were like a weed and had tendrils into everything. No, she'd keep her attention focused on the bits that mattered, the turners and the pages. She had lost sight once. She wouldn't do it again. "If we keep heading this way, we should reach the gnome warren soon. Just say what we practiced and then we can go from there."

"Right."

They continued crawling through the tunnel, keeping their heads low and following Soots's diffused glow. Soon they came before an opening that was just big enough for them to both squeeze in and sit back on their legs to rest. In front of them was a massive wall full of oval openings. The entrance to the gnome area, Bipbipplurg. It was impressive how many holes could fit on the soft rocky wall. Fiona sat up, stretching out her back. Her chest pulled, and she winced at the sharp pain of the fresh cuts. She kept her grumblings to herself, not wanting Gaili to worry unnecessarily about her, and focused on the task at hand. Which tunnel would take her to the right warren? It was supposed to be the third from the bottom, but now she realized there were a few thirds from the bottom.

"I really wish we had a proper door knocker or the like," she said and sighed.

Soots twirled about, lighting up the holes at their eye level. Each tunnel looked tall enough for a small humanoid and was made of packed soil rather than the hard rock they had been crawling on.

A hairless beet-colored head popped out of a hole above them. Another popped out below that one. The gnomes smiled down at them, all pupilless eyes, wide bulbous noses, and toothless mouths.

Fiona smiled up, pulling Soots away from the tunnels and covering their glow with her hands. She turned and whispered to the faun, "Tell them we're here to retrieve the hot black stone. And we have something for them in return for keeping it safe." She didn't want to lie to the creatures, but she also wanted to make this as simple as possible.

Gaili contorted her face, making it longer than it already was. She pressed her nose down and inward to translate the words into Sod and up to the gnomes. It sounded like she was eating a rather crunchy bit of toast but very slowly. The two sentences took forever to Fiona. After Gaili was done, Fiona opened her pack and pulled out a pair of darkened glasses with a head strap. A round cup was attached where the nose would be.

The gnomes stopped grinning. Their eyes widened, and they disappeared from view.

Fiona frowned. "What happened? Did they say anything back? I would think they'd be relieved."

Gaili shook her head. "Not a thing."

A head popped out closer to them on the first level. The gnome walked out of the hole and stood before them silently. Fiona put the glasses in front of them so the gnome could reach them without moving too far. "Tell them we want the Blackstone and in exchange we'll leave them this device to use outside the page. And then explain how it works."

Gaili repeated her message in Sod. The glasses were a lot like the ones Fiona (and almost every turner) used for traveling in Blaze or Depths. Instead of just making the dark areas brighter and the lighted areas dimmer, it would also enable the gnomes to block out the smells of the world around them so they wouldn't be overwhelmed. When Fiona had suggested they needed to bring a gift for the gnomes, Gaili, clever as always, crafted something perfect in a flurry of activity.

Perhaps these glasses would give them a taste of freedom outside their page.

The gnome ran a stubby flat hand over the darkened glasses. They spoke back into the tunnel where another gnome was walking toward them, gesturing for a moment to make some point and then waved, beckoning for them to follow. Fiona didn't have the foggiest idea what they said except for the word *stone*.

"He said his name is Grodlic and that he's taking us to the Blackstone. They're glad to get rid of it, but we're early so they'll have to get some others to help dig it out." Gaili conferred with the gnomes, motioning and smiling in the dim light.

"We're early? Bless Larrakane, we must be just ahead of the Painted Edge." Finally a bit of luck! If they could stop whatever the ripper group had planned for it, then everything just might turn out right. She hoped Dodger was keeping track of Petronia.

Fiona pushed Soots behind her and ahead of Gaili. It would be harder to see this way, but she wanted to make sure they were protected from the gnomes and the gnomes weren't blinded by them. They crawled through the tunnel, finding their way in the dark behind the small gnome who walked ahead. Attached to his belt was a pickaxe of stone and rock and a great many other items Fiona wasn't too sure about. The tunnel shifted down and there were many offshoots from the path they were on. Fiona looked for some sort of sign as to where they were, but if there was one, she couldn't ascertain it. She wondered how far they were going from the pagemark and wished she had remembered to look at her clock before moving on.

They entered a bigger space, another empty pocket. The walls here gleamed with studded gems catching Soots's covered light. While Fiona and Gaili couldn't stand, they could sit up a bit and did so immediately. They saw a few other tunnel openings in the space and a mass of rocks piled to one side. Several gnomes milled around, but they all stopped as the visitors exited the tunnel.

Their guide spoke to the other gnomes in the slow grinding language. They started to move rather quickly to pick up their stone axes and head into a tunnel.

Fiona looked back at Gaili, who whispered, "He just said some soft ones have come for the Blackstone and to bring it out."

"Okay, but it's not going to fit out of one of these tunnels, right?"

"Not if it's the size you told me," Gaili said, looking around with interest at the gnomes, gems, and walls. Fiona could practically see her stitching together a formula in her mind.

There was a sound like boulders tumbling and then a plink, plink, plink. Fiona couldn't tell which tunnel it was coming from, but it sounded close. She began to edge her way back to the opening they'd come from, wary of rock worms.

The ceiling opened up about the size of two gnomes shoulder to shoulder, and a large black stone fell through. The small cavern was warmed instantly, and Fiona scrambled back out of the way as the dark gem hit the packed soil. She had expected it to be made of solid rock or stone, but that had been wrong. It sparkled with its own inner glow. She quickly put on the protective gloves Dodger had loaned her.

Above, hairless beet heads peeked over the hole they had dug. They grinned and waved. Gaili pulled out the darkened sunglasses and spoke to them in Sod, motioning to the glasses and the stone.

Another sound came from a tunnel on the other side of the room. A babbling gnome walked out and stopped to stare dumbfounded at the Blackstone they clearly hadn't expected to be in their way. An irritated but familiar voice ground out words in Sod behind the gnome. Fiona tensed and Gaili made an audible squeak just as Petronia crawled into the cavern.

25

PETRONIA BARED HER SHARP white teeth. "I thought I put you down."

Fiona recovered and smiled, trying to think quickly, "Yes, well, I had a better nurse than you could've anticipated." The blasted tigress was wearing Fiona's beautiful multicolored scarf around her furry waist. Fiona wanted nothing more than to snatch it, but she knew she was in no position to fight. Petronia didn't have to know that though. "A few concoctions and I'm right as rain."

Petronia snorted but shifted a glance behind Fiona.

Gaili began mumbling to herself in her faekin language, speaking too fast for Fiona to make out a single word.

Fiona put a hand on Gaili's furry leg, squeezing it to pull her from her bewildered state.

"What are we going to do?" Gaili whispered to Fiona in her human tongue.

"I'm going to bluff. You're going to run," she said quickly in the same tongue. To Petronia she said, "I don't think your superiors will be happy to know I found where you've hidden the stone. What kind of start is it for the Painted Edge if they can't even accomplish their first goal?"

Petronia had been edging her way crawling to the Blackstone and nudged the still flummoxed gnome to the side. She stopped then, eyes narrowed. "I work for the Guild, you imbecile."

Fiona was relieved to see the pressure in the page had the same effect on her as it did on them making her have to crawl as well. "No, no I don't think you do." Fiona pushed Gaili's leg again to get her moving into the tunnel. "I mean, the Travel Guild is pretty terrible, I grant you, but even they would have done a better job than you at hiding this thing."

Gaili took the hint, backing away, small stones falling as she pressed into the tunnel.

"Once it's clear to everyone that they didn't steal this, you and the Painted Edge will have more than the Guild to deal with. Blaze will retaliate for what you've done to their home."

Petronia began crawling around the Blackstone, hugging the wall. "You're not really convincing me to leave you alive this time."

Fiona moved toward the rock pile in the small cavern. She wanted to keep the Blackstone between herself and Petronia—its heat was the best deterrent she had right now. What was she going to do? She couldn't fight her off, and she certainly wasn't letting her leave with the stone. She had to make her hurt herself on the stone. The tigress had only worn gloves to pick it up and didn't appear to have any other protective gear. Fiona took a breath and tried to distract her.

"Have you figured out how to work my scarf yet? Happy to show you how it's done."

"It wasn't that hard," Petronia answered tartly. She stopped moving toward Fiona and slipped her paw into the scarf, pulling out a palm-sized dagger with a banded hilt that seemed made for her.

Blast. Fiona ducked behind the Blackstone, trying not to touch it, its warmth radiating across her skin as she crawled away. Her only recourse was to escape into the tunnels. But could she count on the gnomes to close the way up behind her?

"Move you, pesky sprite," Petronia said as Soots flew toward her face. She knocked them out of the way with one hand, and Soots hit the wall of the cavern, light casting about erratically. The gnomes yelled and ran, covering their eyes.

"Soots, are you alright?" Fiona called out. She felt the flame sprite's anger push against her and said hurriedly, "No, don't get mad. It'll be okay." The temperature in the cavern increased, and Fiona winced as it blasted against her unprotected body. "Soots, if you get too hot you'll hurt me too. You have to control yourself!"

A paw grabbed the back of her doublet and pulled her back roughly against the dirt floor. She screamed, a mixture of pain as her bandaged chest rubbed against packed dirt and surprise from being jerked back. Petronia's fur was wet with sweat from the heat, but she sneered down at her. "If I bury you here, then I don't have to worry about you following me again."

"Don't, don't do this." Fiona rushed on, trying to stitch the words together. "You don't have to kill me. I know what it's like to take orders. To make sure you're staying in line just to keep going." This woman was prepared to kill her, and for what? Someone else's greater plan. Just another minion in some organization's power struggle. Fiona's hand shook, but she clenched it into a fist. Her voice wavered but she kept going. "Whatever reason you have for doing this, it's not worth it. You were right. In the Thread. About doing what it takes to survive. I understand that. But killing me won't make your survival any easier."

Petronia licked her lips, dagger still in hand, whisker's twitching.

Fiona could see hesitation in her face and then surprise as a blast of cold air, booming in this tiny cavern, rushed in, knocking Petronia away from her.

The blast of chilly air subsided and Gaili appeared next to her, holding a golden-handled azure fan. "Fi," she yelled, grabbing Fiona's hand and rubbing it, "are you alright?"

I'm not dead, was her first thought. Her second was relief and confusion struggling to rise to the top. "Gaili! I thought you were gone," Fiona said weakly. Her back hurt pushing against the stone, and the adrenaline pumping through her made her shudder.

"I couldn't leave you behind like that," the faun said, golden face tight. She looked up quickly and threw open the fan, directing another burst of wind from it above Fiona.

There was a thud and then Gaili shut the fan with a snap and slapped it against her hand. "Oh no, I can't believe I just did that. She was getting up, so I..." She winced. She pressed her hand gently to Fiona's back and grasped her hand, pulling her up to a sitting position.

Fiona grimaced but got up and on all fours into a crawling position away from the stone. She turned around to see Petronia, unconscious, slumped against the rock pile. Fiona raised an eyebrow and then looked back at Gaili. "Well done."

She crept toward the tigress, watching to see if she was going to move. The dagger had fallen to the ground, but Fiona ignored it and made her way to her scarf. She pulled out her manacles and slapped one on each of Petronia's wrists. The tigress wouldn't be able to turn the page by herself with them on.

"Soots?" Fiona called out, her stomach tied in knots. The suit was meant to protect them from the wind but not from being knocked against a wall. She crawled as quickly as she could to where she saw the flame sprite drop and was met halfway by the ball of light flying around the Blackstone toward her. They barreled into Fiona, and she pressed their hot little flickering body against her, letting out a heavy sigh of relief.

The gnomes peered over the edge of the holes above them. Fiona saw their movements in the dim light and called out to Gaili, "Tell them it's alright. We'll be leaving directly with the stone, but I'll be back again later with a friend." The gnomes wouldn't be under the thumb of the Painted Edge anymore, she hoped. But they needed someone who could help them navigate outside influences. Fali might be precisely the right person to negotiate some protection for them. She didn't mind the Followers owing her a favor.

Gaili repeated her words in Sod with a look of confusion. "But then who will take Petronia in?"

"You will," Fiona said, pulling her scarf off of Petronia and wrapping it around her neck. She relaxed with it back on and began to pull out her fire-resistant clothes. "She's knocked out cold, and the manacles will stop her from running or doing anything drastic. I believe in you." She smiled at Gaili. She wanted her to know she knew she could do this, do anything really. "I'm sure Dodger won't be too far behind. But if you don't see him, just take her straight to the Hinge and ask for him. He'll know what to do."

Nodding tentatively, Gaili moved over to Petronia. Gnomes rappelled down on ropes, and Gaili spoke to them. They each took one of the tigress's arms or legs and began making their way toward the tunnel wall as a unit. A couple in front took off their pickaxes and began to chip away, creating a hole. The dirt and stone moved much quicker than Fiona thought possible, and soon there was a hole big enough to carry her through.

"I'll meet you back home," she said to Gaili, finishing buttoning up her cloak. She popped the cork on a vial of shimmering gold liquid and downed it in one gulp. It tasted of ash and smoke, and she realized she greatly preferred the jelly breaths.

Gaili waved. "Be safe, you two." And she followed the gnomes through the hole, holding her fan like a shield in front of her.

Fiona grinned. "I didn't think she had it in her. She's quite formidable when she has something to defend, hmm?"

:Friend!:

"Yes, I do believe that's probably it. She just needed a friend." She ignored the warmth spreading through her as she counted how lucky she was to have found her. She slapped her gloved hands together to focus and moved to the stone. She reached into her pack, pulled out metallic pockets similar to Soots's suit, and placed them on over her gloves. "Alright, Soots. Stay on my shoulder. Don't touch the stone. Do you hear me?"

:Careful.:

"Exactly." Fiona put her hands to the stone, thankful the heat wasn't cutting through the new protection, and then attempted picking it up. It was lighter than it appeared, which explained how they had gotten it here in the first place. Larrakane's luck was really on her side today. She just needed to give it one more go. Concentrating, she let the world around her shift and turned the page to Blaze using the Blackstone as her bookmark. It was time to return it.

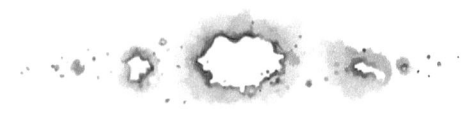

The spire was shadowy and lukewarm as Fiona floated up within it. She shivered. The fire had died down so much since the last time she had been here. Soots pulled her forward, and Fiona bit her lip worrying. If this didn't work, other flame creatures like Soots would continue to be snuffed out.

"Things will be so much better once Blaze is hot again," Fiona said, her voice high. She hoped if she was positive, things would turn out well. "You can stay with me, Soots, but I know you might want to come back home here. And that's okay." Tears welled up and Fiona realized they weren't evaporating. She frowned and went quiet.

She had thought about taking the stone directly to the Ashborn, but she knew that's not where it really belonged. It had a home, and she wanted to see it safely back in its place. The gate was upon them now, and she could make out the metallic sheen in the soft amber glow of the unsheathed flame sprite.

"Flames of a Thousand Lights," she said quietly. The gate dissipated, and she pulled herself through and onto the rough pumice of the small chamber. She walked to the inset, propelling herself with the wall. Soots was right over her shoulder filling the area with light.

She took the Blackstone from the metallic pack she had placed it in, the same clever material that Gaili had used for the mittens and Soots's suit. Fiona placed the Blackstone back in the hole and took a step back. It was small compared to the indent it had come from. Wisps of flame flickered within it, casting shadows in the chamber, but it sat there unmoving. Fiona ran a finger over her scarf as the dancing light glanced off a crack in the stone.

"Oh. I almost forgot." She pulled the shard from the crumbled rock pile. She supposed the pickaxe the rippers had used to dig it out of the wall broke it. She gently placed the shard where it had broken off. The Blackstone was whole now. She didn't know how long she would have before it started to do whatever it was going to do. She just hoped it worked so that the page would be alive again. Fiona moved quickly back to the gate to get out of the way.

"Come on, Soots," she said, lowering her body through the open gate.

:Whole!:

A wave of joy washed over Fiona from within the chamber. Soots flew to the top of the Blackstone, wisps of flame rising and falling in waves as they engulfed the stone. Fire licked at its smooth edges and an iridescent red began dancing and writhing inside the onyx.

Fiona couldn't tell the difference between Soots and the fire around the stone now. There was a cracking sound as if glass had begun to shatter. Another crack echoed through the chamber. Fiona watched, dazed, as the temperature rose. "Soots!" she cried out. What was happening? Where were they?

With a final crack, an explosion of heat and flame rushed her. She dropped through the gate, pushing against the edges of the opening to propel herself into the darkened tower as fire pursued her. A streak of crimson shot out toward her among the amber flames and curled itself around her, encapsulating her. It was warm but not unbearable. She gasped as the flames held her firm.

"You are safe, little one," said a light raspy voice from above. The flame tendril pulled her upward within the roiling fire that surrounded her. She didn't struggle, but her mind was jumbled at the conflicting images and brightness of the spire.

"Soots?"

"If you wish. I did love eating your papers."

The rolling flames coalesced into a massive figure with the shape of a woman and look of Fiona. Their face was as tall as her front door and their hands the size of her parlor floor. Their eyes were ink-blue flickers, and they gazed upon Fiona in their palm. "I can take many more shapes now. Perhaps this one will be less confusing for you."

Fiona laughed, a delirious, uncontrollable sound. "If you think looking human makes this less confusing, you've still got a lot to learn about us." She had no idea what was going on, but she didn't feel like she was in any danger. She studied the creature before her.

"I suppose that is true. I've learned only a little being with you, but it is a vast deal more than I ever expected. You have shown me the Book in a way I never could have seen it. Thank you for all that you've done to keep me safe."

"Did you..." Fiona trailed off, trying to find the right words. "Are you still a flame sprite?"

There was a crackle, and Fiona got the impression that Soots was laughing. A hint of amusement crept through the temperature of the air, like a tickle. "I am the Guardian of the fire page. The Ever-Burning Blaze is my responsibility."

"Oh," she said and tugged at her scarf, "so you're supposed to protect this place?"

"And repair what was broken, yes. I can do that only because of you. I never thought I needed to be more than I was to protect us before, but I was wrong. Blaze will forever be in your debt."

Fiona waved her hand dismissively. She wasn't quite sure how to react, but the tickling of flames scattered around her again. Soots was laughing at her bashfulness. Perhaps she had taught them one too many things.

"Will I ever see you again?" she said before thinking about it. A cold lump formed in her throat. She didn't want them to go away. "I mean, I'll miss you."

"I'll miss you too. You will always have a place here," they said, and this time there was no tickling of flames but a warm cocoon embraced her.

"You will always be my friend," Fiona said, her words heavy on her tongue. She felt she was saying goodbye forever. It wasn't fair. She hadn't prepared for this.

"And you mine. I didn't know I needed one. I'm glad it ended up being you."

Fiona nodded, too overwhelmed to speak. She looked about, trying to think of what to do next, but her focus failed her.

"Don't worry, little one." Soots chuckled in the crackling sounds of a thousand tiny flames popping around her. "I can get you home."

There was a burst of fire underneath Fiona and a sound of ripping echoed throughout the spire. Whipping her head around, Fiona saw the evergreen trees of Spine below her as the world folded in. Of course, it was their page; they could control it however they wanted.

"I cannot travel from here again, but you will always be welcome. My home is your home."

"Thank you, Soots." Fiona wiped tears from her face. She would miss the little flame sprite more than they knew.

The hand of flame holding her pushed toward the folded tear from Blaze to Spine and into the forest with Fiona. The world shimmered as the fire leapt through the air and back into the hole. The blackened Blaze was there and then gone, nothing but forest and trees around her.

Fiona lay in the grass for a while sobbing. The rush and adrenaline from a whole day of mishaps, threats, and violence against her poured out of her into the quiet woods. She had never been one to hold back her feelings about a person or her own thoughts unless she needed to focus. But here, now, it all hurt and she wanted nothing more than for the ground to overtake her, swallowing her whole in its wet, grassy cover.

She didn't know how long she lay there until she heard the clearing of a throat a short distance away. She sat up quickly, hand reaching for her scarf before she realized she didn't have a weapon at all. With her luck, she'd probably hurt herself with it instead of the enemy. She wiped her eyes, glancing around for whoever had made the sound.

From within the trees the Elder appeared and walked slowly toward her. Their warm golden-brown skin looked flushed on their cheeks. The sky-blue linen dress they wore moved around the trees and branches as if it was one with the air around them and could not be snagged. Their hair was unbraided, soft and pine green, flowing behind them. They looked like a nymph from the myths Fiona had read as a child. For a brief moment she thought them a real one until they spoke.

"Hello, Fiona." They smiled.

Fiona tried to remember her manners and nodded her head. "Good evening, Elder. Or...morning?" She looked around, lost. The sky was a bit darker than she'd expected.

The Elder sat down next to her. They opened a pack that Fiona hadn't noticed before and took out two cups and a kettle of coffee. Pouring the mocha-colored liquid into each cup, they handed one to Fiona. "Drink and tell me your story."

Fiona sat comfortably next to them and observed a brief moment of silence as the world around them seemed to still. A bird's high-pitched trill sounded above them. She leaned back, looking up at the amber sky, like a wave rising up to overtake the azure. Taking a deep breath, she recounted all that had happened since she last left the druid's grove.

The Elder lowered their cup and held on to Fiona's every word, not raising it again until she was done.

"You knew about the Guardian then?" Fiona said, ending her recounting with a raised eyebrow. She thought back over the Elder's warning. They must've.

"I knew that the page in itself was the rightful owner. That is all that can be said. The ways of druids are mysterious for a reason." They took a sip, appraising Fiona over the rim.

She nodded and finished her cup. She knew better than to push this one. She suspected there was much the Elder was saying with their eyes, but she was content to be ignorant for now. She needed the break.

After a few breaths, the Elder continued, "The pages were not opened up to the whole Book and left defenseless from the inking. There will be changes now. The Guardians cannot be lax in their duties any longer."

"The Guild won't like that," said Fiona absentmindedly. All the work the Guild had put into creating outposts in each habitable page and floating out their network to be the ones in charge. All that work to find out they weren't even close. She sighed a little, wondering how they would handle it.

"No, my dear," the Elder said, pouring her another cup of coffee. "They won't."

"I'll have to tell the Ashborn about the salamanders. They'll have proof now. What they do with that proof will change the dynamics of the whole page."

"And that change will ripple throughout the Book. People may have been used to the Ashborn being aloof, but if they are going to become the leader they need to be, it has to change."

Fiona pursed her lips at the thought of the Ashborn leading the fire page entirely. A lonelier job she had never thought of, but there it was. Who knew what the future looked like from then. She rubbed her temples. "There's work left to be done."

"As always. But for now, rest." The druid sat back, hands splayed out behind them. They looked calm, relaxed, with their chin up and wilting ears hanging back. But Fiona could sense a tension in them coiled like a snake, ready to spring if provoked. She wondered what could be bad enough to provoke it.

Fiona closed her eyes, listening to the trees and the birds of Spine's forest. Something still nagged at the back of her mind. It wormed its way up like the tendril of a newly planted bulb. She kept trying to push it away, to rest, but she said quietly, "I do have one worrying thought."

"And that is?" the Elder said, voice like whispered wind.

She kept her eyes closed. Perhaps if she didn't look, they would confide in her. A childish thought, but she went on anyway. "What else are these Guardians protecting against?" It couldn't just be organizations like the Travel Guild or even the Painted Edge. Those were products of the inking. They weren't there before the Book opened up to be a threat.

There was a slight shuffle, a sip of coffee, and then their wavering voice answered: "Let's turn that particular page when we get there."

If you enjoyed Between the Lines, spread the word by writing a review! Reviews really help my books get into the right hands, so I'm super grateful for every single one.

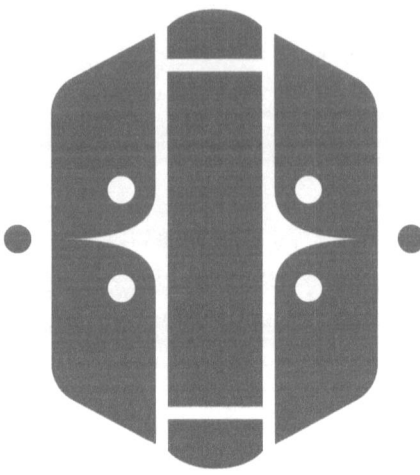

EXPLORE MORE OF THE Planar Pages for FREE by signing up for my newsletter.

Not only will you get me in your inbox with news and giveaways, you'll also receive The Planar Pages prequel HIDDEN WORDS

About *HIDDEN WORDS*

Life flourishes in the Book, a world of stacked realms spanning the ages. Those who can travel between them are page turners, blessed with the power to go from one page to the next.

For investigator Fiona Thorne, turning the page is normal life. Solving mysteries is where the excitement lives. No case is too small to ignite her curiosity, no page too familiar to explore.

Hired by her charming, gossipy neighbor to track down a shipment of rare books, Fiona thinks it'll be easy. She'll search for clues, sort out the issue, and be back in time for her nightly cup of coffee. And her reward? An introduction to one of the most reclusive leaders in Spine, the Druid Elder.

But that dream slips through her fingers as she realizes there's little evidence. She'll have to kick this investigation into high gear if she wants to impress her neighbor and earn her way into a privileged connection.

You can only read HIDDEN WORDS by signing up online for my newsletter at www.dhalerambo.com/newsletter/

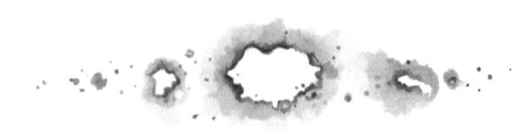

Glossary of The Planar Pages series

Find expanded lore, world information and more at
https://go.dhalerambo.com/tpp

Spine: A realm connected to every page in the Book. All page turners live here and can suffer ill effects for being gone too long. Split into over a dozen districts.

Seven Known Pages (as stacked in the Book)

Elemental Chapter

Blaze: page of fire, contains salamanders, flarions, ragnis, and other fire elementals

Depths: page of water, contains water elementals, merfolk, turtles, and more

Mistral: page of air, contains sylphs and other air elementals

Cobbles: page of earth, contains gnomes and other earth elementals

Mortal Chapter

Restless Rise (Rise): page of humans, contains a central mountain with floating islands all round it

Kerus: page of smilodon, elephas, and ursidon

Court of Copper (Court): page of faekin: fairies, fae, fauns, centaurs, and nymphs

Terms

Aer: language from page of air, Mistral

Aguan: language from the Depths

the Binder: leader of the Guild

the Book of Larrakane (the Book): all the known pages of the universe

bookmark: token from a page, used to travel there by a page turner

the Card: a free leaflet by the Travel Guild

the Church of Larrakane: organization devoted to worship of Larrakane

Claire: a language from page of fire, Blaze

Depth's Door: a lake in Spine

diamonnette paper (papers): universal currency

dusty: used to described a page turner who's ready to retire

elephas: like elephants standing on their hind legs, from Kerus

faekin: fauns, fairies, pixies, centaurs, all from the Court of Copper

Fallen Bubble: a cocktail

flarion(s): fire elementals who live in pools of magma from page of fire, Blaze

the Followers: a subset of the Church of Larrakane

format: slang for rumor

the Gilded: six leaders in the Travel Guild, including the Binder

the Hinge: Travel Guild headquarters

inked: blessed by Larrakane with the ability to turn pages

the Inking: historic event that created page turners

jacket(s): slang for officers of the Guild

kora: fish with an oily excretion from page of water, Depths

Larrakane (she/her): bestows the ability to turn pages and creator of the Book

La'mior: a fire forest in Blaze

pagemark(s): safe places where turners can move between pages

page turners (turners): people who can move between pages

Pestles and Mortar: smithy in the Spine

pulp: slang for creatures from various pages who are not page turners

ragnis: metallic-boned quasi-flame creatures from page of fire, Blaze

ripper(s): slang for thieves and smugglers across pages

Schiflan: a language spoken from page of humans, Restless Rise

skimmer(s): slang for tourists visiting other pages

skips: slang for criminals on the run

smilodon(s): catlike people, from Kerus

Sod: language from page of earth, Cobbles

spotter(s): cartographers

sylph: stark white air creatures from page of air, Mistral

the Towers of Calistino (the towers): prison in Copper

the Travel Guild, the Guild: organization that regulates all the comings and goings of page turners in the Book

the Trussadary Inn: hotel in Court of Copper

the Waterfall Palace: hotel in the Depths

unread turner: slang for someone new to being a page turner

ursidon: bearlike people, from Kerus

Excerpt of Hard Bound, Book 2

Step into the next Page and read Chapter One of
HARD BOUND

About *HARD BOUND*: Someone has stolen from the Court of Copper, the illustrious fae page nestled within the Book. As the fabled Order of Seven, once impervious to discord, tears under the weight of distrust and strife, an innocent risks being shelved, penned as the thief. Who lies at the heart of the crime? Is it a member of the fractured counsel, or could the thief be much closer to Fiona than she realizes?

As the fate of the fae teeters on the brink of upheaval, Fiona and her alchemist ally, Gaili, must delve deep into the tangled mysteries of the page, racing against the clock to unearth the truth and restore harmony to the Court of Copper. Can they halt the rewrite of the fae page before it's too late and keep it from tearing inside out?

Chapter One

It took every ounce of Fiona's self-control not to dump her drink on the scribe currently intruding on her space. It wasn't that she didn't love a good verbal sparring match—she certainly started those enough. Or even that in the past she hadn't daydreamed about giving interviews about her work like all people who wanted someone to notice their intelligence. But here, in the tavern that was like a second home, one of her favorite places in the Book of Larrakane, she simply didn't want to be the one who started the fight. First because every page turner in the place would gossip about it like the hens they were, but second because Mac, the fae proprietress, would tut and look disappointed. Fiona never wanted to trifle with the bond of friendship she had with Mac. Especially not over something as small as this.

The Book of Larrakane, or the Book for short, was the way everyone grouped the seven known pages in the universe that could be traveled or "turned" to by people with the ability to do so: page turners. Fiona was one of thousands or so creatures who had the power to walk through the stacked worlds, turning the page from one to the next. It seemed like a big number until compared to the vast ocean of people who were not page turners. That was somewhere in the millions.

With a deep sigh and a tight clutch on the clay mug holding Mac's latest concoction, Fiona answered another exasperating question as reasonably as she could: "What was it like to help the Guild with Blaze? I didn't help the *Guild* with Blaze. I helped Blaze with Blaze. The citizens did it for themselves. They were quite extraordinary." She motioned with her mug to punctuate the last sentence.

Format had been decided on what had happened a couple of weeks ago, when the dying page of fire, Blaze, suddenly flared back to life, and it was all tangled. She had returned a previously stolen fire artifact to its rightful place in the dimmed page after recovering it from its hiding place, Cobbles, the page of earth. That was true. And though it had been quite the endeavor, she'd had help along the way. Once she got around to asking for it. Fiona liked to think of it as a team effort now. But naturally, the *Card* would get it wrong. The printed booklet was best at spreading the word of everything the Travel Guild did. Made sense, as they were owned by them.

The Travel Guild was a powerful organization that regulated, administrated, and profited off the Book and the page turners who traveled it. They supported them too, of course. When page turners started to travel across the Book two hundred years ago, there was a heady mess of conflict, page versus page, on what permissions the page turners were allowed, who they could take with them to another page, and much more. The first turners quickly dived into the fray and established order out of the chaos, all at a reasonable cost, and quickly the Travel Guild was born. But Fiona knew who to trust when things truly got tough, and it wasn't the Guild.

The reporter, his young voice belied by the crinkles around his eyes and mouth, nodded as he scratched on the paper. She had seen him on the edges of her vision as she moved around the city in the last week or so. It wasn't until he turned up here that she realized he had been dogging her steps closer than expected. If she hadn't been irritated, she may have been impressed.

He scrunched up his face, a habit familiar to Fiona from other humans like herself when trying to puzzle out a scheme, and said, "But the Travel Guild expressed that it was *their* jacket working with you that solved the broken page. Indeed, we made that the headline the next day: 'Guild Saves Blaze.'" He said it quite loudly, making sure to accentuate the headline with his hands as if it were written in front of him directly. The turners on the stools next to him nodded and raised mugs happily. He smirked, seemingly pleased that his show was well received.

"Well, when you print it, you can write what you like, can't you?" Fiona said through gritted teeth. "But I assure you, the Ashborn working together with the other fire denizens are really the ones who saved Blaze." Fiona knew that trying to pivot the story to the exact version would be a lost cause. But she wasn't going to let the Guild earn all the honors just because she had used some of their resources. They would take the recognition and use that for undue influence elsewhere. Well, not if she had any control over it.

Though the Guild worked to regulate the Book of Larrakane, sending jackets from page to page and stepping their foot in every negotiation they could, they were not an altruistic bunch. Dodger, one of her closest friends, and Rockcruncher, a salamander she had gotten to know well chasing down the stolen fire artifact, were about the only worthy jackets she knew. She tried to find the angle the scribe was coming from. Had been for a few minutes. But he was being elusive and wasting her time. "Why are you talking to me if you have all the facts?"

The scribe looked up, blinking. "Format has it you work for them now. There were sightings of you coming and going to the Hinge the day before. A little birdie told me you were offered a job in regulations. And your partner"—he consulted his notes—"Marcius was the one who traveled with you to Cobbles and then turned in the smilodon tigress culprit."

Curse her to the dark edge for writing his name down on the logs. At the time it was to cover her tracks in case anyone was following her. She didn't think it would be evidence that the Guild had retrieved the artifact. An artifact that enabled the fire page to be what it was and had, to her surprise, been part of a friend she dearly missed, Soots. So much had been uncovered by the simple act of restoring Blaze. So much still to discover. Fiona had many questions but so little time in getting to research exactly what a Guardian was, besides what Soots called themselves. Protector of a single page who could control it completely. The page was roiling fire currently, so hot that no one mortal could turn back into Blaze at the moment, so further questions to Soots were on hold. Fiona reasoned that this was Soots fixing the page after she left, but her curiosity made her itch to confirm it with the Guardian herself. She had given full reports to her client, the Elder druid, briefed Dodger, and filed information (obfuscating Soots's involvement naturally) so that the trial for the smugglers of the artifact could begin. Interruptions to research that would answer her questions crowded her like a swarm of ants to sugar, and the scribe was just the latest one.

"Well, format is wrong," Fiona said, turning away from the scribe and back to the counter where Mac stood eavesdropping quite openly. The honey-skinned older fae winked at her, which eased some of Fiona's tension. Though the fae looked like humans, apart from the wilting ears and taller height, their natural beauty made one captivated for a brief second, no matter how long you had known them. She focused on the barest of wrinkles on Mac's face, then sighed. "I don't have anything else to impart and I'd rather like to finish my drink alone. I've said all I'm going to say," she said over her shoulder in a nicer tone.

"If you think of anything else," the unswayed, chipper scribe said, "feel free to stop by the *Card*'s office at any time." A calling card landed beside her on the bar. "And, nice scarf," he said as he departed.

She ignored the card and looked up at Mac, letting out a deep breath.

Mac squeezed her lightly on the shoulder, her perpetually warm hand decorated in swirling cream, indigo, and olive tattoos, like a kite's tail spinning in the air. "Was answering his questions truly that hard? You should've talked yourself up a bit more."

"But it's not about me. It's about Blaze. Or it should be. People should be talking about what matters, not who saved what," Fiona said, her shoulders slumping. She had wanted the connection to the Ashborn for larger cases and a little renown with the leaders of the pages, yes. It would help her expand the investigative work she could do and the people she could help. But she couldn't see anything good coming out of having her name spread across the Book like this and linked with the Guild so tightly.

She had disliked the Travel Guild for most of her time as a page turner. They often made her job more laborious than it needed to be. They touched everything and were an obstacle in just getting a good job done. But she had to admit her grudge against the Guild could make it easy to judge them before their due, as it had in the case of Blaze's stone. She had been so focused on the Guild being the culprit, she'd almost lost Dodger as a friend and fallen into the trap of the real thieves. She wouldn't let that happen again.

She tilted her head. "Besides, the ones I want to know about my work don't even read the *Card*. No sense using that to make an introduction." Fiona wanted to get to know the leaders of Spine, the one place connected to every page in the Book. She often thought it was better to know the people in power so one could help them do better or hinder them from doing worse.

"Well..." Mac started wiping down the polished wood bar like it too was being stubborn to her words. "If it makes any difference, I think what you did to help Blaze is invaluable. I know for a fact that one or two people in the Book are impressed with you, and that may lead to bigger things, you know."

Fiona smiled. Mac was usually so forward and blunt. Why not say who? "That's quite cryptic. Who're you talking about?"

Mac shook her head, her sunglow-gold hair swinging across her ethereal azure-robed shoulder. "Nope. I've said more than I should've as it is. You're too clever, and some secrets are best kept that way—secret."

"Oh, now you're simply trying to poke my curiosity." Fiona had known Mac for the last fifteen years, ever since she was inked and brought to Spine. But somehow the fae still managed to be a bottle of mysteries as intriguing and delightful as one of her drinks.

It was a shame that the Thread was tucked so deep in the turner district. Few people outside of a smattering of page turners even knew it existed. Folks would be as awed by the proprietress as she had been—still was. Mac said she didn't mind being unknown and that those who needed the place would find it. Fiona always suspected she kept the Thread hidden away on purpose for some secret reason. The Thread housed a large first floor boding ample seating for all body types in the Book (which varied from small and winged to large and elephantine). Its robin's-egg exterior was edged in white trimming that gave the appearance of delicate lacework draped upon an elaborate dollhouse. That delicacy belied the showroom for performers, quaint guest rooms, private quarters, sitting areas and so on. With a handful of floors and so much space, there had to be more going on here than met her investigative eye. She had thought once that perhaps it was Mac's experimental concoctions, like the tipsy maelstrom she sipped on, taking up so much room.

Mac waved in Fiona's face. "Stop trying to figure me out. I know that look, and I regret every word. I'm going to go clear tables before you start asking me more questions." Her bubbly laughter trailed after her somewhat as she headed to the other patrons in the room.

Fiona took her advice, tabling her mysterious friend's antics for another time, and focused on finishing her drink. She ought to be getting home soon as it was. She had promised Gaili that today they could discuss future living arrangements, although she didn't think there was much to discuss. Gaili had been staying in her house for the last week at Fiona's insistence that she not continue sleeping on the floor of her small smithy and alchemist shop. It was no wonder the faun was always covered in streaks of dirt and oil. Though she had only known Gaili for a couple of weeks, she felt immediate kinship with her. As that didn't happen often, Fiona didn't treat it trivially.

To Fiona it just made sense that she helped her new friend with a room. Her place was big enough for the two of them and was already paid for by the pension she received as a page turner of Restless Rise, her native home. In the last century or so, page turners from Rise were immediately lifted to nobility and put into the royal spectrum. It was more for the monarchy than them. A measurement of control. But the funds had meant she could give half to her mother, use the rest to purchase her home, and still have a small amount for basic needs set aside. She had no need for Gaili to pay for the space.

And when she could admit it to herself, it chased away the loneliness she had been feeling. That loneliness had threatened to deepen with Soots now stuck in Blaze resuming their role as its Guardian. But Gaili's chatter and inquisitive personality matched her own and made the place incredibly lively, even with Soots gone. If only she'd get over the notion of having to pay for the room in some manner. How much the faun made at her shop Fiona didn't know, but she got the sense from asking circuitous questions it wasn't enough to rent a proper room. What could Fiona possibly say to make her quit the subject?

Fiona meandered through the cobblestone streets of her beloved city. Spine was quite a bit unnatural compared to the other realms in the Book. While there was a clear indication and previous history to understand all the pages had existed separately before the Inking, the Spine had no such history. It was a large city buffered on four sides by an evergreen forest.

There were over a dozen districts, some dedicated to the seven pages in the Book and others to vocations such as crafting or farming. As more page turners were brought to Spine by their power, bits and pieces of the city refreshed over time to match their desires. Spine was at once new but also dated. For page turners, there was no other home but here. No matter how many showed up, there was always room for them, whether in a district similar to their native page or the turner one.

The turner district itself, where the Thread and Fiona lived, was home to most page turners who either had no alliance to their native page and wished to be far from the representative marks of said pages within the city or, like Fiona, had been in Spine since they were young. The mismatched dwellings that marked the uniqueness of the place were more normal to her than anything else. She passed by a small dark stone keep and a wide yellowing circle yurt on the way to her home. The area was less regulated by the Guild, so turners did as they pleased here. There were a few human and smilodon children running and laughing through an alleyway, blissful in their own little world. People strode the streets, intent on places to be and barely glancing her way. Just how she liked it when she wanted to be alone with her thoughts.

She rounded the corner of the street, swaying out of the way of a passing carriage, and went to the side entrance of her house. The front entrance, with her large Thorne Investigations sign and open-eye insignia, was for clients and when she wanted to be seen entering. The side entrance was lesser known and came in handy when she needed to get away without her nosy neighbors noticing.

Unlocking the large wooden door, she pushed it open and was assailed with the smell of fresh bread mixed with an overpowering sickly sweet smell. She wrinkled her nose, pulling up her multicolored and multi-pocketed scarf to act as a bit of a barrier. The two smells mixed together were too much, and the scarf did little to help block them. Taking a deep breath back outside, she strode into the antechamber, leaving the door open to coax the smells out into the street, and went to find the faun and her latest experiment.

Gaili sat on the wooden bench attached to the long wooden trestle table. This had recently replaced the small one Fiona had used to store various items as she passed back and forth from door to door on her way in and out. The kitchen, more cupboards than anything, hadn't seen much use before Gaili's arrival. But now it was transformed. The cupboards held dishes, the counters a mix of cooking and baking supplies on one wall and some of Gaili's alchemical equipment and clay jar ingredients on the other.

A large iron pot stood in the hearth of the open bricked stove above a smoldering fire. Thankfully Fiona had had the place modernized when she moved in a few years ago, so there was a brick-and-stone chimney attached to funnel the smoke up and out of the room. The bread smell was clearly coming from the pot, a quickly becoming usual occurrence when Gaili was working on a project. Fiona turned her attention to the kitchen table, where Gaili was focused on what looked like small hills of bright-pink sand in front of her. They almost matched the color of her curls. It was scattered on the table on one side from end to end. Larrakane help her, Fiona wouldn't be able to eat on that side of the table again without thinking about whatever it was.

Fiona's slippers made no noise on the polished wooden floor as they were meant to, so she cleared her throat to avoid catching the faun off guard.

"Oh!" Gaili said turning around. "Fi, you're back! I mean...welcome home. Sorry everything is well...everywhere. I'll clean it up right now. Do you want any coffee?"

"Please don't trouble yourself about it," Fiona said, smiling gently. Gaili could be an apologetic sort of person for absolutely nothing at all. It poked at Fiona's senses sometimes, but she would never mention it to her. She knew Gaili's strict education and deplorable professor was the cause of her timid ways. "Honestly, Gaili, there's little you could do to upset me, so don't worry so much." She squeezed Gaili's shoulder in reassurance but moved farther away from the table as the too-sugary smell invaded her senses. She took the warm kettle and buried her nose closer to it, inhaling the earthy, chocolatey scent of one of her favorite pleasures, fresh coffee. Though these were the last beans from Rise, they had only somewhat dented the brief pleasure.

As if reading her thoughts, Gaili chirped up as she turned back to the bright powder. "You got a letter today, sent by a postman from Rise."

"Rise?" Fiona repeated, surprised. A letter from the page was most unexpected. She picked it up, examining it. It was thin and nondescript except for a vine of thorns, her family's crest, on the opening. Larrakane be kind, it was from her mother. She hadn't heard from her in months. She dropped it back on the table as if it had bit her. She'd read it later, alone, or perhaps whenever she needed to remember what it was like to be frustrated and young for a moment.

The smell wafted again from the table as Gaili shifted the sand around with a scraping tool, interrupting her thoughts. Fiona said as politely as she could, "So what have you here? It has quite the interesting smell."

Gaili's rose eyes widened in barely suppressed excitement. "I went to the market this morning to get a few things for dinner, and I came across something I'd never seen here before. Fae rose! Well, the stems. It's from the Court. I haven't had access to any since I was inked. Once it's chopped into dust it's great as a binder to other elements for experimentation and creating potions." Gaili scraped up the sand and funneled it into a jar. "It was fairly rare back home too. Only the old fae knew how to grow it."

"I'll take your word on it." An alchemist and inventor, Gaili could see a great many uses for a thimble if given the time. Fiona moved closer now that the sand was gone. "I'm glad you were able to find some if it'll help you."

"And help you too. I'll be able to find plenty uses for your work with this."

Fiona wasn't quite sure when she'd need to clear out a place by stinking it up, but she was sure Gaili already had several ideas for it. The way her mind worked to take something mundane from another page and make it a valuable tool or weapon was amazing. She had met Gaili when trying to find a solution to keep her then flame sprite Soots from burning down the house. Gaili's work had already helped her more than she could properly express to the faun.

"Gaili, I've been thinking about your request to charge you something for the room."

Gaili's hands stilled as she was cleaning up and then started again. "Oh good, did you come up with a price? I'm happy to pay what you think is fair."

"No, no that's not it. I simply want to say once and for all that you don't need to pay me. The house is paid for," she mumbled, feeling odd about it, "my clients are somewhat steady, and I'm happy just to be helpful."

"But that's not the point, Fi. I need to do my fair share around here. The occasional meal cooked or jelly breath for the fire page can't possibly cover my expenses while I live here."

"Your expenses?" Fiona said, raising an eyebrow. "Are you worried that I'll think you costly at some point?"

"Well, yes, of course. Not costly exactly, but I..." Gaili wiped at her bottom lip, smearing pink powder off her hand to her chin. "I simply want to be on even footing if there's ever any particular disagreements between us in the future."

Ah, so it was a matter of equality that she was worried about. Fiona knew the basics of how things ran in the Court of Copper. She had learned during her few years of turner training and personal study on her own as a tour guide that the levels of hierarchy in the Court were very real and very felt among the people there. But she thought it better than the social order of her own native human page. At least in the Court if you worked hard and could show you were educated or intelligent you could rise to prominence and even be elected to their page council, the Order of Seven. When all the pages opened up some two hundred years ago, it upended the lives of everyone, not only turners. When the Court of Copper was revealed, the Order of Seven was created to preside over the Court's connection to other pages. Each member from one of the seven regions in the Court's page. And they had worked hard since the Inking. They were the ones who prevented the Travel Guild from having outposts in the Court of Copper and oversaw all relations between the faekin page and the rest of the Book.

There were not many methods for escaping the status one was born into in Rise. The only guaranteed way was to be inked. And even then, some people would always remind you to mind your betters.

But if Gaili thought she needed to pay rent to be equal to Fiona then she probably thought herself inadequate in some way. Well, Fiona would certainly not let that stand.

"Alright then. We should be equal partners while you're living here." She leaned back, gauging the faun's reaction to her words to make sure she was on the right track. "But you paying rent would be a waste of your paper. So instead I suggest an agreement. You help me run Thorne Investigations. Assist with the clients. Create resources at a discounted cost. Many cases have needs. And most importantly, combine your considerable talents with my rather mischievous ones to do the very best we can at helping others." Fiona held out her hand, a lightness in her chest. "This is where you take my hand and shake it, agreeing to our deal."

Gaili's took a step back, eyes widening. "You can't be serious."

"I absolutely am," Fiona said, waving away the faun's words. "I should think that a bit obvious, given the circumstances."

"Fi, I don't—You barely know me."

"I know enough to understand that you are quite capable, and capable is a good person to have at your back."

Gaili paced the floor, her golden tattooed hand rubbing her face. She sighed. "You're very sweet, but be reasonable. I can make some minor concoctions at best. That's not enough for you to be offering a partnership."

Fiona straightened up and grabbed on to Gaili, stopping her pacing. As if she was reciting the facts of a case, she said, "You have a knack for languages that is entirely useful. I pay quite a bit in the artisan district for potions to travel to the elemental pages, maintenance of my gear, and so on. I must spend time hunting down information and doing research that your thorough education may have already taught you. And your ability to create items of use for unpredictable situations is exceptional. You are invaluable, Gaili, and I'd very much like to work with you."

Gaili shook her head, bright-pink curls swaying side to side. "Oh. But..." She dropped her gaze. "I don't want to bring you down."

Fiona dropped her hand and tried to think of how she could solve this. If telling Gaili that she was valuable wouldn't work, she'd simply have to show her. "At least give it a trial run. What do you have to lose?"

The faun looked up, but whatever she was about to say disappeared as a bell sounded from the front of the house. Gaili turned to answer it, wiping her hands on her apron as she went. Fiona sighed but followed. She would bring the conversation up again later at her first chance.

A faun, tall with gold-leaf skin, deep-brown eyes, and curved black horns stood staring open-mouthed at Gaili's presence in the doorway. Her hands, less tattooed than Gaili's, held the sides of her simple rust-colored woolen dress, fidgeting. She seemed on the verge of running away.

Fiona called out to set her at ease: "Hello there. Welcome. Do please come in."

The faun's attention snapped to Fiona. There was a wobble of the mouth, but it was gone as soon as Fiona registered it. Raising her chin up, she asked, "This is the home of Investigator Thorne?"

Fiona motioned to a large padded chair by her desk. "Please sit. I'm Investigator Thorne."

Gaili took a step back and the faun walked slowly into the parlor-turned-office.

"Would you like some coffee?" Gaili said.

The faun cleared her throat. "Yes. That would be nice." She smoothed her dress as she sat down. "Er, I've never had any before."

"I know the precise way to make it for a first timer," Gaili said, avoiding Fiona's eyes and heading to the kitchen.

"Have we met before?" Fiona asked. There was a lilt to her voice that sounded a little familiar, but Fiona couldn't place her.

"No, no we haven't. I'm Elinor." She played with her dress, entangling the fabric in her fingers. "Format has it you helped some of those fire creatures get back home when the smugglers had taken them. That you didn't think twice about setting them all free."

"That's true." Fiona sat, trying to ease the faekin's anxiety. "Do you need help with something?"

She nodded and broke into fresh tears as she said, "My sister's been arrested by the Order of Seven, and I think you're the only one who can save her."

Continue your adventure and purchase HARD BOUND in your preferred format at www.dhalerambo.com/books/

Also by D. Hale Rambo

A SERIES OF DECISIONS ON KAIRAS

A cozy high fantasy trilogy set in the world of Kairas where the deities may be sealed away but their troubles are not.

Book 1, TOOLS OF A THIEF

How do you stop being a thief? Zizy Zakar assumed quitting her job, stealing from her boss, and teleporting hundreds of miles away was one way to give it a go.

Buy it now: teleport yourself to books2read.com/toat

Book 2, COMPONENTS OF A CASTER

Laysa has always vowed to do whatever it took to learn magic. Can Laysa keep her friends alive and survive uncovering the depths of the unknown? Does she have what it takes to be a Caster?

Buy it now: cast your coins at books2read.com/coac

Book 3, ROUTES OF A RANGER

A family under threat. A perilous journey home. Skinny has spent her life running from her past. Now she must achieve the destiny she was denied before she can defeat the enemy at her doorstep.

Buy it now: steer yourself towards go.dhalerambo.com/roar

THE PLANAR PAGES

A historical fantasy mystery series with investigator Fiona Thorne and her motley crew of friends.

Life flourishes in the Book, a world of stacked realms spanning the ages, like the pages of an epic chronicle. Those who can travel through them are page turners; blessed with the power to go from one page to the next. For investigator Fiona Thorne, being a Turner is normal life. Solving mysteries is where the excitement lives.

Book 0, HIDDEN WORDS (newsletter exclusive prequel)

Cases are ramping up in the Spine and Fiona is in the middle of the action. Hired by her charming, gossipy neighbor to track down a shipment of rare books, Fiona thinks it'll be a piece of work.

Read it for FREE by signing up for my newsletterat go.dhalerambo.com/freestory

Book 1, BETWEEN THE LINES

Blaze, the page of fire, is wasting away. Fire elementals are being smuggled out in waves, but by whom? Fiona is on the job and nothing will hold her, not even the overbearing Travel Guild.

Read BETWEEN THE LINES and buy it now at: go.dhalerambo.com/tppbtl

Book 2, HARD BOUND

Someone has stolen from the Court of Copper, the illustrious fae page nestled within the Book. Is it a member of the fractured counsel, the fabled Order of Seven, or could the thief be much closer to Fiona than she realizes?

The fae realm is only a step away. BUY HARD BOUND at: go.dhalerambo.com/tpphb

Book 3, PRESSED

Between the tangled politics of home and facing her overbearing mother, Fiona counts herself lucky the yearly attendance with Queen Brilliance is only for a few days. But this year, the Queen presses Fiona with an unexpected request—find the mythical Guardian of Restless Rise. Amid schemes and betrayals, Fiona must piece together palace intrigues and myths to discover if the Guardian truly exists.

Join the investigation. BUY PRESSED at go.dhalerambo.com/tpppressed

About the Author

D. HALE RAMBO IS a historical fantasy author whose books transport readers to wondrous worlds filled with magic, mystery, and humor. With compelling and memorable characters at the heart of her stories, Rambo weaves tales to entertain and enthrall.

A lifelong storyteller, she's been writing and creating other worlds since she was old enough to mark them on her bedroom wall.

When she's not writing, you can find her enjoying a stiff cosmopolitan while reading mysteries alongside her favorite pet companion.

Discover more about her wondrous worlds, the versatility of gnomes, and fun fae cocktails at www.dhalerambo.com